DARKNESS AND THE AZURE

DARKNESS AND THE AZURE

TALES ABOUT THE MOUNTAINS,
MOUNTAIN PEOPLE
AND MOUNTAINEERS

BY ANNE SAUVY

BÂTON WICKS · LONDON

Other works of fiction by Anne Sauvy:

FLAMMES DE PIERRE (0-906371-88-0)
Diadem, London 1991 – now available from Bâton Wicks;
Éditions Montalba, Paris 1982;
Presses Universitaires de Grenoble 1993, 1998

THE GAME OF MOUNTAIN AND CHANCE (1-898573-15-8)
(LE JEU DE LA MONTAGNE ET DU HASARD)
Bâton Wicks, London 1995; Éditions Montalba, Paris 1985;
Presses Universitaires de Grenoble 1995, 1998

NADIR
Éditions Glénat, Grenoble 1995

SECOURS EN MONTAGNE
Arthaud-Flammarion, Paris 1998, 1999

Flammes de Pierre received the Prix de l'Alpe (1982), the Literary Prize of the German Alpine Club (1983), and was shortlisted for the Boardman/Tasker Award (1991). *Darkness and the Azure* was awarded the Prix du Salon du Livre de Montagne (1991). *Secours en Montagne* won the Prix Littéraire de la Gendarmerie Nationale in 1999.

Copyright © by Anne Sauvy

Published in Great Britain in 1999
by Bâton Wicks, London

First published in France in 1991 as *Le Ténèbre et L'Azur*
by Les Éditions Arthaud, Paris

Trade enquiries: Cordee, 3a De Montfort Street, Leicester LE1 7HD

All rights reserved. No part of this publication may be reproduced, stored in a retrieval system, or transmitted, in any form or by any means, electronic, mechanical, photocopying, recording or otherwise without prior permission of the publisher.

British Cataloguing-in-Publication Data
A catalogue record for this book is available from the British Library
ISBN 1-898573-42-5

Printed and bound in Great Britain by MPG Books Ltd., Bodmin

CONTENTS

Asphodèle 7

Midday-Midnight 21

Snowball 25

Gingermoon 41

Darkness and the Azure 53

The End of the Season 57

Strange Happenings 69

The Mont-Cervin Hotel 77

Solitude 101

A Day on Holiday 110

The Secret 116

The Fall 122

The Twistleton Hut 135

The Red Sentinel 141

Expeditionitis 155

The Temptation of Philibert Avril 161

The translation was made by Anthea Bell
with the collaboration of John C. Wilkinson to
both of whom the author expresses her
deepest gratitude.

ASPHODELE

'I really loved the mountains!' murmured Ludovic.

Yes, well, I knew he did, but I dared not ask the question that was on the tip of my tongue and had haunted my mind for the last six months: in that case, why did he leave them? What had he been running away from so suddenly? What had happened in a life of apparently rock-solid stability? What fantasy had shaken him off balance – or what wild dream?

Since I couldn't broach that question, the one that I thought really mattered, I chose to keep quiet and say nothing. After all, if he wasn't prepared to tell his secret there was nothing I could do. In fact I had suggested this walk before he left again with a view to avoiding anything that might upset him, any chance meetings or unwelcome curiosity. But then again, wasn't the admission he had just let slip a first reminder of the past? The beginnings of a confidence? Perhaps he wanted to tell someone – me – why he had torn himself abruptly from everything that once made up his life? If so, it would be better not to interfere with the fragile process. I had to respect the rhythm of the memories in which he seemed to be indulging.

In fact I'd been surprised to see him back. He had asked me to carry out the delicate task of re-selling the old farmhouse he had just bought on the Mont des Bossons. After deciding to restore it himself he began, with typical enthusiasm, by demolishing half the internal walls in what spare time he didn't spend climbing. He was full of splendid ideas for the improvements he would make over the next few years. I could still hear his enthusiastic voice last summer telling me how the Brévent would be framed in his bedroom window, and about the door that would open some day on a garden containing a complete collection of alpine plants.

However, it had been difficult to sell the farmhouse in its gutted state, full of rubble and with only one habitable room where the master of the house temporarily camped out. Ludovic had asked me to deal with it in a friendly but brief letter which told me nothing at all about his reasons. In spite of the relatively modest price he was asking it had taken me months to find him a buyer. The first estate agency I approached even refused outright to take the property on unless a minimum amount of work was done on it first. But my instructions were clear: it must be sold just as it was, as quickly as possible, and finally a deal was done. The contract had been signed that morning in the Chamonix notary's office.

Asphodèle 8

Ludovic had arrived a little earlier, with the firm intention of leaving again in the afternoon. We had lunched together at the Bartavel, and since there was some constraint to our conversation, which was confined to what I had been doing last winter and the details of his move into his new home, I had suggested a walk in the April mountains.

We had gone up towards the Floriaz, along a grey earth track interspersed here and there by large chunks of solid snow in the channels made by avalanches. The forest was still in its dormant winter state, but some early signs of spring hinted at the coming explosion of new life. Catkins dangled from the bare branches of shrubs, the twigs of myrtles, though still leafless, were green, and there was a humming in the air. I saw a russet butterfly, its wings rimmed with blue and white. On the slopes, however, last year's old, yellow pasture was still frozen, grass bent by the weight of snow that had now melted, and no green showed except the dark branches of spruce trees and a few bramble leaves that had survived the winter.

Now and then I looked at Ludovic, with his lean form, determined face, keen profile and clear eyes. He had scarcely changed, although imperceptible lines of bitterness seemed to be traced on his forehead and at the corners of his mouth. Nor was I used to seeing him look so pale. Usually he was always tanned from the sun and fresh air. However, his bearing was as precise and powerful as ever, his step firm and extraordinarily sure. This was something I had always admired in him when we went climbing together, and although I did not know just what had torn Ludovic away from the mountains, it certainly wasn't any sudden physical infirmity.

At last we sat down on the fallen trunk of a dead tree. The föhn was blowing, that hot and violent south wind. Its gusts set the tall pines dancing sarabandes in different directions, bowing the tree-tops, bringing them together and then apart again as if they were imbued by a life of their own. The branches themselves swayed this way and that, rising fringe-like in irregular rhythmic waves, and the thousands of smaller twigs seemed to be beating time in all directions to some mysterious symphony. Opposite us, through a gap, we could see the north side, still with much more snow than on ours, its glaciers and needles of rock plastered with powder, and Mont Blanc pale against the clear sky.

Ludovic looked at all this in silence, gazing at the mountains, his mouth slightly contracted by some malaise I could not define. Then he spoke again.

'You know how I loved living here,' he said. 'This valley meant everything to me, from the wildest peaks to the smallest details – just look at these little pine-cone scales scattered at our feet where the squirrels have been feasting! When I was a student and told my family I was going to settle here they couldn't believe it. They knew my taste for all the plays and concerts and other fascinating diversions of Paris, and they thought I'd never be able to live outside a great city with all its intellectual ferment, although I was perfectly capable of it. I had to put up with a lot of banter from my sisters and my younger brother when I told them what I was going to do and said I planned to open a medical centre for functional rehabilitation here. "Good heavens, yes, Ludovic, just the thing for you! What fun you'll have up in those mountains, my dear, vibrant as they are with all the energy of the human mind! Which will you go for first? The Charamillon artistic biennale? The Chosalets *bel canto* festival? The Mouilles literary workshops? The Rocher des Gaillands Institute of Advanced Hittite Studies? The Plan de l'Aiguille cultural soirées? You'll be spoilt for choice!" I laughed with them and let them carry on. I knew I could spend years here absorbed in my profession, my climbing, my discs and my books, until some day I had a wife and children to add even more to a full life. So I settled in Chamonix, and I was happy. Well, you know I was happy. That is, until last year …'

Here he fell silent, and for a while I heard nothing but the roar of the wind in the trees and the creak of branches. I sensed that Ludovic was hesitating, not sure if he wanted to go on confiding in me, and yet some force impelled him to speak at the same time as something else held him back. I tried to remember the circumstances of his departure. He had left while I was away on holiday late last summer, and when I got back it was all over. I had been astonished to hear that Ludovic's medical centre was closed and that he had left the area, lock, stock and barrel. A little later he told me he had found similar work in La Rochelle. His choice of location alone amazed me; I mean, could there be anywhere less like the Alps than La Rochelle? I was absolutely staggered.

'You must have suspected that something happened,' Ludovic went on. 'Something so weird that I haven't told a soul about it. I'm trying to forget it … if I came here to sign the contract on the house I suppose it was because I had no good excuse for wriggling out of it, but perhaps I also wanted to see if I was strong enough to come back and confront the solidity of the life I'm trying to rebuild with some very strange memories and my old love of the mountains – I'd certainly like to get over that. I was really shaken this morning, though! I spent the night with friends in Geneva and set off feeling reasonably all right, but as soon as I looked up above Bonneville and saw the pure, white line of that ridge – I think it's is called the Môle – well, my heart turned over, and after the Cluses ravine with its wooded slopes and the blue planes of the cliffs stretching away, I knew I was home and nothing could ever make up for what I'd lost. Even on the motorway, with my window wound only a little way down, I could catch the wonderful, pure scent of pines, forest fires, hay, snow – it's hard to pin down, but to me it's the smell of the mountains. And then I saw Mont Joly, the first peak I ever climbed, when I was thirteen. I thought of an alpine chalet I know near Rochebrune, where I've sometimes visited friends ... oh, I needn't describe the road. You've been along it as often as I have. There's that moment when the mountains and the sky open out so dramatically. It made the tears come to my eyes. First the great wall of Les Miages, then the North Face of Bionnassay, the Aiguille du Goûter still powdered with snow, Mont Blanc, Mont Maudit, the chain of the Aiguilles up to the Grépon and even for a moment, the Verte and the Drus. It really upset me ... realizing that I might still love the mountains as much as ever but that I was parted from them for good, of my own free will, parted from them absolutely, in a horribly final way.'

'Nothing's ever that final,' I protested. 'I mean, I don't know what made you leave, but I'm sure that in time, when you can stand back from it a bit ...'

'Wait till you've heard my story,' said Ludovic, 'and then we'll see what you say. That is, if you can bring yourself to say anything and you don't just think I'm suffering from some kind of hallucination. Time and again I've wondered if I was in my right mind, and what one's right mind really is ... I do believe I'm perfectly sane and rational, though; it's just that I'm facing something I can't explain. Merely talking about it for the first time, and up here too, upsets me more than you can imagine. But I'm going to. I want to get the reaction of some sensible person like you, and perhaps if I share it that will help me bear it a little better. You don't mind, do you?'

'Of course not,' I told him, getting a little impatient with this long prelude. 'You know you can tell me anything. I wouldn't have asked you, but we've certainly all been very intrigued. The way I saw it, there was no good reason for you to leave, or for all this mystery either.'

'Come to think of it, it happened quite simply,' he said, as if he'd scarcely heard what I said and was merely following his own train of thought. 'And it could just as easily not have happened at all ... Last summer, as you know, I was indulging in the sheer pleasure of rock routes, technical climbing without long approaches, ice, mixed terrain, going to a summit ... just modern routes like the *Marchand de Sable* and *Majorette Thatcher*, *Carmencita* and *Pas d'edelweiss pour Mrs Wilkinson*, *Pioli-piola* and *Symphonie en six majeur*. By the end of the season, all the same, I felt I'd missed out on something that is an essential part of good climbing. Late in September the rest of you had either all left or were busy, so I decided to go up to one of the huts alone and make good use of my weekend before autumn really set in. I don't much approve of climbing alone, but I decided to do it for once, and anyway I was taking hardly any risks. My idea was to go up to the Leschaux Hut because it's right in the middle of the massif and near some major routes including the North Face of the Jorasses ... I have great memories of that. The weather was fine, but to be honest the forecast wasn't too good; in fact it was predicting a deep depression due to arrive on Saturday evening and last for several days. Well, if the weather forecast was wrong I thought I might do the Y Couloir on of the Aiguille de l'Éboulement on Sunday, nothing very special, descending by the ordinary route. Climbs like that ought to be in good condition after the recent snowfalls. And if the forecast was right, at least I'd have stretched my legs and spent a night in the mountains, and next day I'd go back down to the valley in the rain – that wouldn't be a worry.'

I couldn't help saying, 'No need to tell me that!' reminding him of some particularly wet retreats I'd made with him.

'So I set off. Not very early – I was working in the morning, and then I wanted to finish a few jobs on my house. You know, I've just remembered something funny ... I had a letter from my grandmother that day, and I couldn't help smiling. She was urging me never to go climbing in bad weather. She always had a bee in her bonnet about that, probably on account of the newspapers, because she didn't know the first thing about climbing, but you know the sort of headlines that get printed – "Climbers caught by bad weather lost on Mont Blanc", and so on and so forth. Of course I wasn't about to change my plans, and I told myself, somewhat hypocritically, that as it was in fact very fine and the only threat was from the weather forecast I wasn't even rejecting Granny's wise advice. Well, anyway, I packed my sack, shut up the house and finally caught the Montenvers train.'

'And the weather held?'

'Yes, it was still excellent. It was only as I reached the Mer de Glace that I noticed the sky filling up with curious streaked, mottled clouds – a magnificent sight, really. I climbed up the glacier. As you know, when you reach the big central moraine you have to get across it as best you can, so you're fully occupied looking for the right line, keeping an eye on the markers and cairns and only thinking where to put your foot next. Not until I was across did I realize that the weather forecast had got it right. The sky had clouded completely over and was a leaden, livid colour, almost black. In spite of the time of day it was almost twilight. A violent wind rose, and the cloud ceiling came down lower. In fact the atmosphere was remarkable, and once I finally reached the Leschaux Glacier I found myself in total isolation. Not a sound to be heard but the crunch of granular ice beneath my feet, the faint babbling of the surface streams, and further away the dull boom of the glacier streams running into potholes below the surface. Suddenly a flash of lightning lit up the scene, followed next moment by a great roll of thunder. I hurried over the snow slope leading to the hut. The first drops of rain fell as I was at the far end of the track, and I got there just in time to avoid being drenched to the skin!'

'I don't want to stir up our old argument,' I commented, 'but personally I always believe the weather forecast.'

'You have a point,' Ludovic admitted. 'At least it has a statistical chance of being right half the time. Anyway, it was dead right that afternoon, and my prospects of a climb next day looked poor. Still, I had an evening in the hut ahead of me, cut off from the rest of the world in the middle of the storm, and it was quite an attractive idea, although Leschaux is no great fun in bad weather – you could even call it pretty bleak. You know it. It's a very small hut, with a tiny kitchen, the guardian's room and two rows of bunks one above the other on the left, on the side against the mountain. On the right, facing you as you come in, there's a space at most one and a half metres wide, with a rectangular table and a bench. The few little windows in the wall on that side, looking down the slope, give you a wonderful view of the Envers des Aiguilles in good weather. That evening, however, they showed nothing except the rain and hail being flung against them by the wind, and sometimes just a glimpse of the glacier and the grey moraines lower down, lit up at regular intervals by bluish flashes of lightning. And the thunder kept on rolling.'

'I suppose there wasn't anyone else there?'

'Not a soul. The guardian had left around the middle of September, and there aren't many climbers at that time of year. The hut will hold about a dozen people, and you know what an inferno it can be in summer when there's a crowd of thirty climbers milling around. On the other hand it's really comfortable when you're there on your own – at least, comfortable by climbing standards. I unpacked my gear. I'd brought my stove up, because I wasn't too sure what I'd find. It was easy enough to get water; I just had to open the door and hold a billy out! I began making myself some powdered soup, and since I'd expected to be away from home for dinner and perhaps for lunch next day I'd brought ham, rice, cheese, chocolate, a can of fruit in syrup, in fact all the makings of a good meal, and I was feeling very hungry ... Well, I was just sitting down to a plate of piping hot soup and breaking bread into it when I thought I heard a noise at the door. I could hardly believe any other climbers might be arriving in this weather, but I'd come up to the hut myself, after all. I rose and went to open the door. And in the oval of the doorway, by the light of another lightning flash, I saw a young woman, dripping wet.'

'Aha!' I couldn't help exclaiming. 'I somehow thought there might be a woman involved!'

'Don't be silly,' snapped Ludovic. 'There isn't a woman involved. At least, not in the way you think. I was looking at a girl of twenty-three or twenty-four, and I was dazzled by her beauty ... do you mind, please don't interrupt. I helped her to come in and take off her soaking cagoule, and I hung it on a peg. "What luck to find someone here!" she said, smiling. "In such a storm! Are you the guardian?" I explained that I wasn't, that I'd come up on my own for the weekend, and had only just escaped the first of the downpour. Suddenly I felt very glad to have company. The young woman had put her sack down and was looking for dry clothes in it. She put on a kind of thick wool sweater in ochre shades which suited her tawny hair and her blue eyes – they were quite a deep blue. Every detail of that evening comes back to me as if I were still there ... She'd taken off her boots and put on a pair of the rubber slippers you find in mountain huts. I looked for my duvet and put it round her shoulders. In defiance of current fashion she wore her hair in a thick plait pinned behind her head like a chignon, and when she undid the plait to let her hair dry it fell to her shoulders in ringlets. Until now I'd been making do with the light from my stove, but now that night was really falling I lit the candle jammed into the neck of a bottle that was standing on the table. All this time, of course, we'd been exchanging remarks and explanations, and naturally the first thing I asked was whether she was alone or had any companions who'd be following. She told me she was on her own, and it was "a long story". Those were her words, her very words.'

Asphodèle 14

'Didn't you try to find out more?'

'Yes ... well, no, I didn't try too hard. That is, she didn't offer any more information herself, and I had plenty of time to find out more. The main thing was to make sure there was no one lost on the glacier – although I have to admit it mattered to me even more to know that this wonderful creature wasn't going to be joined in our shelter by four or five strapping great bearded, loud-mouthed men. I had her all to myself! I was delighted, naturally. The first thing was for her to get warm, and then for us to have dinner. She had taken some food out of her sack, not a lot, hill food really, dried apricots and nougat. She put it on the table with her head torch, her flask and a small pointed piece of crystal broken at one end that she'd taken out of her pocket. I invited her to share my own banquet. I began by sitting on the bench beside her, but I wanted so much to see her better, look at her fine features and see her smile dimpling her smooth cheeks, that I took the first excuse to move the table closer to the bench running along under the bunks and sit opposite her.'

Ludovic fell silent for a moment. He seemed to be lost in thoughts of a less gloomy nature than before, and there was a light of amused affection in his eyes.

'She was an amazing girl,' he told me. 'Not just beautiful but cheerful, intelligent, out-going, sensitive. We talked climbing at first. She had done some big routes like the Sentinelle, the Arête du Lion on the Matterhorn, the North Face of the Dolent. We felt the same about everything; we understood each other. She loved music, especially opera. She knew a lot about Richard Strauss. She liked Moravia, Dürrenmatt, Yevtushenko, my own favourite authors, and she could bring an original mind to bear on what she knew and particularly liked. I felt more and more certain of something I'd actually known the moment I saw her there in the doorway, smiling in the torrential rain ... don't laugh, but I knew I'd found the one woman in the world for me. I know that sounds silly, like some old-fashioned novel, but you have to admit such things do happen. I mean, there are occasions when time doesn't mean a thing: whole years can go by and they're worth no more than a minute, but quite brief moments can change everything, transforming you. That hour we had spent talking to each other was as good as a lifetime. I felt it very strongly that evening, and I could swear she did too.'

'You didn't discuss it?'

'Well, no! You don't talk about things like that. You feel them, you live them much more intensely than through words. Anything you could say would sound flat, would detract from such an amazing experience. Think of trying to dam up a torrent, forcing it to go a certain way ... no! This was all to do with being together, laughing together, struck with wonder. For instance, just to show you that we were being prosaic, we talked about what we did. I told her at some length about functional rehabilitation and how it differs from kinesitherapy, how I can draw up an anamnesis, make a clinical examination and establish a diagnosis, for the purpose of manipulation or therapeutics that only a doctor is qualified to perform. I love my profession, as you know, I like talking about it, and I believe I conveyed my own enthusiasm to her as I talked.'

'And did she tell you what she did?'

'Yes, of course. She was an interior designer. Recently she'd been working for an architect, building a palace in I forget which of the Arab emirates – she told me some very amusing stories about it. Now she wanted to get back to the mountains, so she was opening an interior design studio in Saint-Gervais and planning to decorate flats and chalets. I was delighted to hear it, and I knew it was all meant to be like this! We'd be practically next-door neighbours; everything was bringing us together. It's the kind of encounter that has to happen just once in a lifetime. I told myself Fate had been waiting for me on a stormy evening in the Leschaux Hut.'

'So what happened next?'

'None of your business ... well, you know I don't chase women much, and it wouldn't be like me to try seducing a girl I hardly knew straight off. You remember Lucile? We were together for a while, but it was all over by the end of last spring, and no one replaced her. Lucile was pretty, athletic, good company, but that was all. Whereas Asphodèle ...'

'Your unknown visitor was called Asphodèle?'

'Yes; odd name, isn't it? The name of a flower. Her parents called her Asphodèle from those two lines in Victor Hugo's *Booz endormi*:

> Sweet fragrance rose from clumps of asphodel.
> Soft winds breathed over Galagala by night.

Her father was in the diplomatic service and she was born abroad, so no one queried her curious first name. It enchanted me: it had the same unusual beauty as she did herself. I don't know if you've ever been utterly under anyone's spell, but I was under Asphodèle's. I don't mean that in some solemn, romantic way, I mean it quite simply. You asked what

Asphodèle 16

happened next, so I might as well tell you. Next we decided to see what the weather was doing. I put my hand on hers as I made the suggestion, and she did not draw her own hand away. We got up from the table, put on our anoraks and went outside for a moment. It was still raining hard, but the storm seemed to be moving away. The lightning that still occasionally lit up the cloudy sky was further off and more diffuse by now. The worst of the storm must have moved on towards Switzerland. I put my arm round Asphodèle's shoulders, and we went back inside ... well, as I was saying, it's not my way to try seducing a girl the moment I set eyes on her, but everything between Asphodèle and me was quite different. We were made for each other, destined for each other, and up there in that little hut battered by the stormy wind I spent the most wonderful night of love in my entire life.'

Ludovic stopped again. I knew I must respect his silence, but my mind was working away to no avail on this new riddle. The story he told, after all, sounded extremely promising. We don't live in a period given to dramas of unrequited love, and even supposing Asphodèle was married, that would hardly be an insurmountable obstacle. Not if I knew Ludovic, and not with the way he described this sudden, overwhelming passion. No, I had to admit I didn't understand it at all.

'We fell asleep,' Ludovic went on. 'I woke in the night, however, and spent some time thinking of my new-found happiness. We hadn't discussed it, but I knew Asphodèle would be my wife, and nothing would separate us all our lives. All our lives ... A last flash of lighting illuminated the hut. I saw Asphodèle asleep beside me, softly abandoned, one hand near my shoulder. I took it tenderly and slipped a ring on her finger, a silver ring I always wore – you may have noticed it; it came from my mother's family. I never took it off except when I was climbing, and then I used to put it in my wallet. It was a kind of talisman. I can't show you how sure I felt about Asphodèle any better than by telling you that I gave her that ring. I thought for a long time after that. I wondered what coincidence or what power had made me come up to the Leschaux rather than anywhere else that evening. I went over all the details of our meeting. I began making plans, and then I fell asleep again. When I woke up a little pale daylight was filtering into the hut. There was total silence. I knew at once that the rain had been followed by snow: thick, endless snow. I turned to Asphodèle, and she wasn't there beside me any more. I called, and she didn't reply. Although nothing about the situation was clear or precise yet, I felt a terrible sense of dread.'

'She could have gone out,' I said. 'Oh – did she fall?'

'No,' said Ludovic. 'Don't try to understand; you can't. Of course that was what I thought myself, that she could have gone out – that's what anyone would have thought once he was properly awake. But I got up, and I saw at once that her sack wasn't there any more, or any of her things. Or no, that's not quite right ... the little pointed piece of crystal she'd taken out of her pocket the evening before was still on the table, beside the bottle covered with candlewax. I couldn't think what had happened. Asphodèle's departure was inexplicable, incredible. I might almost have thought I was dreaming, but everything around me was too concrete and solid for me to doubt its reality. At that moment I heard sounds outside, just as I had the night before. Naturally I thought it was Asphodèle, and I hurried to open the door. You must forgive me if my story seems rather odd, but when I opened the door this time I saw not a pretty woman but two tall men in cagoules, with snowflakes swirling down over them, and I found myself involved in a second adventure. There are days like that ... well, I recognized one of my visitors almost at once as Sergeant Sournia. I'd treated him for a slipped disk the winter before. "Dr Marcevol!" he exclaimed. "I'm glad to see you. Are you alone?" What do you tell a gendarme in the circumstances? That you spent last night in a mountain hut with the woman of your dreams, and she left without a word of goodbye, leaving only a small piece of crystal behind? You can hardly say that to a mountain rescue gendarme, let alone two of them. So I said yes, I was on my own, and I'd climbed up the day before hoping to do a route this morning, but the weather ... Sournia, however, obviously was not much interested in the details. "Too bad," he said, "but it's lucky you're here, and if you're stuck for something to do you can be our back-up doctor." You can imagine my state of mind. Here was I, madly in love and desperately anxious, being roped in by the rescue service. I had no idea how to get out of it. I began doing my boots up and equipping myself to go out while I tried to think how to explain who Asphodèle was, how we had met, and how she had now disappeared. I just couldn't do it. In view of the prosaic turn of events my story seemed thin, almost silly. In brief, my companions told me that the civil guard helicopter had just set them down on the glacier with two other members of the rescue team, and had now gone back to bring up two more and a doctor. The weather was appalling, they said, and the outlook worse, and they were lucky that a helicopter had been able to get up to the glacier at all at daybreak, flying low to the Angle and beyond, because obviously no more air rescues

Asphodèle 18

would be possible for some days with the huge depression still coming in over the mountains. The two of them had decided to use their time waiting for the rest of the team to turn up by checking out the hut for any occupants, and since I was there they thought eight would be better than seven; we could break trail and come up to the Mont Mallet bergschrund from the other side of the glacier. I have to say I was unconcerned by any of this, but felt less and less able to get out of what looked like my professional duty. I ate some bread and chocolate, put on my sack and went out with the rescuers, feeling I was living in some crazy dream.'

'Had there been an accident at the Mont Mallet bergschrund, then?' I asked.

'Apparently,' said Ludovic. 'I told you I wasn't taking any interest in it. This was not my problem, but I had to go along with them and I did, that's all there was to it, although I was fuming inside. The weather was dreadful. The helicopter managed to come in for the second time as we were going down the névé. Then it set off for the valley again, leaving us alone. It's astonishing what pilots can do these days. The doctor who'd been brought up was Michel Sorède. Soon all eight of us were ploughing through new snow in a fierce storm. I was absorbed in my own thoughts, trying to make out what had happened to Asphodèle. It was clear that she'd left at the crack of dawn, but why? No doubt something had forced her to leave, and if she didn't wake me that must have been because I was so fast asleep she preferred not to disturb me. So she hadn't left a word of explanation ... well, not many people take writing materials with them when they go climbing. Asphodèle knew where to find me in the valley, and come to that I knew where to find her. That thought made me feel better.'

'So you still didn't know what had brought her to Leschaux?'

'No, I didn't. We hadn't discussed it – she just told me it was "a long story". I thought that was the key to the problem. Asphodèle's disappearance must have something to do with incidents she'd merely hinted at. I know from experience that some apparently inexplicable delay or complicated situation may have a simple explanation, and once you know what it is you wonder why you failed to guess it instead of worrying pointlessly. I wasn't entirely reassured, as a matter of fact: for one thing I couldn't unravel the mystery without more information, and for another the weather was appalling. But I told myself that there was an area down on the glacier clear enough for the helicopter to fly in, and that lower down the snow would give way to rain, and all things considered the situation wasn't really extreme. Gradually, by dint of logic, I managed to allay my fears, and at the same time I was fully occupied by the new venture into which I'd been drawn.'

'So you still didn't mention your story to anyone else?'

'What do you think? Anyway, we were absorbed by what we were doing. However, the reasons for this unexpected expedition gradually became clear to me from the scraps of conversation I heard my companions exchange when we stopped. Then I asked them a few questions myself, and I managed to reconstruct the situation. Just now the Mont Mallet bergschrund was over twenty metres high, as it very often is. The previous morning a couple of climbers had traversed the Arêtes de Rochefort, coming down via the Mont Mallet Glacier. All went well until the rappel, a manoeuvre they had been expecting to perform. A stake had been placed as an anchorage point. However, when the first climber was in position an enormous block of snow and ice broke off, carrying everything away with it – for whatever cause, human error, perhaps simply fate. The other climber was left alone on the upper rim of the bergschrund, without a rope and calling hopelessly to his companion. He had spent ages looking for an alternative way down, but there wasn't one, and the overhanging rim of the bergschrund hid his view of what lay below. Seeing nothing and hearing nothing, there was no alternative but to go back up again, despite the distance. So he remounted the snow slopes to the Aiguille de Rochefort and then followed the arêtes again. Night and the bad weather caught up with him below the Dent du Géant, and his head was injured by a stone-fall set off by the rain, but he finally reached the Pointe Helbronner, where he alerted the CRS station. The alarm was passed by radio to the P.G.H.M. mountain rescue service. Since the weather forecast was so bad the rescue had to be mounted on foot. They set off as soon as it started to get light, but fortunately the helicopter flight had saved them two good hours.'

'That was the noise which woke you?'

'I expect so, and it was in the faint hope that the other climber had not been too badly injured and had managed to get to the Leschaux Hut that the two gendarmes had come up while waiting for the helicopter to return. We were making our way through the snow in particularly difficult and even dangerous conditions now, and I felt in a peculiar state, what with the effort, exhaustion, and most of all the series of unexpected events I'd experienced since the day before. Finally we were approaching the bergschrund. Slopes that appear easy when you're coming down them in fine weather seem steep and endless when going up in fresh snow. Fortunately, or unfortunately, we didn't have to spend long looking for the site of the accident; we soon found an axe which had caught when the climber fell, and not far away we saw the shape of a body shrouded beneath a layer of powder snow. Two gendarmes carefully disengaged it. The cry I uttered echoed weirdly in the silence, and it must have surprised my companions. Perhaps you've guessed: it was Asphodèle's body. Her hair, which had come undone, was frozen and stiff with ice, but she was as lovely as ever in death. And on her finger – do you hear? – on her finger I recognized my silver ring. Michel Sorède made the medical diagnosis, which was simple enough. The odd backward angle of the neck in relation to the body showed that the fall had been a bad one and death was instantaneous. I was paralysed, not by grief but by fear. For Asphodèle must have been dead when she came and found me. I had spent the night with a dead woman. I had made love to a dead woman. So you needn't ask me why I thought I was practically going out of my mind, or why I left this area, or why I'm afraid to come back. And you needn't wonder why I don't want to spend a night here and why I'm leaving at once, for ever. You do understand, don't you … do you understand?'

MIDDAY-MIDNIGHT

On 5 August 1856 Count Fernand de Bouillé, accompanied by ten mountain men, attempted the most unlikely feat that could then be imagined.

In its time, to be sure, the ascent of Mont Blanc had been a notable exploit, but by now it was such a standard climb that the giant had been vanquished several dozen times, sometimes even by ladies, while the bold notion M. de Bouillé had taken into his head was to mount an assault on the mountain peak dominating Chamonix, which was an absolute symbol of inaccessibility. Its proud, rocky peak and steep sides rose aloft like a challenge. It was known as the Aiguille du Midi because on a certain winter day, at midday precisely, when the sun going on its eternal way behind the mountains reached its meridian, it cast its beams through a natural tunnel piercing the summit. The Aiguille du Midi was indeed a peak of high renown, and to conquer it would call for mad daring, if indeed it could be conquered at all ... You might approach it, of course, by way of the Montenvers, the Mer de Glace, the seracs of the Géant and the immense and still almost unexplored snowfields that dominated them. And you could bivouac overnight in the bitter cold and set off again at dawn. But actually climbing that final rocky peak and reaching its summit – well, only a madman would hope to do it. The poet Malczewski had wanted to try in 1818, but he had to be content with a lesser peak. And now here came M. de Bouillé flinging himself into the venture ... Nine hundred feet of vertical granite, iced up in places, isolated among dreadful chasms! Avalanches of stones fell around the lunatics making the attempt. The party had to stop twenty-four metres short of the summit. Alone and charged with an impossible mission, two guides, Alexandre Devouassoud and Ambroise Simond, set out on the final assault. They were lost from their companions' view for a long time, and they returned trembling and pale as death. They had planted the proud and seditious fleur-de-lys flag which was the expedition's emblem on the mountain summit, but never, they said, never again as long as they lived would they retrace their steps along the perilous way they had just taken, not for all the riches in the world. That incredible conquest had been made once, and once for all ...

Coming down was even more difficult and dangerous than going up. From Tacul, two of the guides left the group and went ahead to carry the

Midday-Midnight 22

amazing news down to the valley. Thanks to these messengers, Chamonix prepared M. de Bouillé the reception and the honours his victory warranted. As soon as the little party entered the town it was welcomed with alternating fanfares and salvoes of cannon fire. Over fifteen hundred tourists staying in the town formed a guard of honour, shouting acclamations and throwing flowers. A triumphal arch had been improvised outside the Count's hotel, and when he stepped under it a wreath dropped on his head. Oh, the glory of that moment! The intoxication of success! The sense of having succeeded in an impossible task! The heroes of the hour could be heard endlessly recounting that they had shown what they could do, but nothing would induce them to try such a venture again. The chief guide handed the valiant conqueror a certificate testifying to the first ascent of the awesome Aiguille du Midi.

'I doubt if there will ever be a second,' said the Count, gravely.

Emotion had given M. de Bouillé a good appetite. He dined heartily on cream of mushroom soup, river trout, a chaudfroid of chicken and a mulberry tart, washing his meal down, perhaps a little too copiously, with a delicious white wine from Yvorne. And as he ate and drank he never ceased telling anyone who cared to listen how remote, pure and fierce the mountain was, and how the wind at such high altitudes had whistled wildly in the ears of the bold men risking their lives in those sidereal spaces.

Was it the excitement of victory, or had M. de Bouillé partaken overlavishly of the Yvorne wine? Be that as it may, on going to bed to sleep the sleep of the just, and having indeed plunged into leaden slumber, he had a frightful nightmare ...

The Aiguille du Midi, his beautiful, stern and noble mountain, had fallen prey to a grotesque carnival of swarming humanity. People came crowding in from all quarters, pushing and shouting as if they were at a fun-fair. Metal cables running from the mountain to the valley continued on their way towards Italy. Those cables might look thread-like in the immensity of the landscape, but they disfigured it as much as one small blister would have changed the face of the Mona Lisa. It was a terrible thing to see. Painted boxes were travelling up and down these cables, crammed with passengers who surged out like an animal tide spreading round the summit, which was now crowned by a kind of gigantic artillery shell. The place was as full of holes as a Swiss cheese, and plastered with footbridges, cement walls, stickily floored corridors, barriers, guard rails, ticket offices, ladders, hooks, ropes, platforms, poles, pulleys, girders, rubbish bins, cigarette butts, refuse and all manner of general detritus. Depending where you were, you breathed in the unattractive odours of urine or burnt cooking fat. People were selling soft drinks, hot dogs, chocolate, chips, gherkins, stamps, badges, decorated souvenir plates, spoons, hats, wood carvings, pipes and stuffed toy marmots. And there was an incessant background noise, from which you could pick out all the silly remarks of which human folly is capable.

'And then you pickle it in vinegar for twenty-four hours ... Oh, here we are!'

'Oo-er! It's ever so scary!'

'You get your money back if there's fog.'

'Hey, Dad, which is Mont Blanc?'

'Bloody hell, what a drop!'

'Oh, what a dear little doggie!'

'I needn't bother to look. My hubby takes very good pictures. I'd rather look at those when we get home.'

'Gissa smile for the birdie!'

'Don't be frightened, love!'

'Wow, is this worth the ticket price!'

'Stop howling like that or I'll smack your bottom!'

'Gary, tell Sharon to come and look at this!'

'See those guys there? Bet you they get stuck in that crevasse.'

'Who's got the tickets?'

'Keep in line like everyone else, can't you?'

And the crowd, perpetually ebbing and flowing, continued to spread, the people in it jostling one another, wallowing in the sun on the terraces, arguing over chairs, tramping down the corridors. The Aiguille du Midi was not a proud peak any more: it was a sewer, a cesspool, a mountain prostituted ...

M. de Bouillé woke with a start, drenched in sweat, nausea rising within him. It took him a moment to pull himself together. Then he groped for his tinderbox, struck a spark and lit the candle. His bedroom was calm and silent, and there was nothing to be heard but the regular ticking of his gold watch, whose hands pointed to midnight. Throwing back his sheets, he rose and went barefoot to the window. Above the quiet valley, plunged in the depths of night, the Aiguille du Midi, still pure and wild, rose against the wide blue sky studded with stars ...

Thank God! Thank God for that! Comte Fernand de Bouillé had only been having a nightmare.

SNOWBALL

The train was due in at the Gare de Lyon at quarter past seven. Or rather, since the language of today thinks it elegant to employ terminology which should properly be confined to a railway timetable but which can fairly be used here with reference to a train, at nineteen hours sixteen precisely.

Christian Paucourt had feared he would be late, but in fact he reached the station a good ten minutes early. He killed time by wandering around the station concourse, glancing idly at the flashy displays in gift shop windows, reading the newspaper headlines from the stand at the kiosk, and above all by alternately consulting the arrivals and departures display and the large round clock with blue roman numerals which once used to mark the long-awaited moment of his departure on holiday. The train he was meeting, due to arrive at platform J, was from Vintimille. Christian listened to the loudspeaker announcements. He heard the dull rumble of the engines, the ringing of bells, the noise from the crowd, the honking of the electric trucks weaving their way around the concourse. He watched all the comings and goings of passengers arriving or getting ready to leave, wheeling suitcases, lugging bags and parcels. He went over to look at the high-speed trains standing side by side, five orange muzzles flanked by large red eyes. Finally he went back to the end of the platform and soon, at the far end of the station, at the very end of the tracks, he saw two yellow lights slowly approaching through the dark.

The train stopped. Passing the engine and the mail van, Christian walked a few steps against the current of the first passengers getting out. He recognized the graceful figure of Sabine from some way off. She was wearing a quilted jacket and large black earrings. A few seconds later she was in his arms.

'Hello, darling!' he said affectionately.

'Hi! It's great to see you, Dad! Where's Mum?'

'There's a case that's been worrying her; she was getting a second opinion this evening. She phoned to say she might be kept quite late at the hospital. So here's the plan: I take you out to dinner in a restaurant somewhere, and she should be home when we get there. How does that sound?'

'Fine.'

'Travelling light, I see. Still, give me your bag.'

'It hardly weighs a thing!'

'Never mind, let me take it. Had a good journey?'

'Yes, excellent. I took the through train from Cagnes-sur-Mer. It's slower, but changing at Nice would have been more of a bother. So I brought stuff to pass the time – work, a good book – and it didn't seem long at all. I'm ravenous, though! All I had for lunch was a sandwich I made before I left. You know what train food's like – not what it used to be! Isn't that what you're supposed to say when you're getting old?'

'Old, aged twenty-three? Yes, sure, your vast experience of life makes you a judge of these things! So how's Cagnes?'

'Fine. I'm doing very well. The job's interesting, and as I was saying on the phone, the studio flat you saw in September is all fitted out now. I'm painting the bathroom at the moment. As you see, leaving home wasn't too big a break, and here I am back in Paris for forty-eight hours! I'll be leaving by the night train on Sunday evening. I might try travelling by air next time. And I hope you and Mum will come and see me in Cagnes.'

As they talked, father and daughter had reached the esplanade outside the Gare de Lyon.

'Well, what would you like to do now?' asked Christian Paucourt. 'Any preferences?'

'None at all! It's good to see Paris again.'

'Would you like to dine somewhere near here? It's still early, though. We could go on into the Latin Quarter.'

'Good idea! The Latin Quarter!'

'Right, then, Metro or bus? Or do we embark on the great adventure of trying to find a taxi in this beautiful capital of ours? Alternatively, we could walk. It's quite mild for this time of year.'

'Let's walk. I've been sitting down all day.'

'Come on, then!'

Sabine and Christian walked down the Boulevard Diderot, still exchanging news, and came out on the Quai de la Rapée to cross the Pont d'Austerlitz.

'You know,' said Christian, 'whenever I walk this way, not that I do so very often, there's an old memory that always comes back to me. Silly, really. I wonder why some things stay in the mind and any number of others, maybe much more important, are entirely forgotten. This must have happened over forty years ago. How time flies! And now I don't even really remember where the hot-air vents in the pavement are around here.'

'What about them?'

'Well, one evening, a very long time ago, I was on my way back from Bleau, where I'd been spending the weekend with my friends. Of course you know Bleau – the rocks in the forest of Fontainebleau. But you wouldn't have any idea how much the place meant to us in those days. We had no cars, of course, so we used to go out to Bois-le-Roi by train on Saturdays, and then it was still an hour's stiff walk to Cuvier and our bivouac.'

'What bivouac was that?'

'Well, originally we just dossed down under a large overhanging slab of sandstone. But we did a good deal of work on the place, fitting it out, making screens of branches and foliage at the sides to keep the weather out. We dug, levelled the ground and then covered it with a good thick layer of dry heather. How can I explain? Well, uncomfortable as of course it was, it was our palace, our kingdom, our own home – maybe more so than the homes where we lived with our parents.'

'Robinson Crusoe's hut?'

'Very likely! Vulnerable to enemy attack, too! You weren't allowed to make bivouacs like that in the woods, you see, and every now and then the forest ranger would wreck the place. His name was Marcellin. We knew him quite well; we sometimes went for a drink with him. As for our wrecked bivouac, well, after the first shock we set about rebuilding it even better. That was the game, and a great game too.'

'You've never told me so much about your young days before, Dad.'

'There are a great many things I haven't told you, my dear Sabine.'

'So what were you up to at the time, apart from making and remaking your bivouac?'

'Oh, we only had to do that from time to time. Well, we lived like prehistoric men for twenty-four hours a week – like savages. It was wonderful! We went out to Bleau in all weathers, rain, wind or snow. In heatwaves and in hard frosts. I once woke up on a winter morning to find the wine frozen in our mugs.'

'Oh, stop it, Dad, you'll make me cry! This is pathetic! Sounds like the retreat from Moscow!'

'I told you you wouldn't understand. Right, let's come back to the present … here we have a choice. Would you rather go up one of the streets beside the Jardin des Plantes or along the Seine?'

'The Seine!'

Snowball

'Good idea. It's no fun walking along those streets lined with laboratories. Let's go along the quays. Where was I? Oh yes, you'd have had to know that period to understand what it was like. A world all our own, you see, all ours! Of course we spent most of our time training on the blocs. We were all mad about climbing. Then on Sunday evenings we retraced our steps almost at a run, back into the forest to reach Bois-le-Roi and catch the train back to the Gare de Lyon.'

'I still don't see what any of this has to do with the hot-air vents.'

'Oh, that was just a minor detail that reminded me of all the rest. Well, one winter evening I was on my way home from the station with one of our gang called Snowball.'

'Called what?'

'A nickname. I'll explain later. We came to the Quai de la Rapée, and Snowball made what seemed to me a really weird remark. Something that would never have entered my own mind, and I still don't know why he said it. Out of some kind of spirit of provocation? Or was it only a joke? Well, anyway, back then, and we were only about twenty, he said, "I'm going to start noticing where the hot-air vents are. You have to think of everything. I mean, I might end up sleeping rough." I was astonished. Every time I go that way I remember what he said. Perhaps you will too, now I've told you about it, so maybe you yourself will associate the place with a few chance works spoken in the early fifties.'

'I might well. But what an odd thing to say! Who was this Snowball? And why was that his nickname?'

'To tell you the truth ... well, you'll think this strange, but despite belonging to the same gang, we didn't really know very much about each other. I don't think we ever talked about what we'd been doing during the week, or what our parents did. We simply weren't interested. We had this other life all to ourselves, away from the rest of the world. We were a bunch of friends, and we never really knew just how we'd come together. So-and-so would bring along someone else, having met him heaven knows where. From doing a route together in summer, or maybe working in the same factory, or in a lecture theatre. We didn't know each others' addresses either. In fact we hardly knew our friends' surnames, let alone their first names. Nicknames were the in thing at that time, both in Bleau and in the climbing world. For instance, my nickname was Pelvoux because apparently when I joined the group I kept on and on about Mont Pelvoux in Oisans. I'd climbed it the summer before.'

'What a funny name! I didn't know any of this.'

'Well, I shouldn't think most people know what their parents really cared about. Not boring you, am I?'

'Not a bit, Pelvoux! I can't wait to hear the rest.'

'I rather think this nickname business involved us even more in a world of our own, a world that non-initiates, known to us as Matthieus or Philistines, couldn't enter. Not that there was anything systematic about the nicknames. They happened naturally or not at all. I can tell you some ... wait a minute while I remember. There was Biscante, Bullion, Three Picks, Ten Sacks, the Baron, Minus, Poince, Old Man, Fat Man, Flower, Roc-Grépon, Young Dog, Stone Marten, Wasp, Chough, Bear Cub ...'

'Good heavens, what a menagerie!'

'There were so many of us ... Farine, Shrimp, Titine and Titi, Big Zig and Little Zig, Moumou, Exo, the Fireman, the Greek, the Mick, Big Boy, Pipo, Zato, Blériot, Toto. Not forgetting the Minets – Tall, Medium and Little Minet. And then there was Cube, Fat Paul, Little Claude, Little Pastrycook, Pin-up, Slow Death, Crazy, Rookie, Bumpkin ... I could go on and on!'

'And Snowball?'

'And Snowball. As far as I know his nickname had nothing, of course, to do with his appearance. It came from his way of skiing, straight on, always falling and getting up covered with snow. His real name was Jean-Sébastien. Some of us got to know each other better later on, as adults, when we went to spend holidays in Chamonix with our wives and then our children too. Others died in climbing accidents, often very tragically. Some just seemed to disappear into the unknown. A few of us went on climbing, and then gradually that tailed off too. I suppose I'm still in touch with only three or four people from that period. Real friends. The others mattered only because they were part of the whole scene, which did give them the indispensable cachet of belonging to the group.'

'It's those nicknames amaze me. What happens to *me* is I find I don't know some people's surnames. So I list them by first names in my address book.'

'Well, that's an original way of doing it!'

'But all those nicknames! You obviously really *did* have your own very private scene!'

'We did indeed. It's a long time ago now. But what I meant to explain is how we could spend every Sunday together like that in the forest of Fontainebleau, or sometimes at Saussois, without ever thinking who we were or what we did in ordinary life.'

'So what did you discuss?'

'Climbing, of course! What do you think we discussed? Climbing, climbing and more climbing. It was our only interest, and more or less every conversation revolved around it ... our last holidays, our next holidays, the climbs and routes we were planning, the grading systems, the angle of the slopes, slab climbing techniques, a ski tour some of us were thinking of doing at Christmas. All sorts of things. Oh, and gear. Footwear, rock-climbing boots, new kinds of soles, anoraks. The comparative advantages of moleskin and tweed. The latest model of hard fuel stove. Where you could get duvets cleaned. Sun creams. Sacks with or without carrying frames. Powdered drinks ... oh, we never ran short of subjects of conversation!'

'Excuse my saying so, but it all sounds very austere.'

'Then I haven't explained it properly. You see, we were fascinated by the whole game, so naturally we found all its aspects fascinating too. We laughed a lot too, I can't remember what at now, but as I remember it we never stopped laughing. Oh yes, I do remember one time when we made an omelette coming back in the last carriage of the train ... no, it's no use, I couldn't explain what was so funny about that. There's nothing more subjective than laughter. It just erupts at a given time in a given atmosphere. Perhaps if I could see us again today I wouldn't think we were quite so funny! I've an idea people's standards change as they grow older. But at the time, you'll have to take my word for it, we were all kindred spirits and we thought ourselves incredibly witty.'

'Okay, then, I *will* take your word for it!'

'Here, let's cross the street and go on up the Rue de la Montagne-Sainte-Geneviève. Well ... how can I explain what amused us? For instance, when we were climbing at Cuvier we called ourselves the Cuvier Academic Club. Funny? And we had our own classifications for climbers. The worst were the Bumblies, the few really good ones were the Pure Rock Luminaries, with an intermediate stage called the Resin Hopefuls. I can't remember the names for the other grades. We ran a magazine off on a duplicator; it was called *Le Bleausard*. And then we played Cave –'

'You played what?'

'Cave. Now and then one of us would chuck something up in the air, anything: an empty can, a boot, a clump of heather attached to a clod of earth, and shout, "Cave!" to warn the others. You had to look up and see what was about to come down and where, and try to get out of the firing line.'

'I see.'

'No, you don't! It's no good, I can't explain. Never mind.'

'I do have one question, though. How did you get in touch with each other if you didn't exchange names and addresses?'

'Well, maybe I was a bit sweeping there. I'm sure we did know some names and addresses. A number of us, including me, were on the phone, which wasn't nearly as common then as it is now. And I forgot to tell you we also met every Thursday evening at the Club Alpin in the Rue La Boétie, where we planned our destination and timetable and everything else for the next weekend's outing. Our Thursday evening meetings weren't just a necessity, they were something of a ritual, and they broke up the monotony of the week by bringing us together automatically; we didn't need to fix an actual date. I think that was how we got to know Snowball. He'd advertised for a climbing partner, one of us got in touch with him, and he joined our gang.'

'And apart from that you never knew anything about him? He must have been a pretty peculiar character, looking out for hot-air vents with the idea that he might have to sleep rough, when he was still only twenty!'

'Oh, I did learn more about him, gradually. One day, for instance, I had to go to Snowball's home to pick up some equipment I'd lent him, because I needed it back. His family lived in Belleville, in a little fifth-floor flat with no lift. As far as I remember it was a very modest, ordinary, spotlessly clean little place. Comfortable and homely, anyway. I've no idea why Snowball said that about the hot-air vents. Perhaps he already sensed some instability in himself.'

'Did he have a job?'

'Yes. I've an idea he was an industrial draughtsman in an office at the time, something of that kind. His parents lived in modest circumstances and had their only son late in life. They thought he was the eighth wonder of the world, although they took a critical view of his climbing. Nothing very unusual there, you'll agree. Something that amuses me is remembering how surprised we sometimes were to find out what someone did for a living. The chap who looked like a student was actually a bricklayer. And the big brute who swarmed up the overhangs so easily and might have been a worker in the Renault car factory turned out to be an intellectual with a father who was a lawyer in the sixteenth arrondissement, with two maids in white aprons to look after him at home. But as I told you, these social distinctions just didn't interest us. We couldn't have cared less about the class struggle.'

'And what about Snowball?'

'He intrigues you, doesn't he?'

'He fascinates me. What was he like? Nice? Good-looking? Intelligent?'

'Good heavens, what a lot of questions! First, I should say he was never one of my really close friends, although I did know him for quite a long time. Nice? Yes, I think so. Remembering that people have different likings, and he was only one friend among many. Quite amusing, rather scatty. Good-looking? I suppose so. Quite tall, well-built, regular features, curly brown hair, blue eyes, a smile always hovering around the corners of his mouth. Yes, I suppose he was good-looking. I've never been able to work out why some men appeal to women so much, but he was one of them, anyway.'

'Intelligent?'

'Well, he certainly had a lively mind and a quick grasp of things – but what exactly do we mean by intelligent? I have a theory that really intelligent people do something useful or original sooner or later, and that was not the case with Snowball. He wasn't stupid, but you couldn't say he was really, brilliantly intelligent. No, about average.'

'Good at climbing?'

'Again, quite good, that's all. Altogether, you know, with a few exceptions we weren't aces. He was reasonable, but he adored climbing, he lived for it.'

'And were you good?'

'Not bad, I must admit. More gifted than he was, but less methodical about it. I didn't train so hard. I enjoyed my studies, loved music, the theatre, the cinema, no end of things. Although that didn't stop me climbing a great deal.'

'So why did you stop?'

'For the usual reasons, my dear! Gradually. I met Danielle, I mean Mum. I married her. You children were born, you and your brothers. I still went climbing during the first few years of our marriage, but a moment comes when you realize you have to stop taking risks. And God knows I did take risks! Then there's your professional life. And that's it ... Well, you still go skiing, maybe climb a bit on Sundays, but you give up real climbing and all that means. You have to make choices.'

'And your ungrateful children have no idea what sacrifices their parents have made for them! Until one day they find out by chance, like me this evening.'

'Well, that's life, and it's unusual for sacrifices, as you call them, not to bring their own sources of satisfaction. Bringing up a daughter like you isn't such a bad achievement. Will that do for a compliment? Ah, here we are. I think there's a fish restaurant opposite the old Ecole Polytechnique. How about that?'

'That'll be fine, Dad. Sorry, Pelvoux!'

And laughing at this, that and the other, father and daughter went into the restaurant and were given a table in a corner of the bay window. Sabine patted the pink tablecloth, smiling.

'Pretty cloth!' she said. 'Pretty plates, too, and proper napkins, not those horrid paper squares you find everywhere. This is nice.'

They were handed the menu. 'Would you like a drink first?' asked the proprietress.

Sabine and Christian declined the offer, and concentrated on the menu for a moment or so.

'Made up your mind?' asked Christian.

'I'll have the menu of the day,' said Sabine. 'It looks good. I'll start with sliced avocado and cockles, and then I'll have the fillet of sea trout with herb butter. I'll think about dessert later.'

'I'll have the same starter, and then the skate with caper butter. It all sounds appetizing. What about wine? Any preferences?'

'I love white Sancerre.'

'They're sure to have some. Okay, let's order. Close your menu to show them we've finished choosing.'

The proprietress came back, and they ordered their meal.

'But you don't wriggle out of it like that, you know!' Sabine told her father.

'What do you mean?'

'I mean we're not through yet. You started a story, so you've got to finish it. I want to know all about Snowball – well, as much about him as possible.'

'Goodness, what enthusiasm! I can at least be glad the two of you didn't belong to the same generation. You'd have been besotted with him, and heaven knows …'

'It's not enthusiasm, just curiosity. I mean, here's someone I didn't even know existed until an hour ago, but I'm intrigued by his character and I want to find out everything about him.'

'I'm afraid you'll be rather disappointed.'

'Never mind that, carry on! Ah, here comes our wine. Taste it and let them serve us, and *then* carry on.'

But Christian did not carry on immediately. Tapping one finger thoughtfully on the tablecloth, looking into the distance, he was gathering fragments of memory together. Their first course had arrived by the time he was ready take up his tale again.

'Well,' he said, 'yes, Snowball had a job when I met him, but he dropped it to try and get a degree in I forget what. In fact he never finished because his climbing came first. He passed the probationary and full guides' courses. He didn't do brilliantly, but he still qualified, so he was able to guide in summer. Freelancing, of course, since he wasn't a local man. He was too undisciplined to join any organization like the UNCM of that time. So he went looking for clients, hung around hotel bars, struck up conversations, and tried to make use of the few connections he had. To my mind he was never a very reliable guide. Pleasant company but a bit disorganized; he didn't inspire you with the same confidence in the mountains as the tough locals who hauled their clients up like an ox pulling a plough, straight along the furrow with an absolutely earthbound sense of security. Snowball had intellectual and artistic aspirations. Some people might like that, some might not, but on the whole he did all right. He spent the winter in Paris. I think he worked in a number of different firms, always changing because he wanted to leave for an extendable weekend, for a ski tour, for some vague plan for a winter climb, for a dash down to the Calanques. I've known a number of people like that, with nothing in their heads but climbing, and they're seldom really successful.'

'Can't people do more than one thing? I mean, it's perfectly usual to have an ordinary life and enjoy sport too.'

'Climbing's different. First, it's much more than just a sport. And second, it means always moving around the place. So one day Snowball decided to leave Paris and settle in the Alps. I met his mother around then. I don't quite remember why. Some material I had to return, I think. She was highly upset, furious. She laid into me. To listen to her you'd have thought everyone in the climbing world was responsible. Her Jean-Sébastien would have had such a brilliant career if he'd stuck to it, and now he'd gone off for some precarious existence in the mountains, living on he himself didn't know what, risking broken bones more than ever. "Do you really think that's a good idea, Monsieur? You people are the only ones he'll listen to, can't you make him see sense …?" Phew! I had difficulty making my escape.'

'So he left to live in the mountains?'

'Yes, of course. He wasn't the first or the last to do so. He lived from hand to mouth, working as a guide in summer, doing this, that and the other the rest of the time. Working on ski tours, as a salesman in sports shops, washing dishes in restaurants. He was never a good enough skier to become an instructor. I rather lost touch with him; I'd stayed in Paris, and it was around then that I married. But we went on spending our holidays in Chamonix for quite a while, and so I used to see him there. Then news got around that Snowball was married too. He settled down to some extent, but his wife had to go on working full time to keep them. She was a plump little brunette, rather nondescript. Why her, after all the conquests he'd made? It was a mystery. Anyway, he seemed very much in love with her, and they had two children. All very commonplace, don't you think, this part of my story?'

'Yes, it is. I'm a bit disappointed. You started by telling me about this young man, who I'm sure was very handsome, amusing, full of great plans, the really adventurous sort. I was imagining him brimming over with energy and wild ideas. Not so? And then your story turns into a boring recital of everyday events.'

'If only you knew how often that happens! I told you just now, didn't I, that I've only kept up with four or five of my friends from those days? Not because I didn't want to, but because you can't really spend time with people who don't interest you just to keep memories alive.'

'So that's the end of your story?'

'No, in this particular case, it isn't, because there were two or maybe three catastrophic events in Snowball's life. Of course there are crises in every human existence, but perhaps they shake someone living outside the usual framework of society more than the rest of us. And a person's own nature is part of it too. Ah, here comes our main course. Shall I fill you up?'

'The fillet of trout for Mademoiselle?'

'Yes, and the skate for me. Thank you … Three catastrophes, I said; well, I'll run over them briefly. The first was the result of a mistake, mere carelessness, if you like, but it had serious consequences. Snowball wasn't a ski instructor, but he skied correctly, and as a guide he had the right to take anyone he liked up into the mountains at any time of year. This particular accident happened at Easter, during a ski tour, but that wasn't really the point. The thing is that as so often, Snowball didn't think hard enough, and this time there were problems. He was accompanying a group in Oisans, and decided to cross the pass of the Clot des Cavales, which he knew in summer, when it's easy, you can use it like a road. In winter, however, it's a high avalanche risk. He hadn't done his homework properly, or consulted the guides, and he was relying only on memory. So he failed in his professional duty. The party set out from the Châtelleret Hut, got quite high up in deteriorating conditions, and then found itself split up and starting to panic. They couldn't make it over the pass. The slope was steep, the snow was fresh and very unstable. They had to risk a retreat and try and get back down. And they set off an avalanche that swept part of the group away. Three people died, including the girl-friend or fiancée of a Chamonix guide, which did Snowball's reputation no good. Anyway, the business caused quite a stir. People didn't go to court as readily as they do these days. You were regarded as responsible for taking your own risks, and there were no grounds to sue, although that was not the point. And no doubt, although it may not appear on the outside, anyone responsible for such an accident will always be seriously affected by it.'

'So I should think! It's not a very pleasant story.'

'I know Snowball's wife felt it particularly keenly. You see, when she married him she thought he was some kind of mountaineering genius: brilliant, hugely gifted. Particularly as he liked showing off to the ladies, and she had no way of really judging him. In the past he'd dazzled her, and now all of a sudden he'd lost his prestige. That wasn't all, of course; after a few years, love wears thin if there's nothing more solid to shore it up. Their marriage wasn't going well. She didn't like having to work and bring up the children while, as she saw it, her husband took things easy. And Snowball can't have done anything to improve matters. I can imagine it: he comes home from a climb, exhausted, gets bawled out, which is no fun, so off he goes to spend the evening somewhere else.'

'Dad, your story is getting very sad, you know.'

'You wanted to hear it, so I'm going to finish it, sad as it may be. Not finding any of the warmth he had a right to expect in his home, Snowball more or less deserted it. He was always short of money, but he still seemed cheerful, as if he hadn't a care in the world, and he chased women worse than ever. Between you and me, it appears that his wife also looked for consolation in various quarters, if more discreetly. The children, who were growing up, openly took their mother's side. She was the one who looked after them, she worked extremely hard, and she didn't mince her words about "that useless Jean-Sébastien". It must have hurt him, because he'd been very fond indeed of the children. Was it around then he began drinking rather more than he should have done? I expect so. I remember meeting him in the street in Chamonix around then, and he dragged me off to a café, speaking in what struck me as a slurred voice. Sure enough, I soon realized he was dead drunk. He couldn't even remember my name. "You *are* Sialouze, aren't you?" he said. "Sialouze, right? You aren't? Sorry, got the wrong mountain. Funny thing, that, getting the wrong mountain! So who are you if you aren't Sialouze? Oh yes, Pelvoux! Of course, Pelvoux! Anyway, you know I like you, right, Pelvoux? Got a long, long, *long*-standing friendship with you. For ever and ever, you know that? You know what a good friend I am?" Well, you get the general idea. A painful scene, but what could I do? I succeeded in getting away from his maudlin affection, but it was an embarrassing incident.'

'Was he like that all the time, then?'

'Fortunately, no! He was still working, more or less, thinking up ideas he hoped would turn out marvellous, although they usually came to nothing. He did contribute to his family's budget, if only in part, but he had really taken to the bottle. Well, the second disaster I mentioned was because, through friends, he'd actually found quite an interesting job. It was in connection with some minor expedition to the Himalayas, with a descent by hang-gliders or skis. This was around the time when sporting stunts began to take off, encouraged by the media. As a qualified guide, Snowball was brought in as a travel courier or assistant or something, anyway one of the team. He was away for two months or more. When he got back he found his house empty. His wife had met a Brazilian. The love of her life, and rather more exotic than Snowball. And the Brazilian had taken them as a job lot, the wife with the children thrown in. They'd all flown off to South America. What's the use of bringing legal proceedings if you're penniless, and much of the fault is yours anyway? Not that the law is much of a help in personal matters anyway. I wouldn't say the Brazilian had been the crucial factor: something of the kind was bound to happen. However, when families break up it's not usually in quite such a drastic way. One of the children may sometimes be kind enough to get in touch with the father later, take an interest in him, even become part of his life. But in this case the break was complete. You know, Sabine, I wasn't thinking about all this when we came to the Pont d'Austerlitz and I began telling you about the remark Snowball once made. Of course I knew the background and the end of the story, but I wasn't dwelling on it as much as I am now. It was your questions that led me into this long account of a disaster … Well, have you chosen your dessert yet? They're coming for our order.'

'What are the baked apples like?'

'Delicious, Mademoiselle, stuffed with walnuts, almonds and raisins.'

'Then I'll have a baked apple.'

'And you, sir?'

'I'll have the same, please ... No doubt you realize, Sabine, that we hold our lives in our own hands. Every action we take matters. Every choice we make for good or ill. Every small act of cowardice or negligence. And at the end of the day, a full life and what may be called happiness depends on whether we gave way or held firm.'

'Yes, I do realize it, listening to your story of one man's life. But what do you think Snowball *ought* to have done?'

'History can't be rewritten. I just think he ought to have pulled himself together. He had a summer job as a guide. Some people do pretty well that way if they take it seriously enough. He could have worked hard to become a ski instructor. He could have looked for a different, permanent job, as a decorator, a mechanic, whatever. No one would have thought it beneath him, far from it. But he always took life as it came, carelessly, making choices only in the light of what gave him most pleasure at the time. And that, surely, is a mistake.'

'Yes, I agree. But you mentioned a third disaster.'

'Correct, and he wasn't at all prepared to deal with it. It happened a little later ... because, you see, there's one thing that can't be denied about the hero of this evening's story, and to my mind it's a great virtue: he really loved climbing. He didn't confuse it with money, he never tired of it as so many other people do, and he was perfectly happy to set out on a climb as an amateur. Well, he was planning a winter climb with a youngster – I don't know where, and anyway it doesn't matter. I expect part of it was a desire to show people he was still good for something. Personal motivation is seldom straightforward. And by the same token, his aims were rather too ambitious. I don't remember the precise details, but anyway, Snowball was leading when he slipped and fell on to the belay ledge, breaking an ankle or a knee, I forget which. Badly, though: bones, tendons, everything. The young man who was with him went for help, and he was lucky to get down alone without mishap, but by then it was dark. No helicopter could go out until next day. Since Snowball had expected them to finish the climb within the day he'd decided to go light and take no bivouac gear. Yet it was winter, freezing. The night was bitterly cold. His leg got frostbite as well as the broken bones. The result was several operations and an infection which lingered on, so that Snowball had to spend weeks or even months in hospital. He recovered, but he was in no state to climb.'

'And you think that was his fault?'

'Not exactly. I don't know. Accidents also involve luck. It's unusual for a climber never to have an accident in the whole length of his career, especially if he's a professional, out and about on the mountains all the time. It would probably have happened sooner or later. But Snowball was over forty-five, and he knew no other profession. That again is nothing unusual. Many other people have had similar setbacks. But in a purely physical job, a bad accident is a real, final handicap. And when you have no back-up it's a disaster, apart from the fact that insurance, compensation, pensions and so on are either tiny or non-existent.'

'I see.'

'Snowball stayed in the Alps for a while and then decided to go back to Paris and his widowed mother, who was getting old. She gave him lodging and found him a job, which he didn't keep long. His mother was drawing her retirement pension and, luckily for her, was in rent-controlled accommodation, fixed in 1948, and almost as good as no rent at all. But Snowball was embittered and difficult to get on with. He was drinking, of course. And he wasn't the kind of person to pull himself together when things went wrong.'

'Did you ever see him again?'

'Yes, as it happens. I don't often have any business at the Club Alpin, but I once needed some documentation when I was going to Nepal with your mother – you remember? So I went to the Rue La Boétie one Thursday evening, when it was open late, and I saw Snowball there. He was unshaven, not too clean, and he smelt of booze. I asked him, tactfully, of course, if I could help him in any way, but he simply avoided the question. According to him everything was fine, and he on the point of getting a very interesting job. I sensed what he needed: he wanted to be treated as an equal, just like the old days. We went for a drink together, and I talked about the past ... Bleau, our memories, our youth, that omelette in the last compartment of the train, all the silly things we did. He was happy for an hour, back with me in our adolescence when the whole future still lay ahead of us all. It was awful to see that man, virtually a wreck, coming back to life with the memory of his younger days. These things are never really entirely lost, you know. We always remember how it felt to be successful, alive, triumphant at some point in our lives. I can't believe that it simply dissolves into nothing – the flame must go on burning somewhere. Anyhow, that's enough philosophy! Here's the bill.'

Sabine remained thoughtful. 'Have you heard anything of him since?'

'Oh, yes. Things didn't work out. How could they? When his mother died he either couldn't or wouldn't keep on her flat. He was on the way down ... ah, here's my change. Put your jacket on; Mum will be expecting us. We'll take the Metro to Monge.'

'Wouldn't it be quicker to go to Cardinal-Lemoine?'

'It comes to the same thing. Let's go.'

A few minutes later, father and daughter were emerging into the Place de la Contrescarpe, which they had to cross. Sabine stopped, and smiled.

'Look – how pretty!' she said. 'Four trees, two street lights, a clock, a fountain, that's all, but it gives the square real charm.'

'You're forgetting the buildings around it,' Christian pointed out. 'They're old, eroded and all different, but they go well together. They have a soul. Imagine them replaced by post-war tower blocks, and in spite of your four trees and two street lights it would look like a Moscow suburb. The making of this place is the complex of shapes and sizes, as complicated as something human, not programmed by a computer.'

Near the centre of the Place de la Contrescarpe there is a hot-air vent where pigeons sometimes go in winter to warm their little feet. That evening the pigeons had been ousted by three down-and-outs who were lying there among an assortment of packages, plastic bags and bottles. On seeing Christian and Sabine approaching, one of them sat up.

'Evening, ladies and gents!' he belched. 'Got any change?'

Christian stopped and looked in his wallet, took out a note and slipped it into the drunk's hand.

'Thanks, mate!' muttered the latter in a slurred voice. 'You're a real pal!'

A little further on, Sabine expressed her astonishment. 'Well, you're feeling lavish tonight, Dad. Five hundred francs! He'll drink it all. Was it because you were remembering Snowball?'

'Good heavens, Sabine, didn't you understand? That was him. That was Snowball.'

GINGERMOON

The most dazzling of dream creatures trying to hitch a lift at the most judiciously chosen spot could not have induced Thierry to interrupt his journey. Or anyway, so he thought. After a sleepless night, weary as he was after a climb linking the North Face of Bionnassay to the traverse of Mont Blanc, he wanted nothing but to get straight back to his room at Vallorcine, take a shower and lie down on his bed, a carafe of chilled water within reach. But when he saw the wretched old woman he hesitated. In doing so he drove at least another fifty metres past the poor old soul. Admittedly, she had stationed herself at the worst possible spot, just where a driver emerged from the Bois du Bouchet after the big bend. You wouldn't see her until you drew level, and once you had wondered whether or not to give her a lift she'd be far behind you. However, the young man's heart was touched by his brief glimpse of this bit of human flotsam, standing gloomily in the oppressive late afternoon sunlight beside the stony causeway where wormwood and dusty thistles grew. The way she looked, he thought, standing in such a bad position, unattractive in appearance and surrounded by an assortment of baskets and packages as she wearily raised her thumb in the air, no one was ever going to give her a lift. And here he was on his way back from the mountains, young, happy, healthy and full of life – wasn't it his duty to help this miserable specimen of helplessness and decay?

By the time Thierry had pursued this rapid train of thought and then braked the car he was past the Arveyron bridge, a tricky place to start reversing, especially as other cars kept coming up behind him. He would have been glad to see the old lady take a few steps in his direction and catch up with him a little further from the bend. However, she did not budge, but merely watched his manoeuvres with a critical eye.

He finally came back level with her. Leaning over to his right, he opened the passenger door and shifted his rucksack and ice-axe to the back seat.

'Where am I supposed to put my things, then?' asked the old lady sourly. 'On my feet?'

Thierry sighed, and saw that he would have to get out. He put his own gear in the boot to make room on the back seat for his companion's impedimenta.

'Careful! That's fragile!' she snapped. 'And there's a chicken in the cage, so don't put those plastic bags on top of it!'

Fleeting as Thierry's first impression had been, it was accurate. There was absolutely nothing to be said in this old lady's favour. She was lame, bony and bad-tempered. Her wrinkled face, enhanced by a pointed nose and reddened, watery eyes, was not improved by the grizzled moustache bristling above her thin lips. A few lank locks of hair tumbled down her cheeks, escaping an ancient turban of an intractably dingy yellow colour. A slight smell of rancid olive oil wafting around this decrepit creature added nothing to her charms. All the same, thought Thierry, at least the pill wouldn't have been so bitter if she'd shown some trace of gratitude towards her benefactor ... but gratitude was obviously out of the question!

'About time too!' she grumbled as Thierry got back behind the wheel and she seated herself beside him. 'Half an hour I've been waiting, and not one of those oafs stopped. I counted a hundred and fifty-nine cars. Incredible! You're all the same, you young folk today! No respect for your elders! No education!'

Thierry gave a start. He did not try pointing out that she was directing her complaint at the one driver who had taken pity on her. His one idea was to get rid of her, fast.

'Where are you going?' he asked brusquely.

'Up above Argentière,' said the old woman. 'I'll show you the way. But I'll ask you to go round by Les Tines first, if that's no trouble. Well, it won't be any trouble. I shan't be a minute. I've a friend there who's keeping me a lettuce. Hurry up, do! I'm late. Your car's nothing to write home about, is it? Just my luck!'

Thierry stared down the road straight ahead. What a bloody fool he was to let himself be imposed on like this! Come to think of it, people were always telling him he was so kind-hearted it made him a real sucker. 'You'd let anyone take you in!' Well, they were right, and here was the proof of it.

He glanced at his companion with some annoyance. Her cross face showed nothing but dissatisfaction and contempt, but her eyes were keen as a hawk's beneath their dark lids.

'Turn left for Les Tines after the crossing,' she told him.

Thierry turned left – what else could he do? – and stopped where he was told to stop.

'How does this wretched door of yours open?' grumbled the old woman. 'Can't manage it with my poor rheumatic shoulder, can I?'

Thierry got out and opened the door for her. This old biddy was a walking nightmare. Ten minutes earlier he had still been in the cheerful mood engendered in him by his climb. His cheerfulness was all gone now. Mixing with other people again after a climbing trip is often a let-down, but it's not usually as bad as this!

The old lady came back, clutching a lettuce wrapped in newspaper to her chest. Without a word, she gave him a sour look which he instantly interpreted. He did not wait for the sharp remark which would surely follow, but made haste to open the door for her again. Then, back behind the wheel, he started the car and made his laborious way along the bends of La Poya, while the old lady took up her discourse where she had left off.

'What a car! I didn't even know any of these old 2 CVs were still on the road. And to think I was waiting for something like *this* to come along! It's always the same. People don't stop these days when they see a woman by the roadside. Nobody knows how to treat a lady now. I'm not saying everything was perfect in the past, but these days all the young men are just bone idle. They think of nothing but themselves. All they're fit for is going on holiday or drawing the dole. Louts, the lot of them! On holiday, are you?'

'No,' said Thierry.

'Unemployed, then?'

'No,' he apologized, humbly.

'Well, you're a climber anyway. You needn't pretend you aren't. I noticed your equipment. Climbing's plain stupid. All it does is risk the lives of folk in the rescue services. I hope you're not proud of yourself … here, don't go accelerating like that! With suspension like yours you'll have all my bags over. I told you, there's fragile stuff in there! But of course you don't pay any attention. Not my fault if I came upon a car like yours, is it? I'd sooner have had a nice big powerful engine, believe you me! Hey, don't slow down like that either! Are you doing all this just to annoy me, or what?'

Only the fact that it would be dangerous to stop on this winding road prevented Thierry from bringing his good deed to a precipitate conclusion and throwing the chicken, the old lady, her packages and all out of the car. But even when he reached the top of the slope he did not feel brave enough to stop, remove the bags and baskets and eject their owner amidst the inevitable torrent of indignant remarks. It was best to stick it out. Since he'd been fool enough to let himself in for this venture, he'd just have to see it through to the bitter end. His friends were right, though. He was too kind-hearted.

A small, worried cluck was heard from the back of the car, and an unpleasant smell filled the interior.

'That was the chicken,' announced the old biddy, evincing an ill-timed propensity for pointing out the obvious.

Thierry wound up the bottom of his window. A few seconds later it fell back, painfully, on his elbow.

Finally they reached Argentière. 'Where can I drop you off?' he asked.

'You can go on. Turn right for Montroc,' commanded the old lady.

'I'm sorry, Madame, but I'm turning left for Vallorcine myself,' Thierry protested.

'Do as I tell you and don't argue. You'd never have the heart to leave me by the side of the road with all these things, not when I'm nearly home.'

Unfortunately, she was right. He really never would have the heart. And having come so far, he might as well go on.

'But I'm not actually going to Montroc,' she continued. 'Go under the railway bridge and then turn right at once for Le Planet.'

He took the road the old lady indicated, but after about two hundred metres she made him stop and pointed to a stony little track climbing uphill to the left.

'I'll never get up there!' he exclaimed. 'It's steep and narrow and full of potholes.'

'Other people get up it,' she retorted. 'Anyway, the great thing about a car like yours is it doesn't have much to lose. I'm saying this in your own interests, you know. You'll go faster by car than on foot, helping me with all this stuff.'

The Citroën climbed the slope with a great deal of jolting. It seemed to Thierry an incredibly long way: the path was full of ruts and stones and brambles grew beside it, their spiny shoots scraping the carriagework with unpleasant scratching sounds.

Finally they came within sight of a hovel overhanging the path, built of cob and old planks. Resigned to anything now, Thierry helped his passenger to get out, extract her bags and baskets, and then carry them to the opening of a dark passage which plunged into the depths of the cottage.

'And while you're here – ' said the old lady – 'well, it would be a shame for you to come all this way for nothing – while you're here, take the ladder and fix that bit of tin on the roof. There's a leak, and you can see I'm not young enough for such acrobatics any more.'

'Now look here – ' Thierry began, determined to show some spirit this time.

'There, there, my boy! Don't make yourself out worse than you are! I've sized you up, I have, and I know you won't leave me with that leaky roof. So take the ladder, I tell you. All lads your age are more or less handy. Anyway, you won't be any more ham-fisted than the next man.'

The repair took some time, and when Thierry came back down he was in a very bad temper.

The old lady, however, gave him a kindlier glance. There seemed to be a small ironic light in her eyes, and her withered lips sketched a smile.

'I may not look like the part,' she announced, 'but I'm a fairy. That's right, no need to look so surprised. I said: I'm a fairy. And it so happens you have behaved to me correctly. Correctly is all, but it's no good expecting too much these days. So tell me what I can do to show my gratitude.'

'Oh, good Lord, nothing!' Thierry hastened to assure her, in considerable distress. 'Absolutely nothing! What can I say? The pleasure was entirely mine!'

'Oh, come along! You must have some reward,' continued the old lady in benevolent tones. 'I mean, I'm making you an offer! Think about it. A little wish, surely? Just one little wish.'

'No, really, nothing,' insisted Thierry, swallowing hard. 'The fact is, I'm in rather a hurry. I'll be on my way.'

'Then surely you'll have a little drink?' she offered with an amiability that struck Thierry as profoundly suspect. 'A little glass of my alchemilla wine? Or my bitter mandragora liqueur, no less than fifteen years old?'

The young man saw the menace of some ghastly magic potion looming ahead. He looked to make sure his car was still there.

'For goodness' sake, don't be so nervous! I haven't summoned a dragon to eat your car! Well, if you don't want to make a wish, and you won't have a drink, I hope at least you'll let me give you a little souvenir?'

Thierry mopped his brow as the old lady disappeared into the darkness of her home. She came back with a wooden-handled knife, the kind of folding pocket-knife known as an opinel, but the handle was an almost shiny emerald green instead of the usual yellow. Thierry dared not refuse to take it. He murmured his thanks, slipping it into his pocket under the old lady's amused gaze. Then he said a hasty goodbye and drove away as fast as possible.

Gingermoon 46

He forgot the incident, or he thought he forgot it. The knife he had been given went right out of his mind, for he had left it in the pocket of the red salopettes he was wearing that day, and he hadn't needed them again. He and his usual climbing partner Bernard devoted themselves to straightforward rock climbs during the remaining weeks of the season, and Thierry dressed to suit those conditions. Then September came. Bernard went on holiday to the south of France with his wife, while Thierry decided to make the most of the last few fine days to do one or two solo climbs. However, he was not particularly keen on climbing difficult rock without the security of a partner. So why not go for the big mountains in the lovely early autumn light? Then, when some neighbours came back from the Norman-Neruda on the North Face of the Lyskamm, enthusing about the conditions they had found, how could he resist having a go himself? Next Saturday Thierry packed his sack for an ice route at altitude; he put on his red salopettes, took his best Koflachs and set off in his little 2 CV to tackle the Forclaz pass. After driving up the Rhône and Visp valleys he parked his car at Täsch, took the train to Zermatt, went some of the way on the Gornergrat railway and slept at the Bétemps Hut that evening.

He set off along the track through the boulders above the hut with a carefree step in the early hours of the morning, but when he came to tackle the glacier he felt he had not thought quite enough about what was involved in climbing a major snow route alone. Of course he would not have cared to venture on a difficult rock climb unaccompanied either, but he had underestimated the pitfalls of the Valais mountains, and soon found himself lost in a maze of crevasses. Well, he thought, it was too late to go back now. Once he had completed the approach, with all the requisite circumspection, it would be a straightforward face climb followed by a good ridge. The game was worth the candle.

He took his time, making his way through the vast, icy labyrinth, sometimes with considerable difficulty. The Lyskamm was a long way off, and the scale of the terrain surprised him. When Thierry finally came out below the bergschrund the sun had long since risen, but he expected to make rapid progress on the face itself, and allowed himself a rest. His breakfast was some hours in the past now, and most likely he would not have another opportunity to stop for any length of time before reaching the summit. He opened his sack, took out his thermos of tea, some bread, sausage and cheese, and then found, to his annoyance, that he had left his knife in the car. Luckily he remembered the old lady's opinel, which he had found at the bottom of his pocket the evening before. He used it and began eating hungrily. An alpine chough was strutting about nearby. Thierry threw a sausage skin its way. The chough seized upon this booty, swallowed it with evident pleasure, came even closer and said, 'You called me, master?'

'What?' exclaimed Thierry, almost choking with astonishment.

'You called me, master?' the chough repeated.

Thierry sat up very straight, coughed, and opened his eyes. He must be hallucinating.

'I'm here to take your orders, master,' the chough explained. 'Don't you remember? The fairy Gingermoon put me at your service.'

'I just do not believe this!' muttered Thierry.

'Did you want something, master?' the chough enquired patiently.

'Oh, get lost!' shouted Thierry.

Evidently this first wish of his was granted. At least, the chough disappeared from sight.

Thierry hurriedly put the knife back in his pocket, not even daring to look at it. He made haste to finish his meal, and within a few minutes he felt sure he had been dreaming.

'The memory of that old biddy is getting me down,' he reflected. 'Good heavens – she was such a pain in the arse it only takes a sleepless night, solitude and the prospect of a north face ahead, and the thought of her sends me round the bend. This won't do! I didn't think I was quite so impressionable. Okay, it looks as if I can get over the bergschrund easily enough to the right, and then I'll be on the Norman-Neruda.'

Thierry was so fit that he did indeed make easy progress over the steep snow slopes, which were followed by a rocky rib with reasonable mixed climbing. Hour after hour passed by. The sense of exposure grew. Thierry felt intense enjoyment of his solitary climb at high altitude amidst such wild beauty. He was almost surprised to notice suddenly that the sky was clouding over, but it did not really worry him. In the haste of his departure he had not paid much attention to the weather forecast; the weather had been excellent for several days now, and when fine weather has held for some time you tend to assume it will last. Anyway, Thierry was a natural optimist, not given to dire forebodings. Surely the weather would hold as long as he needed. The task immediately ahead of him was to climb, and that was what he did.

The face was certainly larger, higher and more complex than he had gathered rather too rapidly from the guide book. But all went well, and he was climbing smoothly when a new section of the route started to pose problems. Thierry found himself at the bottom of a steep bulge several metres high which, because of the altitude and its exposure, was covered with rime. Thierry could not see what lay above it. On the other hand, there seemed to be an obvious solution to his problem in the form of a traverse over to the left, in the direction of a rock ridge which looked easier. He would have to take a few steps across the ice to reach the traverse, but he had anticipated such a contingency and had brought a stout 30 m rope which provided him with the means of self-protection. Within a few moments he had fixed a nut in a good crack, passed the rope through a karabiner and fastened the two ends to his harness. Abandoning the equipment would cost money, but speed and safety are beyond price. When he was fifteen metres higher up, or less, he would detach one end of the rope and pull it through, as in a rappel.

It was a good thing Thierry had taken such precautions. He did not fall, but as he was traversing the ice one of his crampons skated, and he only just saved himself, using his axes. He managed to get across to the rock ridge to reach a good belay several metres further on. He was now hanging on a fairly comfortable sort of spike, from where he could see that a delicate ramp led to easier ground. All he had to do was pull the rope through. Thierry undid one end, and began gently taking the other in, coiling it as it came with a sense of satisfaction in both his handling of the situation and the prospect of finishing the climb soon. But suddenly everything jammed. Thierry swore. He tried playing the rope, carefully at first, then yanking at it and finally tugging it in despair. It had caught somewhere on the other side of the rock ridge. He shook the end he still had, making the rope undulate. He tried to free it with a casting movement; he tried pulling hard. Nothing worked. He would either have to abandon the rope and cross the last few exposed metres unprotected, or else, still unprotected, try to return across the rocks to where the rope was stuck. Both alternatives were equally dangerous and unappealing, with a fall of hundreds of metres below him. Thierry felt horribly alone, and shivered with apprehension.

It was then that a third possibility occurred to him. Glancing surreptitiously around, as if someone might mock the eccentric course of action he had decided on, he slipped his hand into his pocket, took out the little green-handled knife and opened it.

'You called me, master?' croaked the chough.

'Good God!' said Thierry, stunned by surprise despite himself.

'What are your orders, master?' enquired the chough.

'Free that end of the rope for me,' Thierry stammered.

The chough disappeared behind the rock ridge, and silence fell over the mountains again. Thierry could not help thinking he had imagined it all, even when the rope suddenly went slack and he was able to pull it in without further difficulty.

The rest was easy. He had only a few metres of awkward rising traverse ahead. Thierry climbed them with the aid of a new belay and then, rebelayed from above, lowered himself to recover his gear. Ahead of him now there was only a firm slope of frozen snow in which his crampons gripped perfectly. The summit was not far off, but the weather was certainly deteriorating. The wind blew over the arêtes, and hailstones were beginning to whirl in the grey sky.

It took Thierry perhaps no more than half an hour to climb the final slope leading to the summit ridge, but when he got there the sky to the west was full of dark clouds, visibility was greatly reduced, and it was beginning to snow in earnest. He had to get down the mountain, and fast. Bad weather at four thousand five hundred metres is no joke, particularly when you hardly know the area and you're on your own. At first his route was obvious, since he had only to follow the arête going down eastwards, but it would not be easy to see the formidable double cornices said to be found here all the way down. And then what? Would he find a track coming from Monte Rosa to help him negotiate the great snowfields and crevasses of the Grenz Glacier, or would any such track already be buried under a layer of powder snow? Then what would happen? Thierry knew that the difference of altitude between his present position and the hut was seventeen hundred metres, and he had several kilometres of difficult going ahead of him. He felt the situation was close to disastrous.

With his back to the wind, he took some swift refreshment, for he was going to need all his strength. Then he set off, battling through the storm, trying to crampon on the slope below the arête itself, testing the solidity of the ground beneath his feet at almost every step. It seemed to go on for ever. Far from dying down, the storm was getting worse and worse. A real blizzard was sweeping over the mountains. Thierry struggled frantically on. His face was crusted with ice and his limbs numb with cold. He could no longer hope to get to the hut this evening, but at least he wanted to reach the end of the interminable line of the summit ridge. Then he would shelter for the night in some hole or crevasse and wait for morning, when the weather might be better. But he could not stop where he was, so he had to continue making his exhausting way forward, step by step, in an inferno of ice and wind. And suddenly, as if things were not bad enough already, the worst happened. Thierry felt one of his legs go through the crust of a cornice, and in his efforts to recover himself the other went through as well. There was nothing but empty space below. He could stay where he was only by lying on his stomach, his left arm clutching the axe still fixed in a kind of snowdrift – but for how much longer? Then, before he fell, he had one last idea. He pulled the frozen glove off his right hand with his teeth, moved his hand towards his pocket, got hold of the little green-handled knife and managed to open it, but his numb fingers let the knife drop, and it was swallowed up in the snow of the north face. Never mind, the chough was there.

'You need me, master?' it enquired in its obsequious tones.

'Can't you see I do?' cried Thierry.

'May I ask what you wish for at present?'

'Oh, I wish I was nice and warm, and home in bed!' sobbed Thierry.

Putting out his hand, he touched his hot-water bottle. It really was hot, boiling hot. He threw it on the floor. He might have been in a furnace. He pushed his quilt back too. As he did so he realized he was falling asleep and dreaming, while he was actually in a very dangerous situation on the ridges of the Lyskamm. Determined to do something, he gave a sudden start, almost fell, and clutched the side of his mattress. No, obviously he had been wrong. He was at home all right, having a nightmare about climbing a north face! But his legs were as weary as if he really had spent a long day climbing. He stretched, snuggled voluptuously down between the sheets, and fell asleep.

Next morning he woke with a perfectly clear head and entertained himself by rehearsing the amazing details of his imaginary adventure. Then he got out of bed, and was surprised to see his clothes, his climbing equipment and his sack strewn about the bedroom floor. That did make him stop and think. Could he possibly have climbed the North Face of the Lyskamm yesterday, coming back so tired that he had forgotten all the circumstances of his descent and his return home? It was an odd but plausible notion, and disconcerting. Either he had or he had not been climbing, and he must find out which. Thierry's education had inculcated in him a very positive, even positivist attitude which ruled out any phenomenological approach to the complexity of the world. Only the strictly rational would satisfy him, and he was irritated by the present situation. Admitting the possible existence of a supernatural being was more than his mental structures could cope with, and the idea that a climb he seemed to have made was associated in his memory with such preposterous details as a talking chough, sent to rescue him by a fairy called Gingermoon who had hitched a lift with him in the Bois du Bouchet – no, that really was too much! The whole thing must be cleared up in a proper Cartesian way, and now!

He opened his shutters, expecting to see the car parked under his window as usual, a heap of old scrap metal furnishing him, in its material solidity, with clear proof that he had simply forgotten his journey home. The car was not there.

Thierry had the day at his disposal. He took the first train to Martigny and changed at Visp for Täsch. And at Täsch, in a car park now wet with rain, he found his little 2 CV patiently waiting for him. The ticket he had left under the seat showed he had parked it there the day before yesterday. He got behind the wheel and drove back, but instead of stopping when he got home he passed the Col des Montets, turned towards Argentière, turned off again for Montroc, and after the railway bridge turned right towards Le Planet, keeping an eye open for the steep track up to the old woman's cottage. But he saw nothing anywhere. He stopped the car and set about examining the road in detail, on foot. Roughly where he thought he remembered turning up the track there was nothing but a small clearing among the larches, an ordinary picnic place surrounded by large blocks of stone, with a green rubbish bin. That was all. There quite definitely was no path. But tall willow-herb grew there, with purple pods emerging from their surrounding down, and red-berried rowan trees. The larch wood rose above the clearing, and fine drizzle was falling over the whole area. Thierry explored it for a long time without finding anything.

What was the use of looking any longer? He went home, trying to persuade himself it had all been a dream. He wondered if this was how people began losing their minds. Did he need psychiatric treatment?

He got home just in time to welcome his friend Georges, coming up from Les Houches with an electric drill for him.

'I've been trying to ring you for the last three days,' said Georges, 'but there was no answer. Been climbing?'

'Er … yes and no,' Thierry cautiously replied.

'Where did you go?' asked Georges, without noticing the inanity of this reply.

'Um … well … the North Face of the Lyskamm.'

'Congratulations! Good climb?'

'Yes, quite … well, there was bad weather near the summit,' said Thierry evasively, not wishing to dwell on the subject. 'What about you? How are you these days? You look a bit worried.'

'Oh, it's nothing really,' said Georges, half smiling. 'I was thinking of something that just happened to me – I feel I acted like a bit of a bastard.'

'You, Georges?' Thierry protested. 'You'll never get me to believe that!'

'It wasn't much, to be honest,' said Georges, 'but somehow I can't get it out of my mind. Just now, driving up here, I came to the bend in the Bois du Bouchet, before you reach Les Praz, and I saw this poor old woman thumbing a lift. Ancient and dowdy and surrounded by bags and carriers and cages and wicker baskets. And the rain was pouring down. Well, you know me – I'm more likely to give a pretty girl a lift, and in good weather too. The poor old soul made me hesitate, but she was standing at just the wrong spot. I was past her before I really knew it, and then I went on driving. That's all, but it does bother me a bit. She must still be there, raising her poor thumb without any real hope of a lift. A picture of helplessness. That's life, I know, but I feel I ought to have stopped. Or even gone on a bit, turned and come back for her. I could have done a good deed for once, for free.'

'Nothing,' Thierry interrupted him brusquely, 'nothing in this world is ever for free!'

DARKNESS AND THE AZURE

It was that time of day when a new dawn was rising over the Alps in the cool of the night's end. Imperceptibly, the stars were flickering out. It was not yet day, but the first hint of light cast a deep azure glow over the velvet, snow-covered slopes rising to the confines of the sky.

At the same moment, elsewhere, everyday life was starting.

In Rio the last revellers, mouths dry from too much cachaxa, were on their way back to their hotels in taxis, their doors carefully locked, that did not stop at the red lights for fear of being attacked.

In Istanbul, Islamic fundamentalists were leaving a parcel bomb at the home of a professor known to be a supporter of human rights. As this was not their first such attempt, they felt sure that in the end their methods would silence those who dared resist their law.

In Pivovarika, in the Siberian taiga, the three thousandth corpse was being exhumed from a Stalinist burial pit which still held a great many more.

Thousand of tons of toxic dust, emerging from the chimneys of refineries, cement works and many other industries, were falling on Mexico: nothing new in that.

Two men died in the Gaza Strip when the driver of a Palestinian coach deliberately rammed an Israeli car.

A military revolt broke out in the Philippines where a rebel colonel, accompanied by several hundred supporters, proclaimed a 'war of liberation' at Cayagan de Oro. Two T-28s were immediately dispatched to bomb the insurgents' positions.

On the Tokyo stock exchange the market was falling fast in response to the first financial exchanges of the day, and the Nikkei index had dropped 1,138 points, a downward movement of 4.82%, sinking to a new low which gave warning of major disturbances to the international economic equilibrium. Financial experts were concerned.

A Hamburg-born homosexual in his forties who, in search of fresh young flesh, had bought the favours of a young Tunisian boy in Hammamet for a handful of dinars, ended a night of debauchery by infecting him with AIDS.

In Medellin a dynamite charge placed on the ground floor of a building containing a secret laboratory for processing cocaine went off. The case involved reprisals between rival cartels competing for control of the New York market. The explosion blew up the whole building, killing eighteen people including six children, and injuring some forty others.

Peasants carrying a few personal effects were fleeing down a track in Cambodia, their village headman having just been assassinated by a Khmer Rouge commando unit in order to maintain an atmosphere of insecurity and terror.

Not far from Algiers, three journalists had their throats cut in their car.

In Cergy-Pontoise two gangs of black African immigrants known colloquially as 'Zulus' were facing each other, armed with knives and shotguns. There were some deaths, but the government preferred to ignore the matter, putting its mind instead to foreign policy and the manipulation of the electorate.

Some violent rocket firing by the Mujaheddin resulted in eleven dead and over thirty injured in the Kushal-Khan quarter of Kabul.

Off the Canadian coast, eight thousand tons of crude oil spilled from the tanks of an ancient tanker flying the Panamanian flag (and not equipped with a double hull).

Armed Tutsis crossed the Ugandan frontier to massacre their hereditary enemies in Rwanda, the Hutus.

Amid cries of terror, a vessel carrying boat people sank in the China Sea.

Not far from Chernobyl, in a wretched dispensary in the suburbs of Kiev, an eight-year-old child without eyebrows, lashes or hair and a severely ulcerated skin lost consciousness. Yet the same nuclear reactors continued to be used at Kursk, Leningrad and Smolensk, since an output of 50 GW had to be achieved as soon as possible.

In Melbourne, Wallace Bank Rumount Inc, the holding company of one of the largest international cement producers, made a takeover bid for Angus Cement Ltd (ACL), one of the four big Australian cement companies. Kirset, a subsidiary of WBR, was offering 4.85 Australian dollars per share and 5.60 dollars per convertible bond.

All over the earth, the ground was soaking up heavy metals, pesticides and nitrates. All over the earth, river water was being poisoned. All over the earth, forests were disappearing: burnt, cut down or destroyed by acid rain.

The world, in short, was going its usual way. The world as man has made it, as it serves his ambitions and desires, as he has ordered and arranged it, the world, indeed, as he wants it. Our world.

But while these tragic events were unfolding all over the globe, regarded as such everyday occurrences that to list them, far from emphasizing their drama, makes them seem ordinary, two climbers were setting out in the mountains in the small hours of the morning. Escaping for a few brief hours the omnipresence of world news with its jarring words and images, its prohibitions and regulations, its laws, its ministerial decrees, its responsibilities and restraints, its bureaucratic paperwork, its electioneering speeches, its traffic jams and carbon dioxide, its promiscuity, noise, queues and crowds, they were patiently climbing beneath the calm sky.

In the middle of the night they had torn themselves away from the warmth of their hard bunks, all that still linked them to the softer aspects of a universe which knows no values but comfort and facile pleasures. They had slept little, and with hesitant hands had folded the rough blankets which had kept them from the cold, almost reluctantly. Up at last, getting their gear ready by flickering candlelight, forcing themselves to drink bitter tea and eat biscuits which tasted insipid at this early hour, they had prepared to leave the hut.

Then they plunged themselves into the icy darkness of the mountains. The dark sky was framed by even darker peaks. Frost chiselled their expressionless faces and pinched their fingers under their mittens. As they moved, the pale halo of light cast by their head torches made glittering sequins sparkle at every step, only to fall back again behind them in the darkest, impenetrable opacity. From time to time a shooting star crossed the depths of the sky. The silence was absolute, apart from the faint crunch of crampons biting into the hard snow, which fell away down the slope with a rustle of silver.

Then the first faint hints of pale daylight began to drive away the dense darkness of night. The air was colder than ever in the chilly dawn, but the sky had lightened. The stars seemed to melt and disappear into a colourless landscape that slowly revealed itself. Before the day can break the night must die. Imperceptibly, twilight brought forth pallid shapes that gradually acquired a milky whiteness, while in the east the horizon blazed red, and here and there the sky glowed with a pure translucent green. Passes, crests and peaks assumed the clarity of alabaster. And finally, in a shower of gold, the sun rose.

The climbers had paused in their ascent to contemplate the splendour of the day, and for a moment they saw their shadows born and outlined on the snow like fragments of the sky. In the mountains, dawn is the time when shadows are an azure blue. In the glory of the rising sun, in the sparkling play of its rays, the climbers were high above everything. They had escaped the heavy darkness of the world which lay beneath their feet in the depths of the valleys and the plains.

Elsewhere, no doubt, sensible people were making sarcastic remarks about idiots who climbed mountains just to come down again, sometimes at the risk of their lives, and why they did it. The two climbers knew the answer to that. They were free, they were alone, they were filled with joy, dazzled with magnificence. They were richer, happier and luckier than all the potentates of the world.

Nothing existed for them now except a few crampon points, the rope linking them and the white damask carpet of snow on which the frost had left silky serrations. A sudden gust of wind raised slight scrolls of snow at ground level and whirlpools of gilded powder. Then all was calm again in the deep peace of the mountains.

They reached a sharp ridge and followed it. In the depths far below, the ridges, valleys and hollows stretched in blue planes until they were finally lost in a hazy infinity. Yet their route reached higher, towards some undefined end of the earth. Now they climbed along the flank of a vast cornice that seemed to resemble a petrified storm-tossed wave stretching to the skies. Drunk on the limpid light, vibrant all around them, drunk with the altitude, the clear air, the azure, they climbed on over pristine snow, as at the dawn of the world.

THE END OF THE SEASON

It was late when Mathieu Bullet stopped his car at the last bend in the road. He wedged a large stone under one tyre as a precaution; the stone was lying ready to hand, and must have been used for the same purpose quite recently. Then he took his sack out of the boot and hoisted it on to his shoulders with so practised a movement that you could detect hardly a trace of weariness in it. He did not check the contents. He wouldn't need anything up there, or hardly anything, but he would have felt strange without a sack. Walking at his usual strong, steady pace, he turned into the track which climbed upwards, through meadows at first.

By imperceptible degrees, the valley was taking on autumnal hues. A russet aura clung to the landscape, although the leaves had not actually turned red yet. The grass had its late autumn colour, and the tufts of willow-herb standing here and there, their flowers faded weeks ago, were only dry stalks with purplish pods opening to show seeds embedded as if in cotton-wool. Although it was late in the year the weather was still warm, almost sultry. The clear ring of cow-bells sounded through the air now and then. A train went past down below, the rattle of its carriages shattering the afternoon tranquillity. Then calm returned, an even deeper calm than before. The hamlet above which Mathieu had left his car was bathed in the slanting rays of the sun. Great luminous clouds hovered motionless above the Aiguilles, their rocky silhouettes standing out clear-cut against the pale sky, and far away, towards the massif, the setting sun cast golden reflections high up on the north faces that emerged from their shadowy isolation only for these few moments at this time of the year.

When Mathieu entered the forest he noticed the fresh scent rising from the undergrowth, a smell of damp earth and mushrooms. He decided it was too late to leave the path now, but perhaps he might take time to look for chanterelles on his way back tomorrow. Some walkers out late greeted him on their way down, but no one else was going up, and he wondered if he ought to have given warning of his visit. Daniel might have closed the hut already for lack of customers at this season. But it was too late to check now, so Mathieu continued on his way. It wouldn't be the end of the world if he had to turn back in the dusk, or even spend the night on his own in a barn. It wouldn't be much fun, but that was all. The idea made him realize how glad he would be to see Daniel again. So few of the friends of his youth were left these days.

The End of the Season

Some midges, catching the light, danced like little dots of gold in the shade of the forest path. Mathieu automatically scrutinized the slopes in search of edible mushrooms the walkers might have missed, but there was nothing among the yellowing grass but a few clumps of heather, the tiny pale flowers of bird's foot trefoil, and the last harebells, their washed-out blue scarcely distinguishable in the dim light of the undergrowth.

At last the woods grew lighter and the larches and spruces thinned out, giving way to groups of hazel bushes, alders, and rowans with shiny bunches of orange berries. The path was now rising through red-tinged pastures obviously already touched by frost, with downy clumps of pulsatillas here and there. The rays of sunlight merged above the steep ridge that stood out against the sky. The shrill whistle of a marmot broke the silence.

Mathieu walked on for a while through this pastureland, until he saw the wooden slats roofing the hut beyond a small rise. Strictly speaking, it was not really an alpine hut at all, but a collection of disused old farm buildings that Daniel Grandson had converted for his guests, who tended to be walkers rather than climbers. The place was still natural and unspoilt, particularly at this time of year and in the evening. It retained a kind of rustic grace that had almost gone from the rest of the massif.

Daniel was chopping wood on a block outside the door of the hut. Aware of someone's presence, he straightened up, and waved with surprise and pleasure on recognizing Mathieu.

'Can I stay the night?' asked Mathieu. 'Claudine's parents arrived yesterday for a couple of days. They're all right, but rather too talkative for me. I bravely endured the first family dinner, but today I said I had business. They haven't come to see me, anyway, they've come to visit their daughter. So here I am.'

'Good to see you,' said Daniel. 'Whatever the reason, I'm glad you're here, particularly as I haven't seen you since last winter and since ... well, since Christophe's accident. I was going to write to you. I didn't, but I thought about you a great deal. You never know what to say at such times. And then Jenny's death ...'

'Oh, well, you know, it had been all over between us for so long, she might have been living in another world. We'd both of us rebuilt our separate lives. She lived miles away – in the Cévennes. I never saw her any more. I heard she'd been ill for a long time, and Christophe's accident must have hastened things. Apparently she survived her son by only three months, if that.'

'And how's Isabelle?' asked Daniel, anxious to bring the conversation back to less dangerous ground.

'Oh, Isabelle's fine!' replied Mathieu, with a faint smile. 'Did you know I'm a grandfather now? She had a little boy. He's a sturdy little lad – still in nappies, but a real character. None of this makes me feel any younger.'

'You're telling me! Me, I still like the solitary life. I feel like an old wolf who's left the pack. And after all my experiences, in love only with nature. Just look at that sunset!'

There was a view of the entire mountain range and the vast sky above from the doorway of the hut. The mountains were bathed in purple light, and the two friends stood there in silence, watching the flamboyant spectacle that marked the ending day. Slowly, the colours faded, the shadows deepened, and the pale snows merged once more with the ethereal hues of the firmament, making the whole scene a cameo of soft grey: blue-grey, pearly grey and tender grey in which earth and sky were united. What had been all contrast a few moments before – rock, ice, azure sky, brightness, blazing light, splendour – was now united in a vast symphony of monochrome hues. Night was falling peacefully, soundlessly. The sky grew dark, and for a moment the snowy peaks borrowed a tinge of white and gold from the last remnants of the light. The evening star twinkled above a ridge, and the breeze which had risen grew cooler.

'Let's go in,' said Daniel.

The buildings seemed to snuggle into the heart of the mountains as night fell. It was hard to distinguish the larch-wood doors from the rendered walls, so discoloured and softly patinated were they by sun, snow and rain. Lower down, the valleys were already plunged in shadow, while the high mountains seemed to float above them in a last clear, pink light. Daniel went through the doorway, flicked a cigarette lighter and lit a candle.

'You can see how quiet this place is,' he told Mathieu. 'If it's solitude you want, you're sure of it up here. I may not be able to offer an extensive menu, and the lodging's plain, but I know you won't mind. I think I have the makings of an omelette with lardons of bacon. Or wait a minute, I could do a fondue. That'd be warming. And I've got a bottle of Cortaillod just waiting for you to come and visit. Sit down while I see to it.'

'Can I do anything?' asked Mathieu.

'You must be joking. I've sometimes made dinner for twenty or thirty people at a time this summer. Gives me a sense of being useful. Here, sit by the hearth. I laid the fire just now and I only have to strike a match …

there, look at that fine, clear flame. You know, I always like to see a good fire burning in the evening. If you want something to do, you can glance through this little book. I bought it in spring – brought it up here for the season because I couldn't bear to be parted from it. It's a fictionalized account of the life of Marion de Lorme, said to have lived to the age of a hundred and thirty-four. I found it in a second-hand bookshop in Annecy.'

'You still have your passion for books, I see! I need my glasses ... wait a minute, they must be in the lid of my sack.'

'You need glasses too? Damn nuisance! You're always looking for them. When I think how good my eyesight used to be!'

'Mine too,' sighed Mathieu. 'And now I can't see anything close to me. My long-distance vision's not too good either. It's not just a nuisance, it's a real problem. When you're young you think only the very old need glasses, and I can't say I feel old.'

'Apart from your knees, maybe?'

'Apart from my knees sometimes!' Mathieu admitted, smiling. 'Ah, well, let's have a look at your book.'

The fire was crackling. Daniel lit three more candles stuck in small paint jars on the nearby table, and then disappeared into the kitchen. Mathieu turned the little book over in his hardened hands. It was a pretty edition, with a gilded coloured paper binding that glowed in the firelight. The place of publication claimed, no doubt falsely, to be London, and the date of publication 1780. Its text was as fantastic as anyone could desire. Daniel had always had a taste for books and stories. As an adolescent, when they were both beginning to climb, he was already searching flea markets and quay-side stalls. The loft in an old farm down in the valley that he had converted for use as his home in the winter months was groaning under the weight of second-hand books. Mathieu leafed through the little volume, reading scraps of text. 'I felt I was about to be delivered from my sufferings by weakness, slumber or death,' he read, 'when I thought I heard a dull sound. Although I had been on the point of giving up the ghost, that sound held my attention for a few moments. I summoned up what remained of my strength, and distinctly saw a light approach me ...' He smiled, and allowed his eyes to wander round the room.

Daniel had furnished the place attractively. The room was both welcoming and rustic: a large, knotted floor, tables of massive wood with pine benches, steep steps leading to the upper floor, small curtains in red and white check at the windows, a map of the massif on one wall, a panoramic view on another, old skis, a mirror with a frame painted to imitate marble, crampons from the early years of the century, old studded boots, sickles, planes, a coffee mill, bunches of heather and thistles in old stoneware jars. And shelves full of books! Mathieu got up to inspect their titles. They were an eclectic collection: Pagnol, Proust, Tolstoy, a treatise on astronomy, Corneille, Villon, Oscar Wilde, Bouillet's *Dictionnaire, La Cuisine de Tante Marie,* Jules Verne, the sermons of Massillon, Mme Riccoboni, a book on wild flowers, *Manon Lescaut, Premier de cordée, Le Miroir du coeur, La Source noire,* Sempé, Naudé, Musset, Daudet, Heidegger, Newman, Dorothy Sayers, Urs von Balthazar, Samivel, Simenon, St Augustine!

Mathieu returned to the hearth, took some logs from the pile neatly piled beside it and added them to the fire.

'All right?' called Daniel from the kitchen. 'The fondue's nearly ready; I'm just stirring it. You can get the plates and forks out if you like. I've cut the bread.'

A delicious smell of cheese and garlic was wafting through the room. Mathieu laid the table, uncorked the bottle and lit the spirit lamp ready for Daniel to put the fondue pan over it.

'Is there enough light from the fire and the candles?' he asked. 'I can start the generator if you like.' He pointed to the four white enamel hanging lamps with their glass mantles hanging from the beams of the ceiling. 'I light them when I have company,' he explained, 'but I make do with candlelight when I'm on my own. I'm used to it, and anyway I prefer it.'

'So do I,' Mathieu told him. 'I like the huge shadows it creates. We forget these things, with electricity – there's no mystery with electric light! Oh, clumsy of me, I've dropped my piece of bread into the fondue.'

They went on with their dinner in almost complete silence. Young people need to talk and exchange their impressions, comparing them and constructing their ideas. Old people go interminably on and on over the few memories still floating about their addled brains, infuriating those around them by the inanity of their constant repetitions. But there is an intermediate age when talk is unnecessary between old friends, particularly men. You know everything about each other; you have experienced life together, explored the world, shared enthusiasms, passions and dreams, you have constructed projects that you tend to forget when they succeeded, but remember all the more vividly if they failed. You have believed, hoped, acted and suffered together. You have known the same companions, many already dead. You have witnessed genuine disasters; you have seen evolution and change in a world of which you were once a part, a world you thought immutable. What's the point of discussing such things over and over again?

Daniel and Mathieu had reached the age where it is good to remain silent. What was there to discuss that they did not already know? It was chance, or almost chance, that had brought them together that evening, not a need to talk. They shared the memory of heroic ventures in adolescence, they shared an alpine world for which they had both left the city, and they shared the recollection of great hopes whose vanity they could now assess.

Mathieu had wanted to be a guide, and he was. His hopes had been realized, he did not regret it, and could have imagined no other existence, but it sometimes shook him to see that old friends who had followed more traditional paths seemed busier, more active, even younger than he was, and had many interests that the rather enclosed world of climbing had tended to suppress in him, although he thought he was the one who had chosen the more adventurous way of life.

As for Daniel, his ambitions had been different, less personal yet vaguer, more liberal and universal. He too had sacrificed everything in order to live in the Alps, but he had dreamed of bringing great plans to fruition there, projects that would have raised him far above the conventional life his parents had envisaged for him. He was in love with nature, and wanted to write, to paint, to create new and original works in contact with the physical world. But although he had never entirely relinquished such hopes, he knew it was too late now. He had lived from day to day, putting off what he most wanted to do until tomorrow, when he thought he could devote himself to it better. But for those who live in the present, tomorrow never comes, and he found himself rather tired, a little worn, cherishing no illusions about himself but no bitterness either.

The whole evening might have passed in this way, with hardly a word spoken. However, Daniel made an effort to break the silence, not wishing his friend to dwell too much on potentially melancholy thoughts. He gave him a drink and sought for a matter-of-fact question. 'Had a good season?'

'Oh, much the same as usual,' replied Mathieu. 'Anyway, the weather was good. I have regular clients, and there were some new ones this year. I'm not so keen as I was to do big routes, mixed routes. I'm going in for more rock climbing, the technical stuff – the Piola and Rémy brothers' routes; clients like that too, and everyone's rock climbing has improved. It's hard to say who's pushing who.'

'I heard you'd been to the Himalayas.'

'Yes, in late spring. I accompanied a trek to Nepal. I was offered a chance of getting out of the country for a while after Christophe's death – it was something of a necessity, really.'

Daniel bit his lip. This was the very subject he would have wished to avoid. But perhaps Mathieu needed to talk about it?

'You know how the accident happened?' Mathieu went on.

'Yes, just about everyone knew, more or less. We all felt terrible about it. A motor-bike accident, wasn't it?'

'That's right, and it wasn't Christophe's fault, though maybe he was going a bit fast. But he rode into a puddle of oil just before a bend, probably left by some heavy vehicle. Of course he was wearing a helmet; he was meticulous about such things. But that wasn't enough. He ... well, I'll spare you the details. At least he died instantly.'

'I'm sorry.'

'You know, you and I used to risk our lives when we were young, climbing as recklessly as we did, but we felt we were justified ... oh, what do I mean, justified? Our grandparents, perhaps even our parents, were ready to die too, but in their case for Alsace-Lorraine, for France and liberty, for I don't know what ideals, but something they believed in. Young people nowadays don't have such ideals – it seems to me they don't even have the mountains as we knew them in our day, vast, wild and distant, without helicopters always at the ready. What do we offer the young by way of ideals today? Do we expect them to die for some TV programme such as *Ushuaia*? Anyway, they like speed, anything that goes fast, and maybe it helps them forget the rest. They love steep slopes, jumping, falling, and they like motor bikes. With Christophe, it was motor bikes. His bad luck.'

Daniel didn't know what to say. Ideas came into his head, clumsy ideas that he hesitated to put into words for fear of opening the wound. He believed in survival, he believed there was a meaning in the world, but how could he say so to a grieving father? He resorted to expressions of sympathy.

'You know how much I loved Christophe,' he said.

And it was this remark, which he thought harmless enough, that suddenly plunged the evening into an atmosphere of drama unforeseen by either of the two friends.

Mathieu made a sudden movement and sat up straight, casting a sombre glance of obvious pain at his companion. 'Yes, indeed,' he said dryly.

He rose and went to poke the fire brusquely, raking the half-burnt logs and adding more. He knocked against the log-pile as he stared fixedly into the flames. Then, left arm leaning on the mantelpiece, his forehead on his arm, breathing hard, he went on tapping the glowing embers with the tongs he was holding in his right hand. With a last abrupt gesture, he finally made the fire collapse before turning round, features set and eyes hard.

'I'm probably being a fool,' he said. 'Anyway, you needn't think I came up with this idea in my head. It just comes over me all of a sudden. It hits me again, after so long. And now that he's dead …'

'What is it?' asked Daniel gently.

'What is it?' growled Mathieu. 'You and Jenny were in love, weren't you? Don't lie to me, whatever you do, don't lie!'

'Yes, we were,' admitted Daniel. He could not help lowering his eyes.

'And she was your mistress?'

'No,' protested Daniel. 'No, certainly not. I assure you she wasn't.'

'I wish I could believe you, but I can't.'

'This is stupid! If I'd known you were going to dig up ancient history when I arrived this evening … so ancient that it seems to me to have happened to someone else … and I welcomed you in without any ulterior motives.'

'Look, I came up without any ulterior motives myself, I told you – and then I just suddenly needed to know.'

'Know what? Why torment yourself? Jenny and you separated over ten years ago, maybe it was fifteen. She's dead. You told me yourself her death hardly affected you. And now you've just exhumed a story going back quarter of a century, something we never discussed.'

'It was better not to. I'd have hit you then, which I won't do this evening. What exactly was there between you?'

'Nothing. I told you.'

'You told me the two of you were in love. And she was my wife. If that's what you call nothing …'

'All right, I'll explain,' Daniel conceded. 'Though believe me, it's not something I feel happy about. At first, at the start, I didn't know she was your wife.'

'That's impossible.'

'It's perfectly possible. I knew you were married, but you'd married somewhere else, don't ask me where.'

'In the Dordogne, where my parents-in-law lived.'

'All right, but anyway I wasn't at the wedding. Then you were living in that chalet at the end of nowhere. I met you now and then, but I never set eyes on your wife. I knew you had a little girl. I expect I congratulated you, but I didn't see the child either. All our friends were beginning to have children, and babies aren't really in my line. So maybe three or four years passed.'

'Four.'

'Then you went off on another expedition. To South America, with clients, leaving Jenny on her own for several months.'

'Are you throwing that up at me? I had to earn us a living.'

'You'd probably have earned it if you hadn't gone away so often. The fact is that whenever you had an opportunity to travel, you took it, and in a way I could understand that. I was probably one of the few people who really could understand you. Climbing in the Andes, discovering almost virgin mountains, camping, leading a life of adventure is a far cry from hacking up routes you've done over and over again until you're sick of them – routes that were already crowded even then. It can't have been any fun for Jenny, young as she was, left alone with the child and all the domestic problems to deal with.'

'So you came to the rescue!'

'No, I didn't. I didn't know her. I was busy with my own affairs, and the mountains and my friends. So one day I was on a bistro terrace where half the tables were occupied by friends of mine. We were talking and laughing, and as it happens the butt of our jokes, or one of them, was Fat Claude. You remember Fat Claude? He *was* rather inclined to obesity, and worried about it more than was sensible – in fact he was bulimic. Well, so I announced that I'd thought of a good trick to play on him. I got the idea from an old book, something that happened maybe at the court of Louis XIV. To cut a long story short, the idea was to make sure he ate a very large dinner one evening, and then, while he was asleep, take in all his clothes a bit to see his reaction in the morning. Well, to help with this trick I needed women who could sew and were ready to stay up half the night altering clothes. One girl offered at once – Dominique, André Charlant's girlfriend. And then there was someone else, a girl I didn't know. At least, I thought she was only a girl. It was only later that I noticed she was wearing a ring with a stone that hid her wedding ring. She looked no more than a teenager. Her face struck me at once; she was like an Egyptian princess. That jet-black hair, those long, almond-shaped eyes, that sinuous, well-modelled mouth, ironic and tender …'

'Jenny, yes.'

'Well, yes, but how was I to know? I was pleased to have found my labour force, and delighted that the beautiful stranger was part of it. We conspired to get everything perfectly organized. I knew Jenny lived some distance away, but she was going to spend the night in question with friends. There was a spell of bad weather beginning, and everyone was down in the valley. We arranged our dinner, and the rain gave me an excuse to invite Fat Claude to leave his tent and stay with me in the dry. You know, he wasn't even surprised by my solicitude! So it all went as we'd planned. At dinner we kept filling our victim's plate and topping up his glass. Fat Claude ended the evening rather red in the face, and when the others pretended to be leaving he went to bed in the lean-to I'd given him. I don't know if you remember, but he could sleep like the dead. He was famous for it in the huts. So as soon as my man was asleep I went to pinch his clothes. All except his shoes, that is. Dominique and Jenny came back – we'd borrowed a sewing machine, and I helped out as best I could, mostly by unpicking the seams. His jeans and shirt were easy enough, but then there was a lined corduroy waistcoat! Dominique gave up at two in the morning, and I was left alone with Jenny. We were both caught up in the fun of playing the game cleverly and well – there was more than complicity between us. How can I put it? It was a current of feeling, a liking for each other. Perhaps it was already something more … I watched her labouring away at the sewing machine looking like an industrious little girl. I admired her. I wished the night would never end. The valley was asleep, the whole of the rest of the world seemed to be asleep, and I felt as if she and I were the only people left alive there in that brightly lit little room. We must have finished around four in the morning, and she left with a smile. We'd won our bet!'

'I suppose she didn't leave Isabelle alone, did she?'

'Of course not! She'd never have done that! I discovered later that her parents had arrived to stay at the chalet for a while, so that's why she came down the day I saw her in the café, and she could spend the night in town. The morning after our trick everyone came back around eight in the morning bringing any amount of croissants, and we made coffee. Suddenly in came Fat Claude, frantic, trussed up in his clothes, which were creaking with the strain. He couldn't even button his shirt! We managed to keep our faces straight for a while, listening with apparent concern to his exclamations of horror. As a practical joke it was a resounding success, and the story made its way all round the valley. I went on seeing Jenny, but it was only some days later that a friend mentioned the practical joke I'd played "with Bullet's wife". At first I didn't understand, but then I realized Jenny was married and you were her husband. Did that prevent me from seeing her? No, on the contrary. I envied you, I told myself you were a lucky man, and I just didn't see how you could stay away for so long when you had a wife like that. One day I went to your chalet – my excuse was that I'd found a thimble on my floor under a piece of furniture, although it wasn't really Jenny's. Her parents had just left, and I often went up to see her after that. There wasn't anything planned or premeditated about it. Well, you know what love's like. It just strikes, and I don't think there's anything you can do about it. You feel different. The whole world is different. I thought of nothing but Jenny. At first I think I just amused her, and then, gradually, things changed. We were both caught up in a whirlwind.'

Mathieu brought his fist down on the table.

'For heaven's sake, listen, will you?' said Daniel. 'I'm trying to explain. You asked me to! You want to know about it – well, I'm telling you. Just hear me out. We didn't even have to say anything to know how we felt. There was something in the air. It was obvious that we thought of nothing but each other, passionately, painfully, deliciously, madly. One evening I'd gone up to the chalet and we were out on the terrace after dinner, when Isabelle had been put to bed. I took Jenny's hand. She drew it away. I talked to her. Well, we both talked … about us, and about you. She said that whatever happened she would never be unfaithful to you. And she wouldn't leave you either, if only for Isabelle's sake. It was nothing to do with you, and there was no reason why you should suffer for it. I was happy and unhappy both at once. Amazed to hear her say that she loved me. Desperate because our passion couldn't lead anywhere, and I respected her wishes. Jenny wouldn't have been the woman she was if she hadn't been able behave well and keep lucid in such a situation. And lucid she was! What happened between the two of you after that came much later, and I have to tell you it was your fault. But it's true that I didn't stop seeing Jenny at the time. We were neither of us strong enough for that. Then one day you came back twenty-four hours earlier than expected.'

'And I found you in my house playing with my daughter!'

The End of the Season 68

'Perhaps she needed someone to play with her, poor little thing. I'd grown fond of her.'

'And then?'

'What do you mean, then? Then nothing! I visited less and less often. You didn't seem very pleased to see me, or even to see Jenny. And it was better to forget.'

'Is that all?'

'Of course that's all. I sometimes saw Jenny in the valley. She came down when she could. And one day she told me she was pregnant.'

'By me?'

'Of course by you! I thought it was just as well for the two of you to rebuild your life together in the end. How can you ask such a question? You surely didn't think …'

'Oh yes, Daniel, I did. I'm not that simple. You don't find a friend in your home when you come back from a long journey, and what's more you don't find your wife changed, different, sad, without asking questions – even if you daren't ask them directly for fear of ruining everything. I always suspected … and when Christophe was born it was almost worse. He never looked like anyone. Not me, not her, nor you, come to that.'

'How could you think such a thing?'

'How could I? I didn't go poking around. I always suspected, that's all. Look, I remember the first time you came to see him with a present, and that magnificent bunch of flowers for Jenny. I watched the two of you. Sometimes it went to my heart. And the idea that I'd never know … But he was such a lovely little boy. He adored me … and I loved him, Daniel, anyway. I was proud of him. I loved him like my own son, as if he really was my son. I even forgot my suspicions. I loved him.'

'But he *was* your son, my poor Mathieu, he was your son! And I never even guessed you had any doubts! It would have been so easy to set your mind at rest earlier. And so now it's me who has to tell you that it was your own son you lost!'

Silence fell again, in an atmosphere that was easier now. When Mathieu turned in for the night Daniel put out the candles, covered the fire, and went to his own room. Soon he was lying in bed. Passing his hand over his damp forehead, he asked himself:

'Did I sound convincing?'

STRANGE HAPPENINGS
From an idea by Marcel Ichac

If ever a man entirely lacked the spirit of adventure, that man was Léon Picarreau. The son of elderly and extremely meticulous parents, he had inherited their nature and their settled habits both genetically and through the education he received. From childhood, therefore, he was used to an existence that would have made a sheet of graph paper look wildly imaginative, and he never felt the need for any change. He observed the noisy activities of his fellow-pupils at school with cautious disapproval, anxious only to get home as soon as possible, back to the little third-floor flat where evening followed evening with tranquil regularity, with the little boy silently constructing symmetrical castles of building blocks, his father setting out games of patience, and his mother absorbed in re-reading the serial stories from her collections of the *Veillées de chaumières* and *Lisez-moi bleu*, which held no surprises for her. These were their only entertainments. Léon's parents distrusted the dark and germ-ridden promiscuity of cinemas, nor would they contemplate the bold venture of an outing in the country. But for reasons of health they took the same walk every Sunday afternoon. It invariably went past the town hall, round the square, along the boulevard lined with plane trees and past the back of the fire station. The tumultuous world could not impinge on the immutable serenity of such a life.

Adolescence did not trouble young Léon Picarreau at all. He soon followed his father into the administrative staff of the Ministry of Development and was content with his humdrum existence as an unassuming office worker. When his parents had left him for a possibly better but certainly no more tranquil world, he made it his business to adhere scrupulously to the rhythms of the life-style and running of the home he had inherited, observing the same respectful admiration as his late parents for the Henri III sideboard, the embossed leather chairs and the heavy beige velour curtains which the old upholsterer who fitted them had assured Mme Picarreau, his mother, would be very hard-wearing.

He did not even feel lonely. When he came back from the office on winter evenings, he would light an anthracite fire in the ancient stove and watch the flames flickering behind its mica panes, while on fine days he would lean over the balcony in idle meditation, watching the traffic and the peaceful perambulations of passers by. He never deviated from the ritual of the Sunday walk, which always provided such small incidents as the lopping of a tree, a change to a shop's display window or the mending of a pavement. But he knew that he would come home to the comfort of his roomy carpet slippers and the reassuring certitudes of an evening guaranteed to contain no surprises, during which he would play the games of patience his father had taught him or re-read a few chapters by Mathilde Alanic or René Boylesve.

As his retirement approached, Léon Picarreau contemplated the event with the placidity of a man who has never been troubled by distressingly aggressive feelings or the traumatic effect on his contemporaries of being constantly bombarded with media information. Yet a major source of emotion was reserved for this period of his life. In recognition of his many years of conscientious devotion to the good cause of administrative development his colleagues, perhaps moved by some obscure sense of mischievousness towards a companion whose routine and habits they knew all too well, decided to club together and give him a magnificent colour television set.

This item aroused dual and contradictory feelings in its new proprietor: gratitude for the esteem in which he had obviously been held, and dismay at the upheaval the intrusion of so large a rectangular object of such audaciously modern shape was bound to introduce into the never-changing internal decoration of the Picarreau home. But it must be allowed in. He had to move the sideboard and put the little hall table beside it, after clearing it of several small containers that had always stood there and had nowhere else to go. He also had to accept the installation of an aerial, with a white lead that stood out against the grey sitting-room wallpaper. Some of the ministry staff came in to lend a hand the evening it was delivered, and Léon Picarreau opened the bottle of sparkling wine he had bought for the occasion. After that, all the others went home, and the recipient of their gift was left alone with the strange object, filled with uneasiness as he contemplated its dumb and sombre presence, not to mention the avalanche of shapes and colours which he suspected it was about to disgorge. Resolutely turning his back on it, he tried to play a game of patience, and felt that a watchful adversary was counting up all his omissions and mistakes. It was even worse when he tried reading; the silent monster just above his shoulder insidiously spied on every line of his book. Léon Picarreau went to bed early and did not sleep well, which was unusual for him. Next evening he made an abrupt decision, and relying on the superiority of man over machine suddenly turned towards the thing and pressed a button. Tamed, the screen showed him a series of images.

If the ironic intention of the staff of the Department of Administrative Development had been to upset their colleague's regular habits, they failed, for the suspicion and distrust with which Picarreau first approached this instrument of modernity soon gave way to an increasing although carefully controlled passion for it. He bought the TV journal every week the moment it came out, and marked transmissions that might or might not be of interest in blue, green and red. As he gained experience, moreover, the novice viewer became increasingly selective. He very soon stopped watching the news programmes which presented him with an incessant barrage of catastrophes. He thought the transmissions of sports events showing a few people prancing about in front of thousands of motionless enthusiasts ridiculous. He ruthlessly crossed out the showings of recent films, which he disliked for both their systematic violence and their laboured eroticism. Ultimately, the only programmes to find favour with him were occasional operettas, the wild life programmes, and above all old black and white films. Their style and tone were those of the reassuring world he had known, a world that was truly his own.

His life now revolved around the irregular rhythm of such programmes, so that he was sometimes spoilt for choice but often painfully frustrated, and gradually a change took place within him. He found he could not bear to miss a programme he wanted to see because another transmission on another network held his attention, when the two might be followed by a whole series of barren, lonely evenings. At this point he abandoned his previous distrust of modern technology: until he had reached this advanced age his sense of tradition and taste for economy had prevented him from allowing so much as a radio set, an electric coffee mill or a quartz alarm clock into his home, but now he began dreaming with increasing frequency of possessing that instrument of the devil, a video recorder.

The temptation took firm hold on him. He haunted the TV and video departments of large stores, he collected brochures, he dreamed, he calculated, he made comparisons with all the fever of desire. He took his decision when faced with a wonderful evening which gave him the cruel choice between *Brief Encounter* and *Duck Soup*. He bought the video recorder and a large quantity of blank cassettes. This purchase transformed and magnified his life, bringing great variety into it. A huge collection of films accumulated in the bedroom looking out on the courtyard, stored between his mother's old sewing machine and the pitch-pine cupboard. Finding himself a passionate cinema buff, Léon Picarreau became familiar with the least of minor roles and forgotten directors. His time was wholly devoted to this new passion, which enabled him to continue living outside the real world, within his own four grey walls where neither the turmoil nor even the distant noise of modern technology could reach him.

But if Léon Picarreau never went in search of adventure, one fine day adventure came in search of him, through his simply happening to press the wrong button. He had decided to watch and record *Kind Hearts and Coronets* on the evening in question. When the moment came he pressed what he thought was the appropriate button – but when the picture appeared he froze, petrified. The screen was invaded by a huge snow-covered mountain, by sheer blue precipices, ice suspended in unstable equilibrium, slopes descending to vertiginous depths. All this stood out against an intense sky of revolving azure, powered with dazzling light. And on the summit of the mountain there stood a young man, with skis on his feet, the very incarnation of human fragility and audacity, hesitating in suspended action before taking off, as it seemed, into the aerial void below.

'No!' cried Léon Picarreau in spite of himself.

But the man did take off. Powdery snow spurted up beneath his skis. Fascinated, Léon Picarreau moved back to sit in his familiar armchair, his fingers clutching its arms. Heart thudding, he followed the progress of the skier as the man began by taking several precise, quick turns and then came to a change in the slope, where he suddenly lost his balance, fell, and began a long, inexorable slide. Then music began to play, soon swelling to a series of chords, and the titles came up against a background of peaks. Picarreau discovered that the name of the daring skier was Ulrich Gering. It was instantly engraved on his heart.

'He'll never make it!' he murmured, shaking his head sorrowfully. But he was spellbound; he could not tear his eyes away from the screen showing these images.

The film went back to its opening sequences: the high mountain, shaded with tints of blue, the young man who seemed to hesitate even longer this time. Then he leaped into the void, turned to the left and turned to the right, throwing up the powdery snow in a rhythmic dance. Yet again the screen showed the moment when the skier lost control of his descent. He was falling ... and then suddenly arrested his fall with a desperate effort which threw him away from the slope, into the air. Performing a kind of mid-air somersault, he succeeded in landing on his skis as he came down again. It all happened in the fraction of a second. Could he regain his balance? He seemed to. Léon Picarreau was overcome by emotion. The man's disastrous fall had been halted by his amazing reflexes, but now he seemed put ever more at risk by the demands of the slope. Only the constant drive forward and the dynamic of his movements allowed him to escape death through sheer skill. Interminable minutes followed. A large crevasse was now in sight, half-way down the slope, cutting right across it. The young man leaped it with a single bound and landed safely on the lower lip. He carried on down, over slopes that at last seemed not quite so steep, but then the path of his skis set off a snow-slide as he raced downwards, which, facing right, he did not appear to have seen. The entire slope was now shifting in a soft but powerful movement. Was the man doomed to die? Another turn took him back towards the avalanche, and he realized his danger, just in time! In a schuss straight downhill, he tried to outstrip the sliding snow, fleeing on in a mad race, pursued by the avalanche which appeared to be overtaking him. The track left by his skis was almost immediately covered by the steady, white wave from which a cloudy powder was slowly rising. But the man was coming to the bottom of the face; he leaped the bergschrund and continued on, carried by the impetus of his own speed, down the gentler slopes, where the avalanche finally came to rest behind him. On reaching the hollow of a valley he made a final turn and halted, safe and victorious.

Relieved of the anxiety that had held him in suspense for so many minutes, Léon Picarreau heaved a huge sigh, and several times passed his hand over his forehead, taut with the lingering remains of his nightmare. On screen the skier, showing great emotion himself, was being joined by some friends. They were gesticulating, clapping him affectionately on the back. He was seen in close-up, his eyes still glazed, letting the air out of his lungs as he leaned forward on his ski sticks. He took off his cap, ran his hand through his fair hair and drank from the flask someone offered him. Thoughtfully, he shook his head from left to right, no doubt going back over the moments he had just experienced: a venture expected to be no more than a very difficult descent had become a terrifying battle of man against death. The sound-track, muted and almost breathless until this point, was amplified as it took over the image which now ran backwards up the mountain face, retracing the man's descent: the avalanche, the slopes, the great crevasse, the séracs, and back up the slopes again up to the ridge at the top and the sky blazing with triumphant light. The last of the titles came up over a background of the rays of the sun against an azure sky.

Léon Picarreau switched off his set. He had forgotten all about *Kind Hearts and Coronets*. He sat down again, with some care, and spent the rest of the evening immersed in the emotions the adventure had aroused in him. He was thankful that the cassette he had inserted had recorded the skier's perilous descent. He could watch it all again whenever he liked.

This remained the one encounter with danger he ever had. He was no keener on trying to find films about skiing or climbing than he had been before. This single experience, which had left an indelible mark on his mind, was enough. Now and then he would spend an evening playing the tape back. In the same way as a child both wants and fears to hear a story that he knows will scare him, he felt the same anxiety every time as he watched the skier committing himself to the descent and then falling. As the credits came up, and he knew the miracle would be repeated after them, his heart beat as it had on that first viewing. He knew every aspect of the mountain, every part of the skier's route, every gesture, the smallest details of the final avalanche, but he was always enthralled by a similar mixture of fear and hope, astonishment and enthusiasm.

Otherwise, of course, his life had not changed. He went on getting up in the morning, going out to buy groceries which he carried home in his mother's old black imitation leather bag, and polishing the furniture in his flat in a manner she would have approved. Every afternoon he took what had once been the Sunday walk and was now his daily exercise. Finally, every evening, when he had washed and wiped the dishes, he watched or added to his treasured stock of films. He was lucky enough to make some notable additions to his collection that year, recording a number of rare pieces such as *Passport to Pimlico*, *La Cage aux rossignols*, *Goodbye, Mr Chips*, David Lean's *Oliver Twist*, *The Ghost and Mrs Muir*, *Green Pastures*. Yes, it was a vintage year!

And sometimes he would feel a sudden desire to watch his friend Ulrich Gering skiing downhill again. He never tried to find out any more about the man. All he needed to know was contained in that single day of thrills, a sequence he could replay whenever he wanted.

A time came when Léon Picarreau's interests were centred on various retrospective seasons of the work of Marcel l'Herbier, René Clair and Serge de Poligny, and he rather neglected the cassette that was unique in his collection. But one fine spring afternoon during his walk, just as he was turning the corner of the square, he felt an imperative urge to replay it. He could hardly wait until evening. He hurried through his dinner, and then slipped the cassette into the recorder.

Once again the familiar images came up before him. Once again he saw the great snowy mountainside and the blue peaks, the misty chasms, the ice suspended in unstable equilibrium, the slopes descending to vertiginous depths, the intensity of the sky, the powdered azure light ... and there was Ulrich Gering, teetering on the edge of the precipitous face. The snow jetted up from his skis like vapour. He skied turn after turn, and suddenly staggered. Then, to the poignant music of the sound-track, the credits came up against a background of peaks. And back came the opening scenes, up to the start of the fall, the moment when the skier took an incredible, risky jump that brought him up off the slope and tried to recover his balance. But he failed ... just as Picarreau had always somehow obscurely feared he would, he failed! Instead of regaining his balance he fell heavily on his back and went on sliding down the slope, skis now up in the air and now down. In a moment they came off and careered on downhill. Now he was only a helpless puppet caught in an uncontrolled fall, a wretched buffeted body passing over the great crevasse, flung down on the far side, still falling, still bouncing. And it was this disjointed body that reached the unstable snow on the lower part of the face, set off the avalanche and careered on, lost in it, swallowed up by the white, boiling turbulence.

When calm returned to the mountain-side, the screen showed only enormous and motionless masses of snow. They had closed for ever over the temerity of this modern Icarus.

Chilled to the bone, Léon Picarreau got up to switch the TV set off. He could not make out what had happened. Yet the world seemed quite normal in the pale light from the opaline lampshade. His electricity bill, which had arrived that morning, was on the sideboard. The familiar picture of a ship with sails forever billowing on eternally blue waves was still in the bamboo frame above the chiffonier. He could hear a bus stopping out in the street. Léon Picarreau went over to the window, drew back the curtain and watched the bus drive away, blazing with light. He touched his forehead with his fingers – it was slightly damp – and went to bed, his step uncertain. He found it difficult to get to sleep.

When he went out shopping next day he took a detour back home to pass the news stand. He was hardly even surprised to see a headline, *Fatal Accident to Skier*, on the front page of a major daily paper, referring to an article on an inside page. He sought for small change in his pocket, bought the paper, went home, climbed the stairs with more haste than usual, sat down at his table, took out his glasses and unfolded the paper to the page in question, where he was saddened but not at all surprised to learn that the famous Austrian downhill skier Ulrich Gering, known as the Conqueror of the Void, had been killed the day before on the slopes of a distant mountain where he was trying to bring off yet another daring exploit.

Léon Picarreau decided to take the experiment a step further and re-run the cassette, but the tape was now blank. Determined to banish even the memory of this disturbing incident from his mind, he decided to re-use the cassette that same evening to record another film. For it so happened that one of the TV networks had scheduled the showing of a 1937 film entitled *Drôle de drame – Strange Happenings*.

THE MONT-CERVIN HOTEL

I won't go into the circumstances that brought me to Zermatt early that autumn. They are of no consequence for the story I am about to tell. The fact is, I went to Zermatt, and of course I planned to go climbing as I had so many times before. I was offered a chance to relax and took it, that's all I need say.

Zermatt is a delightful place. It's been spared the afflictions from which Chamonix suffers, or almost spared. You could go on for ever about the differences between the two resorts. I love Chamonix, and I do realize that efforts have been made over the last few years to make it a more pleasant place to live in, adding ornamental flower-beds and so forth. But if the centre of the town is improving, as town centres tend to, the surroundings and the local countryside are deteriorating fast. You only have to see Chamonix from above to be surprised – and it is a fresh surprise every time – by the density of its built-up area, with a tide of masonry and roadworks amounting to a kind of industrial landscape. Admittedly the dazzling peaks and needles of the Mont Blanc range rise above the town. But Zermatt can boast the Matterhorn, the most fascinating mountain in the world, and although the valley has too much building in it, and there are some unfortunate suburban features below the village, on the whole it has been preserved, mainly because you can only get there by train. So far, the road-building projects threatened by the enthusiastic supporters of unthinking growth have not had any destructive effects.

There are no cars in the streets, only electric buggies and the smart horse-drawn carriages that take guests to the big hotels. You can scarcely imagine how peaceful that is in the modern world. There are no tunnels here carrying convoys of heavy vehicles, no coaches disgorging crowds of dazed or noisy tourists, no constant traffic jams, no exhaust fumes, no cars parked everywhere, invading the last of the green spots unchecked, no architectural monstrosities in concrete, no towering blocks of flats, very few rented luxury apartments with a fast turnover of tenants, no Club Meds, no fibrocement toboggan tracks, no aquatic serpentines, no supermarkets. Zermatt has remained, if perhaps only for a while, an oasis of dignity instead of turning itself into an urbanized inferno like the developing resorts. You can stroll happily down the main street, past old brown wooden houses roofed with local stone and adorned with wonderful cascades of geraniums and pinks. The church, with its severely beautiful tower, marks the centre of the village, and the local people have been sensible enough to leave the alpine cemetery, full of flowers, charm and history, in its protective shade instead of exiling it to some dreary suburb, as if death itself could be banished. To me, Zermatt is a paradise on earth.

I have known the resort for a long time, visiting it frequently. I've always felt my spirits rise in the same way on arriving, and the miracle happened once again. I'd decided to come on an impulse and had nothing arranged in advance, not even a place to stay. I should mention that the old Zermatt hotels have survived instead of selling themselves off for flats, as is the case elsewhere, which makes me think that the people of Zermatt have succeeded unusually well in remaining in charge of their own living space. I left my car at Täsch, lunched there, and then took the train that would usher me into the promised land. I was free. I thought I would walk around for a while before looking for somewhere to stay, and so I went a little way out of the station, carrying my luggage. Suddenly I saw the garnet-red carriage belonging to the Seiler hotels, drawn by two brown horses with little bells on their harness. I asked the driver if there were any rooms vacant at the Mont-Cervin, and when he said there were I jumped up on the footboard and installed myself, with child-like delight, in the upholstered interior of the carriage. After all, why not realize an old dream? And who hasn't dreamed of spending a few days in one of the old grand hotels of Zermatt, among which the Seiler hotels hold pride of place?

It was from the first of the Seiler hotels, the Monte Rosa, more of an inn at the time, that Edward Whymper set out on 13 July 1865 to attempt the ascent of the Matterhorn, and it was to the arms of his friend old Alexandre Seiler that he returned two days later to mourn his success, since four of his companions had died on the way down. Ever since, the Seiler hotels have prospered, grown and multiplied, but they are still attached to their roots and derive their great reputation more from their past and their traditions than their luxury. That was why I decided to stay at the Mont-Cervin.

I have stayed at other grand hotels in the past – not often, I must admit, and usually when someone else was paying the bill – and have appreciated all the attentions which are part of the deal. But often, in spite of all the care lavished on the guests, you still feel a kind of isolating anonymity, as so often when you are travelling. Comfort is sold at the asking price, no more. Another guest occupying the same space next day will have a similar environment and enjoy similar services, and the people who help to ensure your comfort remain strangers who might just as well be robots. Take the United Nations Plaza Hotel, where I recently stayed in New York. You can't find fault with it; it offers its guests the most exquisite luxury, but you could die there and no one would take any notice apart from dealing with the administrative formalities. I suspected I would find something better at the Mont-Cervin, and so I did. Over and beyond its luxury, the hotel had a soul.

As soon as I entered I could sense the welcoming atmosphere, both solicitous and friendly. I had a room with a view of the mountains. Perhaps I was slightly surprised to find it so modern, but I reflected that if it still had its old-fashioned bed and its china wash-basin, I would have had to ring for the maid to bring me a jug of hot water, whereas I now had the benefit of a very comfortable bathroom which even contained a soft dressing gown. I unpacked and sat on the balcony for a while, reading a recent P.D. James. Then I went out for a walk, looking in the watchmakers' windows and amusing myself with the latest incarnations of the Matterhorn in the souvenir shops, leafing through new mountaineering books in the bookshops, buying postcards, in short, getting the feel of the place by resuming the habits I had already formed at Zermatt. If I didn't observe them, I felt I would be violating a deeply significant tradition.

That evening, in deference to the hotel rules, I dressed carefully before going down to dinner, congratulating myself on having packed clothes conforming to the requirements of the Mont-Cervin, and I went to the dining room. I was given a corner table near the door, which suited me very well, and settled down to order from the menu. You want to know what I ordered? Readers can be so inquisitive! Very well, I had cream of cucumber soup with cumin, then a parfait of chanterelles with tomato fondue, followed by the salad trolley, medallions of venison sautéed with figs, and finally a gratin of fruit with almonds. If I add that I ordered a bottle of Nuits-Saint-Georges from the wine waiter, you will know exactly how I dined. A number of waiters and waitresses ensured that the ritual ran smoothly. I was brought crusty fresh bread, and I was soon beginning my dinner, while I took note of my surroundings: the prettily laid tables with their vases of flowers, the pictures and prints on the walls, and of course the other diners, most of them couples, but there was also a large family celebrating some anniversary.

All was very well here: civilized people in an agreeable atmosphere. High above us, the wind was blowing over the mountain ridges and stars were twinkling in a black velvet sky, but you can't be everywhere at once, and there are earthly pleasures to be enjoyed too.

All of a sudden an old man appeared in this quiet calm. I didn't see him come in, and noticed him only when he was inside the room. He took small steps, one hand holding a stick on which he leaned, and supporting himself with the other hand on the backs of the empty chairs within his reach. He was so unsteady on his feet that I wondered if his strength was exhausted. I noticed his tall figure, hardly bent at all by his years, his extreme thinness and the diaphanous pallor of his emaciated face. Ivory skin sculpted the contours of his skull, emphasizing every plane and depression. The pinched, aquiline nose, the thin lips turning in on his mouth, his jutting cheekbones and discoloured eyes all bore witness to his great age. I reckoned the old man must be at least a hundred, but his undeniable strength of will and the light that still lived in his eyes made a considerable impression on me. The waiters kept discreet watch as he made painful progress: obviously refusing assistance was the final achievement of this frail patriarch whom Death seemed to have forgotten. The maître d'hôtel approached him with a respectful 'Good evening, Monsieur Limbourg!' which made me realize he was a regular guest. Then the old man turned the corner of the dining room, disappeared from my sight, and I devoted my entire attention to my dinner.

As I had no reason to hurry I lingered at my table, and had not quite finished my meal when I saw M. Limbourg again, making his unsteady way back from chair to chair. Several questions rose to my mind. This time I was struck not so much by his age as by his extreme solitude. Had he no wife, no son or grandchildren, no family to share his life and go with him when he travelled? What was he doing in this hotel? Was there no retirement home where he could spend his last days in peace?

I saw him again a little later, in the lounge near the bar where he had seated himself to pass the evening, still alone, fixed in a hieratic posture, his glance absent. I supposed he found company in the mere fact of being here – company and perhaps some consolation before the cruel moment when he would have to retire to his room, take his teeth out, remove the clothes which kept his worn-out body in a state of human comfort, and face one of those long, sleepless and restless nights so common to the old, a kind of infinite desert from which they do not even know if they will return alive.

Shaking off the fascination I already felt with M. Limbourg, I picked up my newspaper, ordered a verbena liqueur and tried to relax in the warm atmosphere around me. How can I best describe the interior decoration? It was a little old-fashioned and very agreeable. No doubt it had been designed in the sixties, and under a curious ceiling of wood and false beams it presented a mixture of styles which amused me, uniting Voltaire armchairs, Louis-Philippe chairs, antique pedestal tables, modern sofas with rose-patterned covers, marquetry tables, turned wooden coat and hat-stands, a recording barometer, some engravings, early nineteenth-century posters and faience chamber-pots filled with flowers and proudly stating their origins in the monogram of the Seiler hotels. Ancestral portraits hung on the walls, pictures of Alexandre Seiler senior, Alexander Seiler junior and Dr Hermann Seiler, handsome moustached men who seemed to be still watching over the destiny of the hotel from their frames.

A little further away, in the dim shadows of the bar where a few candles were burning, a pianist was playing a medley of old-fashioned tunes, running them together melodiously and adding syncopated chords or light flourishes. I recognized *La Vie en rose*, *Douce France*, *Tea for Two*, *The Third Man* and various songs by Montand, Piaf and Trenet. The music suited the atmosphere, providing a gentle and agreeable background.

However, my interest in M. Limbourg must have remained alive, for he was in my field of vision and I noticed when someone approached him. I paid discreet attention. A woman of about sixty had come into the lounge. She went over to the old man, greeted him and said a few words to him. He scarcely replied, making a weary gesture, before resuming his impassive posture. The woman sat down on a sofa quite close to me. She was wearing a turquoise silk dress and a necklace of deep, translucent blue glass. I took to her immediately. She had an attractive face beneath hair that was still brown, and the fine wrinkles on it were obviously laughter-lines rather than the result of any harshness of character. I watched her without seeming to. Of course I wanted to ask her about M. Limbourg, but good manners prevented me.

Chance came to my aid when my neighbour made a clumsy movement and dropped her bag on the carpet. Its contents scattered on the floor, and I helped pick them up. She thanked me, and we entered into conversation, exchanging commonplaces and talking about this and that: the hotel, which she had known for a long time, the changes Zermatt had seen, the beauty of this late end of the season. Suddenly M. Limbourg, who was sitting some way from us, emerged from his apparently fixed immobility and sought his stick, which was leaning against the wall. I thought he was about to leave, but instead he carefully placed the stick closer to him before going back on guard, as it were, in his position of motionless indifference.

I ventured to ask a question. 'Do you know that old man sitting by himself?'

'Not very well,' she replied, 'but he was friends with my father, and I know his story. It accounts for the melancholy, reclusive look you may have noticed.'

'He's a figure bound to attract attention,' I admitted. 'I noticed him a little while ago when he came into the dining room. I don't ask just out of curiosity – I feel real sympathy for him. Such age and isolation can only arouse compassion. It would be nice if someone could show it, if he could have some friends around, but it looks as if there's nothing anyone can do for him.'

'Yes,' she replied. 'You're quite right in guessing that there's a very sad story behind his solitude and his presence here. In fact M. Limbourg's story is no secret. Everyone here must be aware of it. If you're interested, I can tell you what I know of it myself, but I should warn you that it's quite long and you'll have to be patient, since I doubt if I could finish it this evening. I'm staying in Zermatt with my husband – he's a doctor, here for a kind of professional seminar. He's with colleagues at the moment, but he's due to come and meet me quite soon, so I can only offer to tell you the beginning of the story and leave the rest until tomorrow.'

'Please go ahead,' I said.

'Well, as you know, that tall old man was once young. But when I say young you must also imagine him brimming with youth, handsome as a prince, highly intelligent and at the same time cheerful, lively, charming, radiant. I remember what my father used to say about him, and it seemed as if there were no words adequate to describe such a personality. I've seen a photograph of the two of them together at that period. I wonder what became of it … I don't know. But I can assure you that even a yellowed old photograph conveyed the young man's charm. Oh dear, if only we knew what the future holds in store I think we'd often lose any wish to live. Thank goodness we *don't* know. Anyway, Stanislas Limbourg was lucky to have turned out as he did, because his childhood was not a very happy one. His parents died in a railway accident when he was only a few years old, and he hardly knew them when he was handed over to a distant cousin who was to be his guardian. The cousin took little interest in him, sent the child away to boarding school and didn't even have him home in the holidays. These details, as you will see, are quite important.

The little boy settled well at school: he worked and played hard, winning the respect of his teachers and making friends with the other pupils. I can't tell you any more than that, but it's helpful to know what the early years of someone's life were like.'

'This would have been about the beginning of the century, I suppose?'

'Yes, indeed. After passing his first examinations with great distinction, the young man planned a career in engineering, but the 1914 war interrupted his studies. He joined up, and after training the army sent him to the Valais with the troops covering the frontier. After the Armistice was signed he returned to his studies. Nothing very unusual there, of course, but something new had entered the story of Stanislas Limbourg's life, for in the army he had discovered mountaineering, and he now devoted his free time to his growing enthusiasm for the sport. I don't know if you understand what such an enthusiasm means, but it radically changed his life.'

'I can understand very well,' I replied. 'I'm an alpinist myself. The world of the high mountains has nothing in common with the everyday world of those who don't know them.'

'Then we both know what we're talking about! I myself have spent several seasons climbing. And from my father's recollections and what he often said about Stanislas Limbourg at that time, I've gained some idea of what it was like for the two of them. This was in the early 1920s: no cable cars then, the resorts were still simple country villages, small huts seasonally occupied perched high up on the alps, hours away from any habitation, and above them rose an unspoilt landscape, vast and beautiful, violent, pure and wild, frequented only by a few highly motivated initiates. It was the period of people like Lépiney, Ségogne, Lauper and Mallory, a time when it must have been wonderful to be alive, and Stanislas Limbourg plunged into that life with the utmost fervour. I won't repeat all the many anecdotes I heard from my father, but I can tell you that within a few years the young man had done some very fine climbs, for instance Monte Rosa by the Marinelli corridor, the Schalligrat of the Weisshorn and the Zmutt ridge on the Matterhorn. He climbed with friends and without a guide, which was relatively unusual at the time. But even though he did climb guideless, the guides themselves liked and respected him. He was famous for his competence, good sense and caution – and for his enthusiasm and infectious good humour! Apparently he had a great gift for communication and was very lively, making fun of those with long faces. I always remember what my father told me about the time when they were stranded by bad weather in a little mountain hotel, surrounded by fog, and Stanislas Limbourg organized all sorts of games and competitions as if by magic: climbs up and down the stairs, roped parties making a traverse from balcony to balcony, a revue and even, as the final touch, an improvised fancy dress ball using whatever resources came to hand. I imagine he had a way of carrying people along with him – his personal friends, of course, but other people too, young and old, women and girls, not to mention children, whom he adored. He was kind to everyone and everyone loved him.'

'What a portrait!' I said, with some surprise. 'Do such paragons really exist?'

'Not many, I grant you,' admitted the storyteller, smiling. 'But why shouldn't they? In any case, there was one, and his name was Stanislas Limbourg. Don't look so sceptical, because I have more of the same to tell you, and you'll be saying my story is turning into a fairy-tale. One day Stanislas Limbourg met a girl and fell madly in love with her.'

'And I expect she too was an accomplished creature of superior intelligence, pure, good, wise and beautiful. Did I say beautiful? Ravishing, delicious, full of charm …'

'Don't make fun of me!' interrupted my interlocutor. 'As it happens, she was all that and maybe more. The perfect wife for such a man.'

'And she wouldn't have him!'

'Heavens, what kind of a story do you think I'm telling? Do you really think an unhappy love affair could have plunged such a well-balanced young man into the depths of despair? Come along, we're not in a bad novel! Even unrequited passion wouldn't bring such a weight of regret with it. No, what I am trying to tell you is a true and tragic story. Very well: Calliope, for that was the girl's name, returned Stanislas Limbourg's feelings, and they loved each other with all the passion of youth. They got engaged, they were happy, and they married.'

'You make me feel even worse, because obviously there's no happy ending to this story. Perhaps I'd rather you'd told me the tall, sad old man there at the other end of the lounge, lost in God knows what sombre dream, was always a melancholy loner, and his end was like his beginning, whereas all I can expect from your tale now is cruel disillusionment.'

'Did you ever suppose happiness was a natural state?' she replied with some bitterness. 'Just as you think you have it in your grasp it eludes you. I suspect we may congratulate ourselves on those few scraps of it we find in this world. Don't forget, Stanislas Limbourg did have some years of very great, intense happiness. But before I go on, if it won't bore you, I should tell you a few details about Calliope's family. The rest of the story won't be easy to understand without them.'

'I'm hanging on your every word,' I assured her. 'It's all interesting. I'm grateful to you for telling me. You're providing answers to the questions I couldn't solve.'

'O.K.,' she smiled. 'Then let me open a parenthesis explaining what was really a relatively simple situation. Calliope's parents were called Christophore and Hélène Bessarion. They belonged to an international set that used to move between the most brilliant cities of Europe early in the century, and had lived in Thessaly, the Netherlands, Romania, Austria and goodness knows where else before settling in Geneva. I should also tell you that Hélène, who seems to have been a remarkable woman, belonged to the very rich Greek Topalidis shipowning family, and she was the sole heir. The couple had two children, Calliope, the elder, and Alexandre, eight years younger than his sister. Hélène Bessarion suffered puerperal fever after having Alexandre, and survived the birth of her son only briefly. Her husband had the reputation of being a gambler, and one assumes it was founded on fact, for she left him nothing except an annuity – quite a generous one, but relatively modest compared to the considerable fortune that went to the two children and was shared equally between them. Christophore Bessarion did not remain a widower very long, His second wife was a German Swiss girl whose first name was Gertrude. Her dowry was small, and from the first she must have felt some jealousy of the heirs of his first marriage, envying them that fortune, which she considered would have been better placed in her own hands. This hostility grew even worse when she bore Christophore three more sons within quite a short time. Her coolness towards Calliope and Alexandre now became outright animosity. Gertrude Bessarion must often have compared the riches destined for the children of her husband's first marriage with the position of her own offspring, and she seems to have been an extremely disagreeable stepmother. I don't know how much Calliope and Alexandre minded. Like Stanislas, they spent most of their childhood years at boarding school, and like him they did very well there. They also found compensation for the lack of a true home life in their mutual affection.'

'So when Stanislas and Calliope met they became everything to each other?'

'Yes, indeed, only you mustn't forget young Alexandre, then still at school. Stanislas felt an almost paternal affection for the boy. He was twenty-eight when he married Calliope, she herself was twenty, and Alexandre was only twelve at the time. From then on Alexandre spent all his holidays with the young couple, often at Zermatt. I hardly need to tell you they used to stay in this hotel. It must have been very different then, full of the dazzling cosmopolitan society of the 1920s, but with the rather traditional atmosphere that was already a feature of the resort …'

At this point in my acquaintance's story several men entered the lounge, and one of them gave her an affectionate smile.

'Ah, there's my husband!' she said. 'Just as I expected, I'll have to leave you now. I'd never have had time to finish my story this evening anyway. Let's meet again tomorrow.'

She left, and I remained prey to a strange kind of reverie induced by the evening's events: the double coincidence whereby my path had crossed M. Limbourg's, and I had then been able to learn such intimate details of the story of his life. I did not wait for him to leave the lounge himself, but soon went up to my own room.

Next day I went out. I walked to the Gornergrat, still a pretty place despite the cog railway. As I have said, it was the end of the season. Frost had scorched the pastures, and down below the valleys were plunged in shadows of an ultramarine hue. Gradually the immense expanse of tall, snow-covered peaks spread out before me against the pale blue sky. I think I felt more deeply affected than ever by this landscape I knew so well. I stayed there for over an hour, enjoying the view from the top of a small, stony hill above the Gornergrat, well out of the way of the last tourists. My solitude was complete and perfect. I went back down by train, marvelling at the way in which the mountains could communicate such intense happiness as I had just felt to mind and heart, in both action and contemplation.

When evening came I found myself thinking of my story-teller of the night before. I didn't even know her name, and suddenly I feared I would not see her again. I would have found it very disappointing never to know the end of the story she had begun to tell. And although M. Limbourg himself came in to dinner again., I did not see my new acquaintance anywhere, and began to feel some concern. After finishing my meal, however, I went to sit in the lounge, and at last I was pleased to see the lady I was waiting for arrive.

We began by exchanging a few commonplaces about the way we had both spent the day, and I told her how struck I had been, once again, by the grandeur of the icy landscape I was contemplating a few hours earlier.

'That's a coincidence,' she told me. 'There's something in common between what I'm about to tell you and the places you were admiring today, which were the scene of a genuine tragedy. But first I'd better take up my story where I broke off yesterday. So: Stanislas Limbourg married Calliope Bessarion, and they were very happy. My father told me that a mutual friend who met them at Zermatt soon after their wedding remarked that they seemed "too good for this world". Is it tempting fate to attain a state so close to perfection? Oh, I don't know ... But I can tell you that the Limbourgs spent two alpine seasons doing a number of climbs together, either with or without a guide. I described that period to you in mountaineering terms as the day of people like Ségogne and Lauper. It was also the day of women climbers such as Alice Damesme, Gisèle de Longchamp and Dorothy Pilley. Like them, Calliope was a good climber. But in the third summer after her marriage she gave up climbing, for the very good reason that she was pregnant. The young couple's happiness seemed complete, and it was a very small thing that spoilt it.'

At this point in the story I could not help casting a brief glance at M. Limbourg, who had resumed his melancholy watch in the same armchair as the night before. I found it hard to imagine him as he had been described to me in the flower of his youth, and felt rather apprehensive about what I still had to hear. But my curiosity was all the stronger, and I glanced back at the woman sitting beside me.

'That summer,' she told me, 'while Calliope stayed at the hotel and contented herself with walking in the fields and the woods, Stanislas went on climbing. One day he decided to do a classic traverse which he had been planning for some time: he wanted to climb the Matterhorn by the Arête du Lion, the Italian Ridge, and come back down to Zermatt by the ordinary Hörnli route.'

I could not help giving a start of surprise. 'I thought you'd be mentioning Monte Rosa or the glaciers around the Gornergrat,' I said. 'You said just now –'

'Oh, we'll come to that part of the story,' she assured me. 'I'm only halfway through, and it all takes place around Zermatt. As you know, the traverse of the Matterhorn presents no great problems, but it does require stamina, and it certainly did in those days, when of course the Théodule col had to be crossed on foot to reach Italy. Calliope got into the habit of going to meet her husband when he came down from a climb. They would carefully co-ordinate their timing as far as possible so that they could meet, and on this occasion they agreed that after completing the traverse Stanislas and his climbing partner would sleep at the Hörnli Hut, waiting until next day to come down to Zermatt, when Calliope would go up to meet them. As the weather turned out to be good, all went according to plan, and the young woman set off early with Alexandre, who was then about fifteen. They took the path going up to the Lac Noir. Calliope was only four or five months pregnant; she still walked at a brisk pace, and she went quite a long way up the mountain. The two parties met. Stanislas had enjoyed his climb enormously, and the four young people happily set off home. All this is commonplace stuff, and as I said just now, there's no real reason why life should not have gone just as before. But during the descent Calliope slipped on a piece of rock, and fell backwards with some violence. Almost at once she felt shooting pains in her stomach and loins. When she tried to go on the others had first to support and then carry her, and finally they fetched a carriage to get her through Zermatt. The day had suddenly turned to tragedy because of the loose sole on a shoe, or perhaps one false step.'

'It happens so often,' I commented 'When you've seen car accidents or climbing accidents at close quarters, never mind which, or indeed a severe illness, you know how easily disaster can strike.'

'You're right,' she said. 'But to my mind the most prominent feature of the story I'm telling you is the contrast between such great happiness and the sadness that immediately followed. I've told you those details I know, but I suspect they're not really essential. Calliope could just as well have been knocked over in the street, or fallen downstairs, and the result would have been the same. But I have such a vivid picture of that group of young people cheerfully walking down through pastures full of wild flowers in the beautiful sunlight of a summer morning: the two climbers happy after the previous day's expedition, with the light in their eyes that I've often noticed in mountaineers, Calliope radiating health, love and all the promise of the future – and the adolescent Alexandre too, delighted to be with those he loved. In that context, you see, the accident seems even worse. Of course I wasn't a witness of the scene. I wasn't even born at the time, but I still feel as if I'd been through it myself.'

'I suppose it ended badly, then?'

'Very badly. Zermatt had no local doctor on permanent call at that time, but Dr Bayard used to come up from St Niklaus and stay for the summer season, so immediate help was available. Given the speed of ensuing developments, could modern medicine have done any more? I'm not sure. There was no way of preventing the miscarriage. Calliope haemorrhaged violently, collapsed and died. Such cases are rare, but they still occur today.'

We remained silent for a few moments. It is always unpleasant to dwell on unhappiness. I was expecting some such ending, but it came as a shock all the same.

'And Stanislas Limbourg never remarried?' I asked.

My interlocutor looked at me in some surprise.

'You know, I never asked myself the question in those terms. No doubt he could have rebuilt his life as the years passed by, gradually casting a veil of oblivion over the tragedy and muting it. But the marriage had been quite exceptionally happy, you see. Stanislas Limbourg felt such grief that his friends feared something terrible might happen. Apparently at the funeral, which was here at Zermatt, he looked so stricken, distraught and pale that everyone who set eyes on him remembered it. He had suffered such a cruel bereavement that he only recovered very slowly and with great difficulty. I believe there was just one thing that kept him going, and that was his duty to young Alexandre, who himself was dreadfully affected by his sister's death. Overcoming his own distress, Stanislas Limbourg tried to rebuild the boy's confidence, developing his liking for his studies, sport, music, travel, anything that can interest an adolescent. As I'm sure you know, thinking of someone else is the only way to shake off a great grief. Stanislas devoted himself to the boy, who had no one but him in the world. I may have forgotten to tell you that Alexandre's father, Christophore Bessarion, had died, I'm not sure just when or how, so on that side of his family Alexandre had only his stepmother and three young stepbrothers whom he hardly knew, and who showed no liking for him.'

'Who inherited Calliope's fortune?'

'Ah, I was just coming to that, and it's the nub of the matter. The law is a human artefact and does not by any means always coincide with true justice. In the absence of a will, legally, and absurdly, the stepbrothers would have had the same claims as Alexandre to Calliope Limbourg's fortune, that is to say the Topalidis money, although there was no real reason for the children of Gertrude and Christophore to get their hands on any of it. However, it turned out that following her mother's example, Calliope had made some very explicit arrangements. The Topalidis women certainly had their heads screwed on! Calliope had divided her property in two, half to go to her husband and half to her brother Alexandre. Since he had already inherited half of Hélène Bessarion's fortune in his own right, Alexandre would possess three-quarters of it when he came of age, while Stanislas would have the fourth quarter, which of itself made him a very rich man. I won't say that money meant nothing to them – money means something to everyone – but I do sincerely believe they saw it as a minor consideration. Stanislas had inherited little in the way of personal property from his parents, yet he had married Calliope entirely for love, not money. He would certainly have taken her without a penny to her name, and he insisted on continuing to work after they were married, although he could easily have given up his job. He went back to work after the tragedy, too, and obviously he did his utmost to instil good moral principles and a preference for exertion rather than idleness into Alexandre.'

'I imagine the wicked stepmother Gertrude didn't like to see such wealth escape her sons?'

'She certainly did not, but there was nothing she could do about it, since as soon as Calliope was old enough she had made everything absolutely watertight. Gertrude undoubtedly brooded and let her rancour mature, as subsequent events showed. But some years of calm now passed – I won't say years of happiness, since happiness was dead for Stanislas anyway, but years of calm. Alexandre finished school and decided to study medicine. His brother-in-law encouraged him, and when the boy was eighteen years old he took him climbing. Alexandre had always longed to climb. I should mention that, thinking of the safety of the boy he loved, Stanislas engaged guides for every climb that was not a simple hill walk, although his own technical skills and experience put him in the top rank of climbers himself. I won't bore you with my father's long list of the climbs they did, which shows not only Stanislas Limbourg's ability but the fact that Alexandre too was becoming good. His natural aptitude and his fitness made him as experienced a mountaineer as could be expected at his age. That's sufficient, and all you need to know to understand the unfortunate accident that happened later.'

'When was that?'

'I can't tell you the precise date, although I'm sure it could be found in newspapers of the time. It was about eight years after Calliope's death, since Alexandre was twenty-three, so Stanislas must have been approaching forty. But before I describe what happened, I must go back to the financial aspects of my story and mention some steps Stanislas Limbourg had been induced to take with the very best of intentions. You mustn't think that the fortune involved was the reason for the incidents I'm about to describe. It so happens that there was a fortune involved in this particular case, but I expect you know as well as I do that greed and generosity are a matter of temperament, perhaps sometimes of education, but never of social class. I've met the avaricious and the very open-handed in both easy and very modest circumstances. Stanislas came into the category of those who are naturally disinterested and obliging, but he knew his way around the world. At the end of the spring I'm talking about he had a health scare, and realized that if by any chance he died intestate his money would go to his distant cousins by blood, the children of the guardian who had neglected him as a child. Here again we have a case where the law had juridical but not moral weight. There was no reason for these distant relations to get their hands on what he had inherited from the Topalidis fortune. Stanislas went to see a solicitor and put everything in order, making Alexandre his sole heir, which in this case would mean reuniting the fortune of Hélène Bessarion in the hands of the last descendant of the Topalidis family. As I told you, Alexandre was only twenty-three at the time. It was likely that he would soon start a family of his own, and the measures Stanislas had taken were sensible and logical, but he made the mistake – an involuntary mistake, and one with consequences he could not have foreseen – of telling Alexandre what he had done.'

'I don't quite see your point. Why was that a mistake? I took it that Alexandre returned Stanislas's affection? I can't imagine that he immediately started coveting the rest of his sister's money.'

'No, of course not! Alexandre was indeed deeply attached to Stanislas. I'd even say he loved him as a father, an elder brother and the best of friends rolled into one. Paradoxically, that was the cause of all the unpleasantness that followed. Anyway, Alexandre said nothing to Stanislas about the steps this confidence caused him to take. On his side, the young student had completed his university year with great distinction, and he would soon finish his medical studies. As usual the two men set out for a new season in the mountains. They'd planned various climbs with guides, but first they decided to go up to the Cima del Jazzi on their own to get themselves fit for altitude climbing.'

'Yes, I know it. I've done it twice on skis. It's one of the most accessible summits in the range, on the Swiss side anyway. You can get there from anywhere over a succession of snow slopes above glaciers. You can call it a climb if you like, but it's almost more of an approach march.'

'Exactly, but it's a vast area, and all above 3000 metres. It was a good idea for a first training session, particularly in those days.'

'I suppose Alexandre and Stanislas set out from the Bétemps Hut?'

'No; they wanted to vary their itinerary a little and had decided on a kind of détour. They planned to sleep at the Gornergrat hotel, leave early, follow the easy rock ridge up to the Stockhorn, then come down to the Stockhorn pass and finally climb the snowfields at their leisure up to the Cima del Jazzi, which as far as I remember is 3,880 metres, or thereabouts. They were planning to do the standard descent over the Gorner glacier, probably without going round by the Bétemps Hut, making straight for the railway at Rotenboden.'

'Not an outing with any special problems.'

'None at all. But the unexpected can always happen in the mountains, and it did so that day in the form of a violent storm, although it seems that the evening before and the morning itself had been wonderful. There was no sign or warning. These days the weather forecast puts out heaven knows how many daily bulletins, satellite pictures and so forth. Of course there was none of that at the time. And although bad weather often sets in slowly and progressively, it can strike suddenly, and it did on this occasion. Everyone out climbing that day said so: the storm broke extraordinarily suddenly. The sky turned from blue to a kind of leaden colour, without looking really threatening, but a few moments later the storm was raging and it was snowing hard. As you said, the route they had planned to take was not difficult, but vast expanses of featureless terrain provide no landmarks in fog or a blizzard. The two men spent hours trying to find their way. Sensibly, they always took a compass and a map with them, but even with those aids it was very difficult to steer a course in that part of the range and in such conditions.'

'I know about that kind of thing from personal experience. Sometimes visibility's so poor that you can't even make out whether you're going uphill or downhill. It's very frightening, and in such vast areas it's a real skill not to get lost in bad weather.'

'Well, Stanislas and Alexandre almost succeeded in getting down all right, making their way through the fresh snow, although they may well have wandered around. But somewhere, no one ever knew just where – probably at around 3000 metres or a little less, but anyway on the Gorner glacier where it joins the Grenz glacier – there was an accident. The two men were roped but keeping their distance, as you must on a glacier. Alexandre was leading, and Stanislas, as the more experienced of the two, followed some metres behind him carrying coils. I told you this was the beginning of the season, the end of June or early July, I don't know which. The snow bridges which cover the crevasses in winter are beginning to weaken or collapse at that time, and you can't always tell what's below. Moreover, the layer of powder snow or hail that had just fallen must have concealed any irregularities in the terrain. Whatever, the snow suddenly gave way under Alexandre's feet, and he fell straight into a crevasse. Stanislas was taken unawares, and the coils ran out, as you might expect.'

'Of course. It's only very recently that people have taken to walking on glaciers without coils, keeping a very long rope between climbers, and even now a good many don't do it. There wouldn't have been any question of it at that time. Climbing manuals advised exactly the procedure you've described, point by point. I think I've read somewhere that climbers were told not to hold the coils as we do now, but as hitches held in the hand, so that they'd uncoil more readily in the case of a sudden pull. And the accident itself was as one might expect. In bad weather of the kind you're describing, the two men couldn't be roped very wide apart; they'd have had to stay reasonably close so that they could see and hear each other. Furthermore, spotting a hidden crevasse in poor, diffused light in a white-out is just about impossible. The only way would have been for Alexandre to probe ahead of him with the point of his ice-axe at every step he took, but in such a huge area it would have been stupid to lose so much time. They'd never have moved.'

'It does seem that no one made any mistakes and it was sheer bad luck. Alexandre was almost in the middle of the bridge when it broke, and he fell free. Stanislas felt the coils slip out of his hands and was pulled off balance and dragged. He tried to brake and finally managed to stop not far from the hole. He got a belay around his ice-axe and approached the abyss – for it seems that it really was an abyss.'

'The crevasses are huge in that sector; people say they're big enough to swallow up a cathedral. It's difficult to believe even when you see them.'

'By what I suppose one should call a stroke of luck Alexandre, who had fallen at least a dozen metres, had come to rest on a sort of snow bridge lower down, but empty space yawned around him. He was suffering from shock, but seemed to be safe and sound. He still had his sack, but he had lost his ice-axe. He had some pain in his ankle, probably a fracture or sprain, but nothing more. In fact he was generally all right, and for a moment the climbers congratulated themselves that nothing worse had happened. But they were swiftly disillusioned. The side of the crevasse was smooth, vertical ice, overhanging at the top. Obviously Alexandre couldn't get up it, and Stanislas was unable to extricate him. As you know, a man weighing seventy-five kilos can't be hoisted up by simply pulling. It takes a team of people and special equipment.'

'So all Stanislas could do was leave Alexandre and go for help.'

'Which is what he did, and as you can imagine with great anxiety. First he took all possible precautions, trying to make Alexandre absolutely secure. He cut a step in the slope above the crevasse, sank his ice-axe into it as far as possible and fixed the rope to it. I should add one detail here: when he tried untying the rope around his waist he couldn't, and he had to make up his mind to cut it with his knife so as not to waste time wrestling with the uncooperative knot.'

'That's not surprising either. The hemp ropes they used in those days would swell with water and freeze, and went absolutely rigid in bad weather. In addition, the shock of Alexandre's fall must have tightened the knot, and it would been gone solid. Something had to be done fast.'

'Yes. So Stanislas left alone, in the middle of the storm which was still raging, risking a fall into a crevasse himself, which would probably have meant the end for both of them. But he succeeded in reaching the junction of the glaciers at around 2600 metres, and took stock. He had a choice of actions. He decided to go up to the Bétemps Hut to see if he could find help there, and so get back to Alexandre that evening, or at least before nightfall. But the hut was empty. Was it guarded in those days? I don't know. Anyway, there was no guardian at that point in the season, and certainly Stanislas found no one there. His efforts had merely resulted in lost time. He had to go on down as fast as possible, despite his fatigue, and he did not reach Zermatt until quite late in the evening. Once there, distressed, haggard and exhausted, he told his story. Some witnesses noticed the cord hanging at his belt. He explained why it was cut. The reasons were clear enough to you, as they would be to anyone experienced, but it's true that there's something disturbing, to the ignorant, about the idea of someone cutting a rope tied to his companion. I only mention this because some of those who saw Stanislas come back that evening got the wrong impression. Stanislas himself had nothing on his own mind but the organization of a rescue. It was too late to try anything that evening, but a considerable number of guides and volunteers were alerted and would be ready to leave early next morning. Stanislas absolutely insisted in accompanying the expedition, and in fact it would be useful to have him there to help locate the crevasse, especially as the bad weather looked like holding and the valley was lashed by rain. He hardly rested at all that night, and set off with the convoy in the morning. At his own expense, he had engaged all available guides who could be contacted, so as to increase the chances of a quick success. All the material was ready: a number of ropes, and a stretcher in case Alexandre was too weak after his night in the open to come down under his own power. The rescue set off at dawn. It was still snowing high up, and Stanislas's tracks were covered. The team divided to explore, section by section, the part of the glacier where they believed the accident had happened, but they searched all day in vain. You can imagine how Stanislas felt. He promised huge rewards to anyone who found his young brother-in-law. He himself joined in the search all that day. Night found the whole convoy at the Bétemps Hut. Next day was fine, and the search began again, with a much greater chance of success. They scoured the Gorner glacier in all directions. The ice-axe and belay rope which should have marked Alexandre's position were nowhere to be seen. They probed crevasses. They shouted. They did everything that could possibly be done, but they failed. Stanislas kept the search going for several days, refusing to lose hope. After a week, however, he had to acknowledge the facts and admit that Alexandre was dead and his body had disappeared.'

'What a dreadful story!'

'That wasn't the end of it. The accident had been duly reported to the officer in charge of the local cantonal police station. Preliminary enquiries were opened. In line with regulations, the cantonal police officer interviewed the man who had survived the accident in order to get a detailed statement down on record and signed. He also interviewed the leader of the rescue team about the conduct of the search and its failure. Finally he sent the results of his enquiry to cantonal police headquarters at Sion. This procedure is routine in all climbing accidents, particularly when the body can't be found. The officer who receives the report can then either file it, which is the usual course of action, or send it to the examining magistrate if anything still needs clearing up and the incident seems to call for further enquiries. You may remember that after the Matterhorn accident of 1865 there was an enquiry into the conduct of the Taugwalders, resulting in the decision that there were no grounds for prosecution. But these things can be extremely unpleasant. Suddenly a rumour began going round Zermatt to the effect that two days before his death Alexandre had made a holograph will – a will in his own handwriting, I mean, dated, signed and all in order, probably drawn up with the assistance of the local magistrate. This privately made document had been deposited in a sealed envelope with the nearest local notary, at Brigue.'

'But who started the rumour? Hardly the lawyers involved, I suppose! Alexandre Bessarion was assumed dead, but his death wasn't official yet.'

'No, the person who began talking was a young man, a friend or relation of Alexandre, a somewhat irresponsible character, who was staying at Zermatt at the time and in whom he had confided. On learning of the arrangements recently made by Stanislas for his benefit, Alexandre had decided to make sure that his brother-in-law's gesture was reciprocated. Once again, their curious family situation was involved. Alexandre Bessarion thought his three stepbrothers and his stepmother had no right to his mother's fortune, even if the law said they did. He decided to remedy the situation by taking the necessary steps himself. He evidently felt enormous gratitude to Stanislas, who had done so much for him, for with the impulsiveness of youth he had also taken out a life insurance policy worth a considerable sum in his brother-in-law's favour.'

'But from what you say about the Topalidis fortune, there was no point whatsoever in that.'

'Indeed there was not, but the fact is that Alexandre took out the policy, perhaps prompted by some insurance broker. Anyway, he did it. Alexandre hadn't told Stanislas, either for fear that he would object or because he hadn't had the time. The young man I mentioned, probably trying to appear important through his close connection with such a spectacular drama, told a journalist about the policy. In those days climbing accidents were less frequent than they are today, and the press seized avidly upon them, particularly if they involved mysterious and more or less tragic circumstances. This story instantly caused a great stir. Think how it could be presented: the heir to a large fortune had robbed his family – such were the terms employed – by leaving it and a huge sum in life insurance to his sister's former husband, who took him out climbing two days later and came back alone, a cut rope still hanging from his belt. With no witnesses, Stanislas could tell any story he liked.'

'But that's crazy. There was no proof!'

'Of course not, but you must admit that the whole affair looked odd to a public not aware of all the details, and it even looked odd to the law. There was an atmosphere of uncertainty which made it impossible just to file the original report. Then Gertrude Bessarion, acting in the name of her sons, hired a lawyer known to be particularly litigious. She said she was sure that Stanislas had done away with Alexandre on purpose, profiting by a situation which made it impossible to discover the truth. You know that saying, usually misattributed to Beaumarchais, to the effect that slander always leaves some stain behind. Well, Gertrude spread slander for all she was worth, for you see, even if Alexandre's disappearance was considered in due course as being equivalent to his death and the legality of his will was recognized, it could still be challenged by the previous legal heirs. I don't know how conversant you are with the law?'

'Not very!'

'Nor am I, but it was through this business that I learned certain kinds of heirs can't be totally disinherited and will necessarily receive part of an estate. They comprise ascendants and descendants, and in some cases spouses, but not siblings. In this particular case, since Alexandre's parents Christophore and Hélène Bessarion were dead, and he himself had no children, he could leave his property to anyone he liked. Note that on the other hand, if Christophore Bessarion had still been alive he would automatically have had a right to all or part of the fortune, I'm not sure which, and through him it would then have passed to Gertrude and their three children. But as Christophore had died first, Alexandre was at liberty to make his own arrangements. Do you follow me?'

'Yes, indeed, although Gertrude Bessarion's conduct in trying to get hold of the inheritance through Alexandre's accident seems to me pretty unspeakable.'

'It was unspeakable. From all I've heard Gertrude was a rapacious, heartless woman, and couldn't be expected to show any mercy. But there was another aspect of the question I haven't mentioned yet. The insurance company was far from happy about Alexandre's disappearance two days after signing his life insurance policy. They got together with the Bessarions' lawyer to try to avoid paying up.'

'How did Stanislas react?'

'Badly, as you can imagine. For the second time he had just been cruelly hit by the death of one of the only two human beings he dearly loved. You probably know that the bereaved always feel a kind of remorse. It's only natural. Stanislas wasn't implicated in Calliope's death, but she had that fatal fall because she came to meet him while she was expecting his child. It's likely that at the time he thought about the accident over and over again, imagining how it might have been avoided. Alexandre's case was even harder. Although Stanislas had made no errors, and nothing was to blame but bad luck, he had been so closely involved with the youngster's death that he was bound to dwell on the circumstances, brooding on the decisions which might have prevented it from happening. He was very deeply wounded, life seemed to have no more value, and now came these monstrous accusations. He defended himself angrily, feeling not only grief but also shock and indignation.'

'So what happened?'

'Oh, there was an interminable series of legal proceedings. First of all, of course, events took their natural course as a consequence of the fact that since Alexandre's body had not been found there was presumption of death, but not confirmation. Probate could not be officially granted. The tribunal had to publish a summons requiring anyone with anything to say about the missing man to come forward. This is done in cases where a person has disappeared in circumstances entailing danger of death, or when there has been no trace of him for a long time. If death seems probable the judge dealing with the case can declare him missing at the request of those who have claims on his estate. But it has to be at least a year after he was seen to be in danger of death, or five years after nothing has been heard of him, before such a declaration can be made. At the same time there was an enquiry. The examining magistrate was the local Visp magistrate to whom the cantonal police had given the file. The whole thing was very long-drawn-out and very complicated, because Gertrude Bessarion was so tenacious. You see, if it had been found that Stanislas was responsible for Alexandre's death then his previous legal heirs could have the will annulled in a civil court.'

'But they'd have had to prove that Stanislas committed the crime.'

'Of course, and they couldn't. However, Gertrude also tried to show that Stanislas had committed a serious offence against Alexandre by cutting the rope that linked them and abandoning him. A serious offence resulting in death could also lead to annulment of the will. I don't know in exactly what order all this happened. Proceedings were adjourned, there were new developments. I think I remember ... wait a moment; yes, I do! When she really had to give up trying to prove that any crime had been committed, Gertrude claimed to have received a letter from her stepson and said he was alive somewhere in Italy. Expert opinions and counter-opinions were given. I'd say that woman did everything bitterness and malice could prompt her to do. All the same, and rightly, Alexandre was officially declared missing. At this point Gertrude Bessarion brought an action to get the will annulled. Her chances of success were slim, but she was waging a particularly nasty war of attrition. Yet again, this is only a rough outline, and I may have been wrong about the precise order of events here, but I think years went by before Gertrude finally gave up. The inheritance then went to Stanislas Limbourg, who also received the proceeds of the insurance policy, but he wouldn't touch it.'

'Then what did he do with it? You don't mean to say he handed it over to Alexandre's stepbrothers?'

'Certainly not. They had no right to it. But to Stanislas, who had suffered so much from having his innocence questioned, the legal decisions that led to his getting the money cleared his name. After adding to the sum what he had inherited on Calliope's death, he left it all in the hands of bankers, and acted as if he were not in possession of such a fortune. He even left Europe before the Second World War and went to Africa to get away from it all, living entirely on his own earnings as an engineer. He had found the atmosphere after Alexandre's disappearance intolerable, and a number of personal links were severed. People didn't turn their backs on him, he was never really under suspicion, but he'd been the subject of a legal enquiry and sensational reports in the press, which always produces unpleasantness. As it happens my father had supported and befriended Stanislas from the first, and he reacted with vehement anger when the infamous rumours began going round. The two of them remained great friends until my father's death, but they didn't see each other much once Stanislas left Europe. However, he regularly came back once a year, except during the war, to visit Calliope's grave. He used to stay at Zermatt, but he wouldn't visit or talk to anyone. He was a broken man, and he'd lost all belief in happiness and faith in other people.'

'So now he lives here?'

'Wait a minute! My story's nearly over, but there's one last detail to be added. About thirty years after Alexandre's accident, when Stanislas was about seventy and had difficulty in supporting the African climate, he retired to Lausanne, and one evening he had a telephone call telling him a body had just been seen in the ice at the bottom of the Gorner glacier by a solitary walker, who told the police. It might well be the body of Alexandre, and they were going to exhume it next morning. Stanislas went up to Zermatt that night. By now, of course, the rescue teams used helicopters. The cantonal police and the examining magistrate arrived at the same time as the guides who were to get the body out. It was in a remarkably good state of preservation, and hadn't been mutilated by the movements of the glacier, as sometimes happens. And it was indeed Alexandre's body. He was perfectly recognizable, and even had his identity papers in his sack. This discovery, of course, confirmed everything Stanislas had said. It was likely, although this is just a hypothesis, that the snow bridge had collapsed before the rescue party arrived, flinging Alexandre to the bottom of the crevasse and ripping out the belay.'

'Even the best belay wouldn't stand up to a shock like that.'

'Alexandre must have been killed instantly. He showed no external injuries and looked as if he'd fallen asleep in the youthful vigour of his twenty-three years. No doubt he had been smothered and buried under the weight of the snow. The hemp rope had fallen on him, intact, one end tied round his waist and the other to the ice-axe which also rested on his body, lying across his legs. There couldn't have been a clearer explanation of what happened. But it came too late. Stanislas had suffered so deeply from his bereavements and the hurtful suspicions cast on him that he couldn't get over it now. Perhaps he drew some small comfort from being able to bury Alexandre in the same tomb as Calliope. He visits it every day.'

'So he does live here?'

'Not all the time, and the hotel's closed in the off-season periods, but when it's open he stays here. Since Alexandre's body was found and Stanislas Limbourg was finally cleared of all suspicion, he has agreed to make use, though very sparingly, of the fortune he inherited – he's left it to some charity, I don't know which. He lives on the Lake of Geneva in spring and autumn, in an isolated house on a hill with some kind of manservant who looks after him as his only companion. When the Mont-Cervin Hotel opens again he comes back to it. He wants to die in Zermatt, but death, which strikes down so many who fear it, keeps sparing this old man who wants nothing more. This hotel is his real home; he's known, respected and admired here, and the staff look after him like a very old friend. It's a place full of memories of a time when life still smiled on him.'

I glanced towards the man whose story I had just heard, but he was no longer there. He must have left the lounge without our noticing, absorbed as we were in conversation. But I saw him next day when I skirted the church before going down to Visp. Leaning on his stick, looking even older and more fragile than ever, he was in the cemetery, gazing at the tomb of those he had loved and whom he would soon join.

SOLITUDE WHERE I FIND A SECRET, SWEET DELIGHT

It actually began in Paris, at the Café Balzar in the rue des Écoles. Bruno, who was still studying, had arranged to meet Roland there. Roland himself had recently moved out to the country. This was a day in early December, one of those cold grey days that herald the real coming of winter. People out in the street were already wrapped up warm, and had gloomy expressions on their faces. The brasserie staff were getting tables ready for the evening, spreading them with white cloths, while a few small groups of customers lingered in conversation over tea or steaming hot toddies. When the door opened, a bitter gust of north wind reached anyone close to it, and Bruno regretted choosing a table almost facing the entrance. He had arrived first and was keeping a watchful eye on the pavement. Suddenly Roland appeared, smiling broadly, sat down opposite his friend and took off his bomber jacket and scarf. The two young men shook hands warmly. They had not seen each other since the summer and their last climbing expedition.

'You okay?' asked Bruno.

'Oh, not too bad,' conceded Roland.

'Same here,' agreed Bruno, without enthusiasm.

A waiter came over to their table; he was dressed in the old-fashioned style, long white apron almost down to the floor, black waistcoat and a starched shirt front adorned by a bow tie.

'A hot chocolate, please,' said Roland.

'I like the atmosphere in here,' remarked Bruno. 'Mirrors everywhere, and those palms in their retro china pots. That's what I call style. Well, at least it makes a change from McDonald's!'

The two friends exchanged a smile, but Bruno's disenchanted expression soon returned. 'City life,' he explained. 'the crowds, the packed Métro – it's really getting me down. I'm fed to the teeth. See all that traffic in the streets, and people jostling and ignoring each other. My God, the North Face of the Ciarforon seems a long way off! I keep thinking about it these days. I imagine the wind blowing the powder snow around at this time of year, up in all that solitude –'

'Oh, by the way,' said Roland, 'I brought you some photographs.'

Taking a large envelope from his briefcase, he found a bundle of photos in it.

Solitude 102

'Look at that! Great, isn't it?'

Leaning over the pictures, passing them to each other and commenting now and then, the two young men relived some of those moments when space and time seem to have been annihilated. They were far from crowded city life, back in the best days of their last holiday together, making their way over the slopes of the Mont Maudit in sunlight ... crossing the Argentière bergschrund ... doing a balancing act on the sharp crest of the Arête de Bionnassay ... struggling against a stormy wind on the Piz Palu. Happy memories came flooding back to them, and naturally enough those memories led to new plans.

'You know what I've been thinking?' asked Bruno. 'About next year – guess what I'd like to do first? A training climb to get us fit again – the Midi-Plan. Yes, I know it's commonplace and you've done it before, but I can't stop thinking about it. When I'm in a packed lecture hall or a crowded Métro train, I think of that exposed ridge, with the Chamonix valley on the left and the high mountains on the right.'

'If it's peace and quiet you want, you'd better think again!' pointed out Roland. 'There'll be hordes of people swarming all over the place, from the moment the first Aiguille du Midi cable car of the day arrives.'

'Well, exactly, but you see, this is my idea: we bivouac somewhere near the start of the ridge and set off at least two hours before the cable car gets there. Then we can do the route by ourselves, while the mountains are still deserted, the way they would have been in the old days.'

'Why not? Yes, I know I've done it before, but I remember I enjoyed it. It's a fine ridge, not all that easy. It's recommended to beginners because of the easy access, but I reckon that's a mistake. It's quite varied climbing, and fairly sustained. Worthwhile, too ... yes, I'd happily do it again, but only if we do it the way you suggest.'

'Great!' said Bruno. 'That makes me look forward to it even more! Our little bivouac beneath the vast and starry sky! How I wish we were there now!'

'Going all poetic, are you?' mocked his friend.

The day finally comes when plans turn to reality, and one fine July afternoon Bruno and Roland, laden with large sacks, cheerfully left the cable car at the Aiguille du Midi, crossed the footbridge, went through the tunnel and the ice cave and then down the first part of the ridge. A few other climbers were preparing to bivouac at the Col du Midi, but no one else seemed to have exactly the same plan in mind as the two friends.

Roland had brought a small high-altitude tent, which they put up on a snowy shelf at the end of the col where skiers put their skis on in winter. The sunset cast a glow over the mountains as the two young men carefully shared out the packet soup that had been simmering in their billy, the local ham and a chocolate bar. They waited to go to bed until they had seen the mountain range bathed in moonlight.

Getting up very early indeed in the morning while it was still pitch dark was rather less exhilarating. The idea of sleeping a little longer was very tempting, and every gesture seemed laborious when they had to emerge from their sleeping bags, get their gear on, drink hastily warmed-up and not very palatable coffee, pack their equipment and fold up the tent.

'God, I feel like a total novice!' grumbled Bruno, trying to fix the straps of his crampons with stiff fingers by the light of his head torch.

'Don't worry, you're doing fine!' Bruno assured him. 'I mean, you've actually got the spikes pointing the right way, down at the snow. What a fantastic memory! What experience!'

'Get lost!' said Bruno. 'If you feel like cracking jokes at four in the morning, I don't! Pass me the rope. It'll be better once we get going.'

Sure enough, the idea of starting the climb several hours ahead of anyone else turned out excellent. The mountains were cold and wild as dawn approached. Following old tracks, the two companions made rapid progress, while myriads of ice flakes glittered from the hardened snow in the beams of their torches. A shooting star fell from the still dark sky.

Bruno made a fervent wish to himself. 'If only this solitude would last for ever!'

The sky was imperceptibly lightening in the east. A cold, grey light replaced the nocturnal shadows. A breeze rose, and pale light spread over the mountains.

'I call this real happiness!' said Roland.

'Solitude!' recited Bruno. '*Solitude where I find a secret, sweet delight!* Isn't that Racine? Good stuff, nicely balanced, says everything! I love that line.'

'How does it go on?'

'No idea. Can't remember ... no, sorry, it won't come back to me. Maybe it will in a moment, but never mind. It's still a great line on its own. *Solitude where I find a secret, sweet delight!* '

'Yes, great.'

With the line of verse still running through their heads, the two friends went on climbing. Day gradually dawned, and the stars flickered out.

Finally, above the Cirque de Talèfre, the sun cast its first rays into the purity of a glorious morning.

Passage followed passage of their climb. Roland remembered that it was advisable to skirt the first rock outcrop on the left; he had lost a lot of time there before when he had tried to go straight up it. The route as a whole was in reasonable condition. Here and there cornices overhung the north flank, and there was a fairly delicate passage where they had to traverse on ice to get into the couloir going up to the Rognon du Plan. Up there the two of them stopped for a rest. It was getting warmer now. Roland brought out their flask.

'I've remembered what comes next!' Bruno announced triumphantly.

> *'Solitude where I find a secret, sweet delight.*
> *Places I always loved …'*

He sighed with pleasure, looking round at the mountains where he was back.

'*Places I always loved,*' he repeated.

'I must say this poem of yours seems more and more apt,' commented Roland. 'So what comes after that?'

'My mind's gone blank again, but the rest of it will probably come back to me bit by bit.'

'Had enough to drink? Sure you're not hungry? Okay, I'll just take off my duvet and we'll go on. I think I remember we go down a system of little couloirs, ledges and chimneys. Ready? Let's get moving.'

'Sure, but just one more look at that view. Amazing, isn't it, wherever you look at it from?'

Advancing through the morning light, relishing their solitude as if the mountains were all their own, Bruno and Roland went on their way, enjoying the familiar gestures, passing an ice axe behind the shoulder of the sack, pulling a strap tight with a firm tug … At last they reached the Col Supérieur du Plan and then went on along the snow-covered ridge to the foot of the last rocks. By now the warmth was becoming almost heavy.

'We'll leave our crampons here for going up to the summit of the Aiguille. Last time I was here there were ropes getting tangled up everywhere, there were so many people going up and down – four ropes on the way up, with three on their way down.'

'Ghastly.'

'Well, overcrowded certainly. Still, everyone was quite cheerful. There must have been twenty or so people picnicking here on the col.'

'Not my scene,' said Bruno. 'But our idea of starting out ahead of the crowd was absolutely brilliant!'

'Even the guides haven't caught up with us!'

'I must say, we've gone fast and efficiently!'

'It was the idea of being on our own that spurred us on.'

'Oh, and speaking of being on our own, I've remembered more of the poem, and I think it's La Fontaine, not Racine:

> 'Solitude where I find a secret, sweet delight,
> Places I always loved, shall I no more enjoy
> Far from the bustling world, your coolness and your shade?'

'Far from the bustling world it is! *And* far from its noise. This silence is incredible. Just the sound of the odd stone falling. You can't even hear any noise from the valley. Nothing but the mountains and a stream somewhere, I'm not sure where. The coolness and shade bit isn't quite right, though. The sun's pretty hot already. Come on, let's get to the top quickly, so we can get back down before the snow softens too much.'

The short climb that followed was quickly done. On the peak, the two of them had a brief rest. Bruno was still reciting scraps of the poem.

'Far from the bustling world. ... Places I always loved ... Solitude ... secret, sweet delight! I can't get it out of my head. I've an idea I've read some other poems about solitude. I was mad keen on poetry when I was fifteen, learned reams of it by heart. Okay, pass me the packet of dried apricots and let's start the descent.'

Coming back down to the Col Supérieur du Plan, he remembered something else.

'Here we are,' he exclaimed. 'Listen to this:

> Ah, how I love this loneliness!
> These places sacred to the night
> Remote from daytime and its light
> Pleasing to my uneasiness.

'So who's that by?' asked Roland.

'Haven't the faintest.'

'Not exactly night, is it? The sun's blazing down, and the light vibrates as if you could touch it. But I'll tell you something, that line about uneasiness comes rather close to the mark. No, honestly, don't laugh. I'm starting to feel a bit uneasy myself, not seeing another single soul.'

'That's what getting used to crowds does for you. You can't do without them now! You've been brainwashed, that's what it is. A few hours away from other human beings and you start to feel bad. So this is what civilization does for us! Personally, I appreciate not seeing a single soul, I really do! This is what we wanted, right? I can breathe freely at last!'

'Okay, but all the same, you know, it's not just that no one else has joined us, I can't even see anyone climbing on the ridge in the distance.'

'That's because we did the climb so fast. Terrific! Come on, then, let's get back down to the valley if you miss the world and all its works so much! The first slope's steep, but it's still firm. Kick your heels in well, or you may get down faster than you want.'

The descent took some time, for the Envers du Plan Glacier was already extremely tortuous and complex. Every step they took sent a short fan-shape of wet snow slithering over the surface of the slope. The track wound around, sometimes going up again, weaving a skilful way between the séracs and the vast crevasses with their stratified walls. A real labyrinth of ice. The snow was starting to ball up under the climbers' crampons, and they had to keep tapping their boots to knock off the clogging lumps. A bridge had fallen since the day before, and they were forced to find another way round. The sun was beating down on the glacier now, the heat was becoming oppressive, and they had long ago emptied their water bottle. Now and then Bruno picked up a small handful of melting snow and carried it to his mouth, enjoying the pleasure of contact with the cold lump of ice that formed against his tongue and teeth, gradually dissolving into cool water in his dry throat.

'You shouldn't do that,' said Roland.

'Why not?'

'I can't remember, but it's supposed to be a bad idea. You could get a stomach-ache or a throat infection.'

'Oh, come off it!' said Bruno.

'Okay, just as you like, but don't expect sympathy from me ... you know, I really am surprised there's still no one on the slopes above us. I mean, we're taking our time over the descent. Strikes me we're the only people on the Midi-Plan at all today!'

'Maybe the 'phrique has broken down.'

'Or else it just happens no one else fancies climbing today. I must say, it's rather a shame to think we don't owe all this peace and quiet to our early start and our speed!'

'Absolutely infuriating! Well, never mind, it's been fun, although I wouldn't say solitude was much of an advantage just now. If there were several of us looking for the way through this maze it would be a help.'

'Hey, just look at that crevasse! Ginormous! I don't like the look of that bridge. Shall we try it, all the same?'

'Yes, I'm getting fed up with always having to climb back up again. Go on, I'll give you a good belay. Let's get out of here fast. I can't wait for the beer I'm going to have at the Requin Hut when we get there! Can't think of anything else. Right, you can go now. Delicately, though, so that I can get across the bridge after you.'

Their descent went on in this way. By now both Bruno and Roland were keeping their curious impression that the mountains were totally deserted to themselves; their sense of solitude was growing all the time, but they hesitated to say so. When they finally reached the Requin Hut they suffered a severe disappointment. There was no one there, and the place was closed. Written on the door in white chalk was the enigmatic and somewhat absurd announcement, 'Closed on account of absence.'

'This is a bit much!' exclaimed Roland.

'Incredible! What do you make of it?'

'It must be like we said. The Aiguille du Midi cable car has broken down. Maybe there's even been an accident. And the warden was told by phone and took the chance of going down. I mean, most of his customers come in on their way down the mountain, not up.'

'Well, if we wanted solitude you have to admit we've got it. Too much of it, actually. It's going to be at least another two hours before we get to that beer. I need a beer, I really do, you've no idea! My legs are tiring too. We've gone quite a long way for a first climb!'

'Listen, I can hear running water – somewhere round the back, I think. I'll go and fill the flask, and we'll finish off the rest of our food. And let's not be ungrateful. We ought to be glad of the chance to have the mountains all to ourselves for a whole day. Then we'll go on to join the jostling crowds at Montenvers.'

'Good idea,' agreed Bruno.

No sooner said than done. Twenty minutes later the two friends were on their way down the path leading to the Mer de Glace, still without meeting a soul. As they moved over the deserted glacier, a genuine sense of anxiety took increasing hold of them. They did not even feel like exchanging their impressions any more, and despite their fatigue they went up the ladders and along the track leading to Montenvers as fast as they could. The station was closed and empty, apart from one train standing at the end of the tracks, with its doors closed.

'What do you make of that?' asked Roland.

'No more than you do. Maybe the train broke down, so there wouldn't have been anyone coming up to the hut from here, or any tourists either.'

'Even on foot? And you reckon the Aiguille du Midi cable car broke down this morning too?'

'Let's get to the hotel, quick. Surely there must be someone there who can explain.'

But there was no one at the hotel. Its doors and shutters were carefully closed. Bruno tried shouting. His voice had a lugubrious ring to it, and was echoed only by the sound of water falling on the slabs and moraines on the other side of the glacier. The sky was azure blue; the mountains looked magnificent. A large rock rolled down the scree slope opposite, carrying others away with it and raising a little dust. Then silence fell again.

'What on earth is all this about?' muttered Bruno. 'I mean, it's crazy, right? Totally crazy!'

'Suppose war's broken out?'

'War? What war? Did we hear about any threats of war when we set off yesterday? I'd only just been listening to the news. The world was just the same as usual.'

'Well, maybe a nuclear bomb went off somewhere close to here.'

'A bomb? Did you see any bomb explode? Stop being so daft!'

'Then what *do* you think happened?'

'I have absolutely no idea. Not the faintest.'

'Or maybe it could be some ecological disaster? I mean, some kind of huge pollution problem.'

'Maybe ... but all the same, we wouldn't be the only people stuck here in the mountains. There'd have been other people coming down from the Couvercle, the Charpoua, Leschaux, everywhere.'

'Then what the hell *do* you think happened?'

'No idea, but one thing's for sure, we must get back down into the valley, fast. I mean, this is really worrying. Come on, let's get moving.'

Legs weary, shoulders sore under the straps of sacks that had been weighing down on their backs since morning, wilting under the heavy heat, and feeling extremely worried and upset, Bruno and Roland made for the path leading to the valley. One behind the other, in total silence now, they hurried towards Chamonix.

'A car at last!' exclaimed Roland.

Sure enough, there was a car parked at the side of a field, not far from the road. They looked at it with considerable affection and continued their downward climb, very much aware, all the same, that they could not hear any noise at all, no engine anywhere, not a human voice. Only their footsteps echoing on the dry, stony ground.

Other cars were parked further down the slope, but there did not seem to be anyone around. The two young men crossed the Route Blanche and the railway, went over the bridge and came to the station. There were no trains or cars moving, there was no sound, there was not a living soul in sight.

'Let's go to the Place de la Poste!' said Bruno in abrupt tones. 'If there's anyone around at all it'll be there.'

They hurried to the town centre and made for the Place de l'Église. Roland stopped in the middle of the square. Bruno passed him and then stopped too. He ran a hand over his forehead, which was dripping with sweat, brought out his handkerchief, wiped his brow and studied the square around him. All that could be heard was the dull roar of the river Arve filling the valley, emphasizing the otherwise total silence.

Bruno wondered if he was dreaming. He dug his nails into the flesh of his arms so hard it hurt, and examined the marks they had left.

'This is crazy!' he told Roland. 'Ridiculous! And I don't think we're dreaming, either. What on earth has happened? What ought we to do? What …'

He turned to his friend, surprised to receive no reply. But Roland was no longer there.

A DAY ON HOLIDAY

That morning's grey sky had gradually cleared, and now the only clouds drifting above the Aiguilles were of the fine weather variety: round and white, looking as if they were rimmed with warm radiance. By now Marcelle felt sure that Raoul would not be back before evening. When she woke up she had expected to see him quite soon. It must have been raining when the sun rose, so she thought he would have called off his climb. But if he had, he would have been back by this time. Even if he slept in for a while at the hut where he had spent the night and then came down at his leisure, he would have been back for lunch.

Well, never mind! She would have a little peace and quiet all to herself. Women never do have time to themselves, not even on holiday, certainly not during the rest of the year. As everyone knows. It's a fact borne out by all research into the subject. She for one certainly never got any respite except for these few days her husband spent in the mountains. The rest of the time she was always busy, chasing about, looking after other people. You could say theirs was a successful life, maybe, but thanks to what? Thanks to her and her own hard work! Raoul did his job as a broker, visiting clients, discussing deals, and once he was home he sat down at the dinner-table and unfolded his napkin. Everything, absolutely everything, depended on her. She had to get up first in the morning, open the shutters, make coffee, bring her husband a cup in bed. She hardly had a moment to sit down for a bite to eat herself before it was time to start again. And over quite a long period she had also had to get the children ready for school and take them to the school gates too. These days she tried to get ahead with her cooking in the morning; she spent more time on that than she used to. Then she set off for the office and the job to which she had been promoted, or you could say she had got it by sheer hard work, having begun at the bottom of the ladder. When she arrived home in the evening, long before Raoul, she started getting dinner ready, watered their little garden, did a bit of housework. She dusted the furniture and wiped the window panes every day. You wouldn't find a house as clean as theirs anywhere else in the neighbourhood. Everything was impeccable: tidy and polished. The fact that they had a house at all was thanks to her too, the result of her good management and thrift, her untiring efforts to find somewhere you could get the washing done for a franc less or buy cheaper vegetables. And she used to sew or knit almost all the children's clothes herself. She had ... oh, there was no end to what she'd done. Raoul was not a bad man, of course. He didn't drink or gamble or chase other women. Not that she'd have put up with any of that. All the same, he was a man. An egotist. All men are egotists. She could certainly understand modern young women with their women's lib and all that. In her own time there simply weren't the same facilities. No disposable nappies, no baby-sitters, no Pill either. She'd had three children straight off, just like that. Even though she was being careful. And she hadn't wanted the last baby at all. She might have thought of getting rid of it but for Raoul's principles. As it happened, that child was the one who'd turned out best. He'd been to the Polytechnique, had a wife with a degree in philosophy, a fine car, a second home already. No one could say she hadn't brought her children up well. In the sweat of her brow! The fact was, Raoul had simply made life more complicated.

'Isn't there a shirt ironed?'

When he knew she got the washing done on Saturday and did the ironing on Sunday!

'Have you seen my cufflinks?'

He didn't even notice she was stirring porridge! He always chose the most inconvenient moments to bother her.

'Could you give me a hand to move the workbench back into place?'

When she'd just that moment sat down with a magazine after her day's work!

'There's a football match on TV this evening.'

And she'd wanted to watch that old film with Charles Boyer and Danielle Darrieux.

It was no use telling Raoul any of that. The next chance he got, he'd go back to thinking of no one but himself. Male egotism will always come to the surface, that's the burden a woman has to bear.

And now that they had this little chalet at La Joux, tiny as a doll's house but their own, they owed it to her as much as to her mother-in-law's legacy, since when the legacy came it was thanks to her, Marcelle's efforts that the mortgage on the house in Bondoufle was almost paid off and they were able to put all the money into a holiday home.

Her own preference would have been a studio flat in the south of France, down by the sea, so that at work she could talk about their place on the Côte. But what with Raoul's passion for his mountains, she might have known he'd get his own way, dwelling on the fact that it was his mother's money. Raoul and his mountains! Why on earth did he have to

A Day on Holiday 112

go on climbing? Escaping, you might say, from the world of cleanliness and security she worked so hard to create around them. Coming back with his face sunburnt, his nose peeling, his lips cracked, his trousers tattered, and after experiencing heat, cold, thirst, perhaps fear. All of which could be avoided if he stayed quietly at home with her down here! And he spread about the place his damp, dirty equipment – his torn cagoules, his soaked sleeping bags, his ropes, soaked and encrusted with grit, his muddy boots, his felted socks with holes in them yet again. Sometimes, dropping with weariness, he would collapse on his bed in the middle of the afternoon, when they could have walked around town with the children. All with that happy, abstracted air that she couldn't abide. As if he were coming back from another world where there was no room for anyone else, not even herself.

Well, there were things a woman had to bear. Of course these holidays in the mountains had their good moments, like today, in fact. Now the children didn't come with them any more she could have some peace and quiet, be mistress of her own time, spend her leisure as she pleased. She had better make the most of it, because if all this talk of early retirement came to anything she'd soon have Raoul around the whole time. In her younger days, she'd been keen to claim the right to early retirement herself at union meetings: 'They ought to lower the age. People have a right to some relaxation. They work till they drop. It's too much for them. That's no kind of life!' Yet now that retirement was approaching she did not look forward to it. She was in excellent health, the children were grown up, she could have gone on working for quite a long time. And she knew the job, she enjoyed the company of her colleagues, she liked having a good heart-to-heart with the other women at slack times of day. Suddenly she began to feel she was being shunted off. Look at it in that light, and retirement was the last port of call before death. There'd be nothing more to expect but growing even older and then dying, and that was a fact. Raoul was very fit and well too – just look at the way he still went climbing. But they'd be stuck with each other, just the two of them, twenty-four hours a day, living on a reduced income. And Raoul would create chaos about the place with all his do-it-yourself stuff.

So she'd better take her chance of enjoying a long, quiet day like this, not a common occurrence in her life. She washed her hair, put in rollers, covered them with a nylon net and sat out in a recliner on the sunny balcony, reading a women's magazine. She perused, with interest, an article on the financial exploitation of women doing equal work for less pay, which echoed her own opinions, and then another entitled *Twenty Summer Salads*. Thinking of salads, she hoped Raoul would be back in time to go shopping for this evening's dinner. They had got into the habit of his doing the shopping on holiday so that she could have a change from it. She had finished up the leftovers yesterday evening and at lunchtime, and now the fridge was almost empty.

Around five o'clock the woman next door dropped in to borrow her electric whisk. They had a chat, and it was almost six when the neighbour left. Raoul still wasn't back, so Marcelle had to go and do the shopping herself. Luckily he had arranged to leave her the car. She ran a comb through her hair, went up to Argentière, had difficulty parking and bought stuff to make a quick meal: a can of palm hearts, a tin of ratatouille and a couple of caramel custards. No one wanted to slave over a hot stove in this warm weather.

Raoul still wasn't back when she returned. She put her shopping away, left the key under the pot of geraniums and went round next door to see if they'd finished with the whisk, rather hoping the neighbours would keep her there until apéritif time, as indeed they did.

It was nearly eight-thirty when she got back, expecting to find the door open and the balcony cluttered with ropes and clothing. But everything was still shut up. It was unusual for Raoul to be late. He usually hurried back, afraid that she would have been left alone too long, that she might be worried, might start making a fuss about his climbing.

The two rooms of the chalet were empty and almost painfully clean and tidy. There was nothing to be done in them. Not an ashtray for her to empty, grumbling. Not a jacket thrown untidily across a chair. Not a toolbox drawer turned upside down because the particular kind of screw Raoul needed seemed to have gone missing.

She ate her dinner on the balcony, feeling rather bored. Then she switched on the radio for the nine o'clock news, and turned it off again almost at once. What was the point of all these wars here, there and everywhere? People got what they were asking for, and one had quite enough problems of one's own, thank you very much, without bothering about other people's!

If Raoul had come home in time she would have taken him off to the cinema. She didn't fancy going on her own. You wanted to be able to discuss things in the interval and talk about the film when you got home. She picked up her knitting, switched the radio on again and searched in vain for an interesting programme, but all the wavelengths seemed much

A Day on Holiday 114

the same, and at this time of evening they were broadcasting nothing but jazz, rock and pop. By now she was getting very anxious to see Raoul back. He would give her a brief explanation of what had happened, tell her what had kept them, and then she in her turn would tell him what the neighbours had told *her* about the plans for a new pedestrian area.

And suppose Raoul had had an accident? She had long ago got used to the idea that things didn't always go smoothly in the mountains. He assured her he was very careful. But there'd been helicopters overhead all day. If he'd had to spend a second night in the hut, why didn't he phone the neighbours? What could have happened? It was ten o'clock now, and night was falling. When someone had an accident, how did you hear about it? Did Raoul have his address anywhere in his sack? It was probably the police who had to come and tell the family. And then, oh God, then what? She would have to identify the body, tell the children, all that. And then there'd be the funeral ... they hadn't even decided where they wanted to be buried. And after that she would be alone. Alone – alone in the house in Bondoufle for the rest of her active life. Alone for the holidays. Alone in her retirement. Would she even have the heart to go on keeping house so well without him? To carry on dusting the furniture and wiping the windows every day? To water the garden? Who would she do her hair for? Who would she clean the tops of the wardrobes for? Who would she live for? And what about the rest of it, too? Who would deal with the paperwork, all the tax and insurance? Who would do things about the house? She was a good housekeeper, but she'd never been the do-it-yourself sort. What about the fuse that blew, the leaking U-bend of the sink, a dripping tap, an unexpected noise in the car engine? Raoul coped with all that. What happens to old women on their own? Who do they talk to in the evening about their rheumatism, the autumn rain, their memories of the past? What does a button off a shirt really matter, a pair of boots left lying about, a cold pipe in an ashtray, a bathroom splashed with water from the shower? They're not really important. They even have a kind of charm about them, the charm of daily life ...

Night had fallen. There was nothing to be heard but the sound of the river, and a car going along the road now and then. Marcelle dared not move. Raoul wouldn't be back tonight, or perhaps ever. The neighbours wouldn't be getting any phone calls at this hour. And no doubt the police didn't come to tell people about accidents in the middle of the night. How suddenly the most ordinary holiday can turn to tragedy! Was it her turn now, after hearing of so many other people who suffered disasters and she hadn't even felt sorry for them?

She rose to her feet, with difficulty. Her temples were throbbing. She took an aspirin and then a sleeping tablet to help her forget, swallowing them with a little water from the washbasin tap. Then she went to the bedroom and got into bed, but in spite of the sleeping tablet she lay awake a long time, listening for the slightest sound.

She was sleeping deeply when she became aware of a violent noise. Opening her eyes, she saw a large shape outlined against the window.

'Is that you?' she asked stupidly.

'Yes,' whispered Raoul. 'I hoped not to wake you, so I was getting undressed in the dark. I dropped a boot.'

'What happened?'

'Nothing. The conditions were bad, and the climb took some time, and then we got the route wrong. I came down from the hut by the light of my head torch, so as not to worry you. But then I lost my way on the glacier. And it was a long walk … my legs were aching by the time I got back. I'm done in!'

'Have you had anything to eat?'

'Oh, yes, I've been nibbling this and that all day. Don't worry. I need to sleep, that's all.'

He lay down beside her, heavily, and she soon heard him breathing rhythmically, fast asleep. Everything in her world clicked back into its proper place. It was all right again. She smiled and relaxed, for this brief moment acknowledging that she was a happy woman.

THE SECRET

Most mountains have their history, but some are much more deeply charged than others. Such is Mont Blanc which, long ago, fuelled a burning ambition in a youngster called Horace Bénédict de Saussure, and was finally conquered after twenty years of much effort and numerous attempts. Such also is the Matterhorn, whose fantastic pyramid was the object of fierce competition and whose conquest ended in the well-known tragedy. Everest is another, for since the start of the century its height fascinated and like a mirage drew the ambitions of climbers of the age to it.

Everest! Chomolungma! The Mother Goddess! The highest summit of the globe! 8848m! 29,002ft! With what amazement the British expedition of 1921 regarded it when first they saw the mountain close to. George Mallory describes the dramatic vision which slowly appeared to him and his companion, Guy Bullock, as they tried to pierce the gloom at the end of the Arun Valley: 'Suddenly our eyes caught a glint of snow through the clouds; and gradually, very gradually, in the course of two hours or so, visions of great mountainsides and glaciers and ridges, now here, now there, forms invisible for the most part to the naked eye or indistinguishable from the clouds themselves, appeared through the floating rifts and had meaning for us – one whole clear meaning pierced from these fragments, for we had seen a whole mountain range, little by little, the lesser to the greater until, incredibly higher in the sky than imagination had ventured to dream, the top of Everest itself appeared.'

But how well do we know the long and marvellous history of its conquest? It offers a peculiar characteristic, remarkable for an epoch of certainties, in which books of records vie to describe, locate, and date in the fullest detail the most trivial of exploits, that a mystery should still subsist over the first ascent of the highest summit in the world …

It was through Tibet that the early expeditions passed. Can we conceive today what that meant? More than a month of sea voyage, followed by a long journey by steam train, and finally an endless approach march in which an army of porters, assisted only by a few mules, had to force a way with a heavy and voluminous quantity of material in wooden cases, special receptacles and jerry-cans, filled with petrol, paraffin, kerosene, hundreds of tins of food, scientific instruments, canvas tents, rucksacks, stiff waterproof capes, woollen breeches, jackets and waistcoats, hob-nailed boots lined with fur, innumerable hanks of hemp rope, heavy cast-iron crampons with leather thongs, long ice axes with ash shafts, candle lanterns, not to speak of a highly cumbersome and primitive oxygen equipment. For weeks all that had to be transported before base camp could be established and the real business begun. And then to get back, the approach march had to be reversed to reach the railway which brought them to the coast and the boat home. An expedition lasted about seven months. And when, as was the case with Mallory, that meant leaving behind a professional job, a wife and three children, one begins to realise the sacrifices climbers were called on to make in an epoch when there were no sponsors and why the mountain was only for totally devoted amateurs.

The first expedition was in 1921. It was led by Col. C.K. Howard-Bury and had eight other members. It was basically a reconnaissance trip and the lead climbers, Mallory, Bullock and Wheeler had to retreat at 23,000ft, that is some 7,000m, due to the violent snow charged winds. Without further ado in 1922 the British determined to profit from the favourable attitude of the Tibetan government to mount a new assault, but this time not in autumn but the following spring. And Mallory, who had written to his sister on the 10th November 1921 from Marseilles that not for all the gold in Arabia would he leave again the following year, was unaware that there was already a letter in the post telling him of the project and requesting him to join it. There was no need of Arabian gold to convince him, for he could not resist the appeal. He only spent three months in England before re-embarking ... The 1922 expedition had 13 members and was directed by Brig-Gen. C.G. Bruce. It was a vast caravan which now took the route through Tibet for, in addition to the Europeans and an interpreter, there were five Gurkhas, forty Sherpas and a vast train of porters, drivers, mules, oxen and yaks. Despite this huge force, the assault party, formed by Mallory, Somervell and Norton, had to retreat from a point which their altimeter read as 26,800ft (8168m). The summit was still 700m above and Everest remained unconquered, inviolate in its immaculate purity, an ever more coveted goal for those who believed they were capable of attacking it.

Two years now passed before there was a new attempt. The story of the 1924 expedition has passed down in history as the perfect paradigm for pure adventure.

Mallory was once more part of the team, ten men this time and again under the direction of Bruce. Amongst the newcomers was a youngster of 22, Andrew 'Sandy' Irvine, with little alpine experience but chosen for his other qualities. A fine sportsman and a natural athlete, he had been in the Oxford Eight which beat Cambridge in the famous Boat Race. A top class skier, he had also shown himself a good climber, leading routes on Welsh rock. He had also practised ice craft in the Oberland. And in the preceding year he had taken part in an expedition to Spitzbergen where he had shown outstanding physical toughness and endurance, proven himself a good team member and almost a genius for solving mechanical problems. Already, on the way out to India he had spent his time putting to rights the faulty oxygen apparatus, even though his personal view was that it was preferable to climb a mountain without such artificial aid. As soon as he arrived in the Himalaya he gave evidence of exceptional acclimatisation and climbed rapidly between camps. Andrew Irvine, despite his youth, was proving an outstanding recruit.

As for Mallory, the veteran, now thirty-seven years old, he was so well known for his resistance, ability and his Alpine and Himalayan experience that he was considered the best mountaineer of his time. He had started climbing in the Alps in 1904 when eighteen, under the eye of Graham Irving and had succeeded in doing Mont Blanc in his first season. He was bitten and climbed actively whilst at Cambridge, where he read History. It was there he met Geoffrey Winthrop Young, with whom he climbed first in Wales and then in the Alps. And it was at this period that Lytton Strachey described him as having the body of an athlete by Praxitiles and a face with the mystery of a Boticelli. In every way George Mallory seems to have been an outstanding person, all the more so since he managed to combine mountaineering with working as a schoolmaster at Charterhouse, and enjoying a family life with his wife, Ruth Turner, and their three children. Throughout the war the memory of his climbs served as a solace in the trenches, and as soon as it was over he was back in the Alps for the 1919 season. Then in 1921 started the Everest adventure.

Doubtless other members of the expedition, of whom less has been said, were also remarkable, for all top mountaineers are in different ways. But Mallory and Irvine formed a special team for the highest mountain in the world, experience and daring, strength and beauty, passion and enthusiasm, power and grace, which made the story of that particular rope pass down into history. And God only knows what happened ...

Conditions in 1924 were execrable. It was bitterly cold and there were violent storms over the Himalaya. Camp V was eventually established at 7,800m. Norton and Somervell spent the night there on the 2nd of June and in the morning of the 4th left without oxygen and got beyond the point reached in 1922 but had to give up. Thereupon Mallory decided to have a final try and chose as his partner Irvine, the only one of the newcomers up to trying the summit bid. The 5th June passed in preparations at Camp IV, which Mallory and Irvine left on the 6th at 8.40 in the morning with eight porters, who went up with them to Camp V, four of whom returned. On the 7th they reached Camp VI and Mallory sent back notes for Odell and Noel with the remaining porters: 'Perfect weather for the job'.

On the 8th in a clear morning the two men left Camp VI. Towards midday clouds began to cover the top of the mountain, but Odell, who had gone up to Camp V on his own, saw the summit and ridge leading to it in a sudden clearing, with two tiny figures moving upwards at around 8,600m, on a small snow crest near to the great rock step. Shortly after the clouds rolled back in again and that fascinating vision was the last anyone saw of them. Their bodies were never found. Had they reached the summit? Odell never wavered in the belief they had.

It would have been nice to have let it rest a mystery and left the highest mountain in the world for ever in grandiose isolation with its secret. But uncertainty does not please modern man who wishes to leave his mark everywhere on the earth. It was better to believe, that whatever Mallory and Irvine had done, Everest remained unconquered and make a further attack, this time with a clear, properly established outcome, rather than leave a disquieting doubt.

It is noticeable over the years, after the initial impact had faded, that a hardening of opinion developed with a gradual eradication of a favourable judgement. Even the view of Odell was bit by bit undermined. Various reasons were found to show why the climbers could not have succeeded. Efforts were made to emphasise the difficulties still remaining to them. Their timetable was taken to pieces. It was said that Irvine was too young, too inexperienced, to make such a climb, forgetting that he had nevertheless come within three hundred metres of the goal. In the end it was preferred to leave the epic as a mystery and consider it a regrettable, but certain failure, and so start thinking of further expeditions which would present all the hallmarks of the criteria which human reasoning required.

In the meantime Tibet had closed its frontiers and it required eight years of diplomatic negotiations for them to be reopened. At last in August 1932 a permit reached Britain and an expedition left the following spring. It was two of its members, Wyn Harris and L.R. Wager, when climbing beyond Camp VI who found a long, wooden shafted ice axe made by Willisch of Täsch, belonging to either Mallory or Irvine. The discovery of this axe, which is kept at the Alpine Club in London, threw new light on what had happened for it was found further down from the point where the climbers had been last seen. Many explanations have been advanced and still are. Had the ice-axe been deliberately left behind on the way up? Unlikely, when one remembers the hundreds of metres remaining in mixed ground. Was it evidence of an accident on the descent? Most probably, but was it a descent after failure or when at the end of their strength after having made the summit? Or again, had Mallory gone for the top solo having left Irvine to return alone, and both died in separate accidents? That is the recent idea put forward by Tom Holzel, but it runs counter to the traditions of the time, for in the Twenties the sense of a unified rope was much stronger than it is today. Whatever, nothing sure has emerged from all this speculation.

The 1933 expedition also ended in failure, thanks to the bad climatic conditions. The Dalai Lama's death shortly after it returned seemed a bad omen to the Tibetans. A new boy had to be found for his successor, and the uncertainties of the regency were scarcely propitious to issuing a new permit. Then followed a further upheaval in Europe which relegated all thoughts of climbing in the Himalayas into the realms of fantasy.

When the war ended, old plans began to resurface, but in 1949 it was Nepal which opened up while in 1951 Mao Tse Tung's Chinese troops invaded Tibet and systematically destroyed its marvellous civilisation, indeed its very people. So it was via Nepal that various reconnaissance trips and two Swiss attempts were made, before finally the British 1953 expedition, led by Brig-Gen. John Hunt, produced the success which has become so famous.

With the strong support of the whole team the New Zealander, Edmund Hillary and the Sherpa Tensing left Camp VIII established on the South Col on the 28th May and erected a tent at 8,500m where they spent the night. Waking at 4 a.m. on the 29th they saw all the high summits, already lit by the brilliant light of dawn silhouetted against the dark backcloth of the Nepalese valleys. They left at 6.30 along a sunlit ridge leading to the South summit and climbed the avalanchy slopes below it. Beyond was a corniced but well frozen arête interrupted by the serious problem of a rock step which might well spell failure for them. Cutting steps they moved slowly but surely forwards climbed the rock step and reached the final fore peak. Suddenly the ridge steepened up in front of them and there remained only the few final steps to reach the highest summit in the world.

The details are well known. They can be read everywhere. One however, cannot. For, before climbing that final narrow crest which separated them from their goal, they took a photo of that last ridge in its pristine purity. A gust of wind at that moment raised a swirl of fine snow and as the shutter functioned there was a shimmer of fine particles dancing around the white cone of the summit. Then having cut the final steps, Hillary and Tensing found themselves on the summit in an indescribable joy. They shook hands, gripped each other, hugged in the pleasure of their victory. Taking off their oxygen masks they looked out over the huge little known landscape which stretched out at their feet. Hillary photographed Tensing brandishing his ice axe embellished with a string of pennants, then took pictures of the surrounding mountains and the North ridge. Tensing meanwhile had placed various offerings to the gods, which all pious Buddhists believe inhabit this great summit, and then in his turn Hillary placed a small crucifix which John Hunt had given him.

So the two climbers started back down, carefully and efficiently. They were particularly concerned about the large avalanche-prone slope. Had they disappeared there a new legend about Everest might have been born ... But the snow held. And the exhausted victors pushed on to join their companions and announce their success.

It was principally at advance base at Camp IV where the entire team was reunited that the general rejoicing took place. James Morris hastily drafted a dispatch to tell the press of the successful outcome of the expedition, and he was very conscious that the news could coincide with the great event that was about to take place in Britain. Accompanied by Mike Westmacott, he straight away set off down and the news that Everest had been climbed reached London for the coronation of the Queen.

Amidst all this euphoria and celebrations of victory, one can imagine the shock to the members of the expedition when, shortly after their return home, their photos were delivered from the processing laboratory. The majority were certainly good and publishable, but one of them it was agreed should be kept secret. Doubtless it was a trick of the light ... An optical phenomenon ... Perhaps a Brocken spectre ... But on the photo taken just before the summit there appeared quite distinctly through the light haze of ice particles, firmly ensconced on the snow summit, Mallory and Irvine with their arms extended in affectionate greeting to the second ascencionists.

THE FALL

Curiously enough, they had been talking about it the night before, with Pascal and Bertrand, whom they had met by chance at the hut. They had eaten at the same table, and the subject had come up because someone spoke of a recent plane crash, and another had said how terrible it must have been for the passengers going through those last seconds of shattering terror.

'There are people', Pascal observed, 'who see their entire life when they are at the point of death, complete in every detail.'

'Rubbish!' Paul Froidvent exclaimed, 'I don't see how you can believe such nonsense.'

'It's you who are wrong!' Thomas Levernois, his climbing partner, retorted sharply. 'I tell you, you are quite wrong. I actually know someone it happened to ... To avoid a car that was coming at him head-on, he was forced off the road into a ravine, and was lucky to get out alive. He says that in that one instant he relived his whole existence, second by second. It affected him a great deal.'

'I met a ski-instructress' added Bertrand, 'who lived through something similar, when she slid out of control down a hard rutted snow slope'.

'And me,' Paul retorted, 'I've got a logical, positivist mind, Cartesian if you want, and I repeat it's all a load of bollocks!'

He was wrong. However, the events of the following day happened so fast that he had no chance to revise his cherished opinions.

From the very start, the atmosphere of the climb was grim, almost frightening. The face turned out to be much more icy than they had expected from general conditions. And when Paul set off up the pitch of rotten rock he knew that Thomas was only giving him a psychological belay, across his shoulder, and that his partner was not tied on. It had been impossible to find any spike or crack to take protection.

Not that that was anything new, he just had to be extra careful. It simply required care. So Paul was keeping his cool, inching his way up on the rugosities which passed as holds, scraping away with his fingers ice and frozen grit before trusting his weight on the flattening. He was concentrating on reaching a slanting crack a few metres away. Once there they would be safe ... But suddenly his foot shot off and there was nothing he could do to save himself. He remembered the hundred metres of the face that they had already climbed and the steep glacier below it. He even saw, in a flash, the grief of Edith, who would be widowed before her child was born. He began to fall and felt the jerk of the rope as it came tight on Thomas who failed to hold him and in turn was pulled off. Paul Froidvent then had the lightning revelation that time did not exist, that it was a personal creation and that its unfolding could be reduced to a flash, in the same way that the huge mass of a star can collapse into a 'black hole'. Then the process they had argued about the previous evening took over, but by some strange dislocation, it was not the past that unrolled before him, but the future.

The whole future ... He saw the gritty surface of the glacier as they went back down to the valley a little later. He felt the pain of a blister which was forming from the rubbing of his left boot on his heel. He heard a chough cawing ... That night he enjoyed his dinner with Thomas and Edith ... There followed several wet days, the dull grey mountain rain when banks of cloud hang around the middle mountain in amongst the firs ... Then came the day they had to go home. And the fright they got when the right front tyre blew out. But he had managed to stop on the verge. Edith was all right, but he would always remember the pallor of her frightened face and bloodless lips. Under a steady downpour he changed the ripped tyre. The trucks and cars roared by on the main road, splashing him. He drove slowly to the nearest garage and it was not until the middle of the night that they reached Paris. It was a different homecoming from the rest, since soon Cyril or Bérangère would be born.

It turned out to be Cyril. Paul experienced all the delights of becoming a young father, never tiring of looking at the details of the sleeping baby's face, the line of his lashes on the delicate skin, the puckered mouth contracting, unconsciously sucking, the minuscule fingers with a dimple at the base of each. Edith was radiant. Paul was doing an intern's job, but he did manage to spend a couple of Sundays repainting the drawing room and redoing the electricity in the kitchen ... He worked frantically on his books and lecture courses, learning by heart hundreds of medical facts and definitions. Clinical forms of typhoid fever. Symptoms and treatment of rectal cancer. Possible problems in blood-transfusion. Complications of gastro-duodenal ulcers. Post partum haemorrhages ... He had to study, study, study. At last came the competitive exam. He made it through to the oral and in a tense ten minutes replied almost mechanically, thanks to the months and months of effort he had put in. He felt as though he were someone else. Was it really him who was waiting for the examiners' results? ... Out of 450 who passed the written exam, only 120 got past the orals, and his name was on the list ... He still did not know whether it was reality or dream ... His friends dragged him off to drink champagne. He heard the popping cork as it shot out of the neck. What he wanted more than anything else was to sleep. But, that night, in fact he slept very badly.

    He got back into shape for another season in the mountains. He climbed at Fontainebleau, where the recent rain had made the holds sandy. He lost a briefcase. He bought a pair of black shoes. He gave roses to Edith, which she arranged in the crystal vase. He read *Les Trois mousquetaires*. He had a night out with his friends in a little restaurant on the île Saint-Louis. He was insulted by a yob trying to pick a fight ... He went on holiday with Edith and Cyril. He slogged up moraines. He drove his ice-axe into the upper rim of a bergschrund dripping with enormous stalactites. Then there was that thunderstorm on the North Face of the Piz Badile. The hail bounced off all over the place. Thomas and he had scarcely got their cags on when the sky darkened alarmingly. The storm broke right away. The lightning struck close to them. They might be hit at any moment. All they could do was wait, huddled together on a narrow sloping ledge, tied to a single piton, their heads hunched into their bowed shoulders, neither daring to give voice to the fear that possessed them as the lightning flared through the half-darkness, the sharp cracks of thunder so close that they hardly reverberated, the streaming rain sheeting down the face. In a moment what had been a pleasure climb had become a nightmare ... The pervasive terror. The fear of not getting out alive ... The intolerable discomfort. The hail which had quickly succeeded the downpour. The noise, the cold, the harsh necessity for patience, the pain of staying still, the inevitable bivouac. The weather that appeared set on destroying them, the relentless storm. It went on for hours. Night fell. Paul and Thomas tried to light the stove, but no match would stay lit in that tearing wind. The cold was making them stiff, but it was almost impossible to move on their narrow platform. After a momentary lull, the wind blew more fiercely than ever. The night dragged on and on and on. Now the snow fell, fine, dense, penetrating, covering them in a blanket which they had the greatest difficulty in shaking off. When at last the dawn came, frozen and sluggish, they had to call up every last ounce of will to get off their ledge and get moving again. They managed to do so and bit by bit fought their way up the wall. When they got out they felt they had lived through centuries.

    Life again seemed sweet. What matters a blown fuse, a lost sweater, a tooth-ache or a parking ticket after such an experience? Everything becomes relative ... Paul appreciated every moment of the life that had been given back to him. There was Cyril's first smile, and his first word, which was 'Dada'. The day came when he began to walk, wobbling and tumbling, full of the extraordinary energy children have. There were nappies to be changed, baby food to be slipped between uncooperative lips. There was Grunt-Grunt the teddy-bear, and the two rag dolls, oddly named Kakouk and Boudoum. There was that bitter winter when Edith got tonsillitis. There was the disappointment over a roll of film that should have been wonderful, but got stuck in the camera. There was the swallows' arrival in a luminous spring sky. Then the death and burial of a beloved grandmother who had died of a heart attack. All this time Paul kept plugging away at his medicine, having decided to become an E.N.T. specialist. He finished one training period of six months, and then changed hospitals and started another. He studied hygiene and forensic medicine. He chose as his thesis subject 'the etio-pathogenesis and the physio-pathology of arachnoiditis of the pontine cerebellar area.' One evening he took Edith out to dinner on the banks of the Marne, and having reviewed their short life together, which to them seemed vast, decided to have another child. Paul felt ready and able to take on a larger family. Another summer went by, but the weather was so poor that he got no serious route done. Bérangère was born in March.

Bleau ... Climbing in Fontainebleau. The special smells of its forest. The fine sand around the boulders. Dry ferns and shrivelled heather. Wind shaking the bare branches. Grey clouds racing in a dark sky. Rain splashing on the sandstone. *Bleau, Bleau, Bleau* ...

A drinks party at the hospital in honour of old Charpuis's retirement and a glass of claret spilt down him because someone had carelessly bumped into him. Paul was irritated by the purple stain on a light-coloured pair of trousers, just back from the cleaners. He was told to use white wine on the spots, to neutralize them. The incident put him in a bad mood, but a single phrase suddenly changed the whole tenor of the day. It came from his head of department and was short and sweet, 'Tell me, Froidvent, how would you like to take over a clinic?' Would he like? It was what he had been dreaming of ... Life seemed to be shaping up well.

He had less time for climbing, but he enjoyed all the more the precious moments when he could get into the mountains ... The sunsets seen from the hut door. Ice slopes opening up beneath ones feet, a receding perspective framed between ones gaiters. The sharp granite of the Aiguilles. The alpine campions opening their rosy stars at astonishing heights, on tiny cushions of moss. There was also the day when an avalanche came down from below the col of the Tour des Courtes just after his party had passed by.

Cyril was an introverted child, sometimes violent, but very affectionate. Bérangère delighted everyone with her pretty almost ladylike ways. Edith had given up taking her degree in Italian, but she decorated, painted, sewed, cooked, dusted and sang with untiring energy. The apartment became too small and the Froidvents moved, in the usual muddle of crates, cartons, straw, wrapping-paper and dust.

A close friend died abroad in an earthquake. Their neighbours were burgled, a daring job which for long was a topic of conversation locally. Paul had a quarrel with Edith for no good reason, and they exchanged such heated words, and took so long to make the peace that for several days they thought that something had gone irreparably wrong with their marriage. The resentment blew over and as time passed Paul took a major decision: to abandon hospital work and enter private practice. When he put up his plate, he felt he had come to an important milestone in his career, and was striking out in a new and risky direction, where he would be in sole charge. Patients, however, appeared, and he was happy with his decision. A few months later he had to take the children to their grandparents, Edith having been told to rest, but it did not help, and Paul spent a sad evening holding her hands, wiping the tears from her tense, wan face after she had suffered a miscarriage. He took time off to spend a restful week at the beach with her. A year later both were overjoyed by the birth of Jérôme.

As he lived through these major events of his life, Paul seemed also to sense all the innumerable details which make up the fabric of existence, from the least significant to the most revealing, from the most uplifting to the humdrum. He was kept waiting interminably in an office with blue linoleum on the floor. He listened to a Bach concerto. He enjoyed the twinkling set of lights he had put on the Christmas tree. He felt the snap of a shoe-lace as he was rushing to catch a train. His mind on his tax-return, he looked, unseeing at the bare wall of the building situated to the right of his office window. He tasted the fog during a country walk in winter. He read all the books he was to read, saw all the films he was to see. He braked for thousands of red lights and absentmindedly went through one, barely missing another car.

He heard with sympathy the screams of children over whom he bent to drain their infected ears, when piercing 8,257 eardrums. He slid a speculum 639,772 times up patients' nostrils. He yelled at people consulting him for their deafness, listened attentively to laryngectomy patients who had lost their voices. The collection of foreign objects that he had removed from the nose, throat or ears of his clients kept increasing: beads, bits of toys, bones, pebbles, safety pins, coins, buttons, drawing pins, dried beans, paper clips and other oddities. His family was amazed at the variety.

He climbed on skins up frozen snow slopes, driving with his poles. He made Cyril recite his multiplication tables. He was the life and soul of a mad New Year's Eve party. He brought a lost kitten home for his daughter. He heard raindrops hitting the tin roof of a hut. He filled his lungs with the sharp thin air at 4000m. He pricked his finger while pruning a rose bush. He spanked Jérôme for putting a gold watch in the toilet.

Slow, steady and infinitely varied, time was passing. Then suddenly the major crisis of his life erupted, catching him up into a myriad of details, pleasant and unpleasant. It started with something of a decline in his relations with Edith, largely due to over familiarity with each other. Then a new patient, Patricia Kilkenny, who was half American, came to consult him about a troublesome cough. She lived in the same building he had his office in and she was lively, unaffected and amusing. From time to time their paths crossed in the entrance hall and they chatted for a moment. He liked to hear her laugh.

That would have been the extent of it, had he not finished early one day. He was getting ready to go home, rather reluctantly. Cyril had acne and was walling himself off in hostile isolation. Bérangère was trying to gain her independence by yelling a lot and slamming doors. Jérôme was messy and noisy. Edith herself was in a sour frame of mind, everything seemed to irritate her, and she was enthusiastic about a group of militant feminists he couldn't stand. She was going out to dinner that evening with a distant cousin whose Marxist views exasperated Paul. He could hardly bear the thought of the evening in front of him and he started home unwillingly. Just as he was double-locking the office door, Patricia happened by and spoke to him. She invited him in for a drink, he accepted gratefully and spent a relaxing hour with her. The next day he brought her flowers. A regular habit grew up, pleasant meetings, which they pretended were more innocent than, in fact, they soon became.

For months Paul divided his time between a home that was burdensome to him and a mistress he found endlessly fascinating. Edith became suspicious, and one evening, having found him out, who knows how, she accused him point-blank of deceiving her. Things went from bad to worse to a point where Paul found himself torn between his two lives, neither of which he wished to relinquish.

He agreed to go on holiday for several weeks with his family, during which time he made a conscious effort, but it was not a success. As soon as they returned he found a replacement to take over his practice and took off again, this time with Patricia. They went to Ticino and found a quiet hotel near Lugano, whose flowered terraces ran down to the lake. Paul loved gazing at the hills rising out of the shimmering water, the villages clinging to their slopes, the flowering oleanders, the ochre-coloured villas with their green shutters, the baroque fronts, the classically shaped urns, the marble columns overgrown with roses, the pergolas, the grape vines, and all the harmony of blue water, blue mountains and blue sky merging in a misty harmony that was already beginning to hint at autumn. He heard the gulls crying as they dive-bombed the lake to pick up scraps of bread. He was happy. He and Patricia had no thought for anything but each other, took boat-rides, walked hand in hand like young lovers, discovering charming little eating-places in their wanderings ...

Then, two days before they were due to leave, he realized that the trip had solved nothing, and that he would soon be back in his previous state of uncertainty. It came to him when they were sitting in the sun on their balcony, after a swim. Patricia was reading a detective story. He began to think of his work and of the scenes at home. He tried to say something, but Patricia asked to finish her chapter, in a coaxing voice like a little girl's. While he waited, he studied her face, her clear-cut profile, one golden lock over the forehead, and for the first time he was struck by her resemblance to Edith. It dawned on him that he had found himself with the same woman, only ten years younger. Was it really sensible to start over again, in that case, or was it simply more fun? Where would it take him and at what cost in ruined lives?

Patricia was still reading. Unknowingly, she was allowing him the time to think things through. He leaned on the balustrade. The landscape was swimming in shades of grey-blue that touched his heart with their beauty. The lake, the steep hills that rimmed it, and the now overcast sky glowed behind a milky blue mist. He thought of a Chinese painting, or of a view in some other world. The first lights came on in Ostenso on the opposite bank. Patricia saw nothing and flicked over a page of her book. She must have started on a new chapter. What would Edith have done? Being more used to forget herself and to respond to others she would most probably have put her novel down, however reluctantly, sensing that he wanted to share his thoughts with her … What was she doing now? What would she have told the children? As far as that went there would be no problems, she would have wanted to spare the younger ones. 'Daddy needed a bit more holiday … '. But what about Cyril? He knew, Paul was sure. Thinking of the boy he felt his throat tighten … He felt a new love welling up in him for Patricia, but he needed the respect and affection of his son.

A few drops of rain fell on the balcony, and Paul stepped back under an awning, while Patricia, still reading, went inside and lay on the bed. The storm quickly broke, violent. Flashes lit up the landscape, the lake surface was ruffled by the beating rain, thunder echoed back and forth between the surrounding hills. No! Nothing had been settled by this escapade … And when Patricia finally emerged from her book he looked at her with new eyes. That was the moment she chose to declare that everything would be so simple when they got back, and they would live together. Paul made a non-committal gesture and heard himself reply that it would not be as easy as all that. The rest of the evening went by uncomfortably.

When he got home, Edith welcomed him and said nothing in particular. Her eyes seemed to him more deep-set, and her face thinner. He felt responsible, but still could not bring himself to a decision. It was Cyril who did it. For such a shy adolescent it must have taken a lot of courage to go to his father, request a talk and advance his own opinions. Simultaneously irritated by this invasion into what he regarded as his own business, and amazed to realize that his son was almost a man, Paul endured in silence the disorganized appeal, of which every word was painful and yet touching. Cyril had wound himself up and now was pouring out all his feelings, interrupting himself, swallowing, but getting back to his main point each time. He had probably planned to follow certain arguments and now discarded them under the stress of the moment. Paul stared at the self-conscious yet determined youngster, who was throwing all of himself into this and knew suddenly that he would stay, above all for the boy's sake.

It was far from easy. He had to withstand Patricia's sobs when he told her he was breaking it off. And Edith's quivering and sombre expression which seemed no longer to believe in anything. His efforts to remain in control of himself were hard, but Cyril's knowing confident look gave him strength. It was a wretched, long-drawn out winter. Once again, he looked to the mountains for solace. He made the snow fly from under his skis, he felt the ice under his crampons, barely covered by a thin layer of unstable powder. He laid his cheek against a rock, warm from the sun. He shook off the hoar-frost a sudden storm had left on his hair.

One evening, almost a year after the end of his affair, he took Edith out to dinner at the Albert Premier restaurant. With no other idea than simply to pass a few hours. The half cordial state of their relations was artificial, largely maintained for the children's benefit, and others close to them. Dinner began in the uninspired, awkward politeness, which appeared to be all they had to look forward to in each other. Had they perhaps reached a point at which their mutual sacrifices could change things? Or was it the restaurant's atmosphere, or the well-being brought about by the setting, the refined food and quality wine that made them relax and warm towards each other? Paul unbent. Edith smiled. They touched hands and suddenly realized that the storms which had divided them were past and gone. To their astonishment they realized that nothing had changed and that their life went on together as before, joined by common memories and the rediscovered solidarity of being a couple.

The days and years passed. Paul went to funerals. He worked and he continued to advance in his field. He lived through a host of incidents. He saw plane-tree leaves silhouetted against a light sky as he came up from the metro one night. Staring into a fire, he watched the glowing embers disintegrate. He retained on his palate the complexities of a bottle of Chateau-Grillet. He visited the Neuchâtel library. He stayed with the family of a godson at Caudéran. He lunched at a restaurant in Wimereux. He crossed Siberia by the slow train which allowed him to see for the first time the frozen blue of Lake Baikal and the endless Mongolian steppes. He saw the Amur river in flood, Mount Etna erupt, the mosque of Kairouan and the Sydney Opera house, the palaces of Marrakesh, the Syrian desert and the slow-flowing Amazon.

That New York sunrise! From his hotel window, Paul got up early to watch the day breaking over the city. The dark gave way to a greyish half-light, to reveal the rising tiers of buildings and towers, stretching into space in an unbelievably subtle play of delicate colours as the dawn broke. Rose-pinks, beiges, light browns, ochres and a range of greys ... Paul never expected to find such tender colours in such a great metropolis. He wished he could paint, as he watched, marvelling, the metal spire of the Empire State building outlined against the pale sky, while the gigantic masses of the Twin Towers at the end of Manhattan seemed to float above a band of early morning fog. The East River was silvery and glinting … He remembered that he was suffering from four hours of jet-lag.

And time was still passing. Bérangère married. Then Cyril. Later Jérôme. The laughter of visiting grandchildren enlivened their home, where he and Edith were now alone. Paul did his last route, although he did not know it. He sold his practice and one evening treated his last patient, this time he knew.

Paul and Edith did their best to prepare themselves for a happy retirement, in so far as those two words are compatible, for in the short time given to Paul to live his life in advance, he experienced all the little sufferings of old age, as they came along. The first white hair, then the rest; crows' feet wrinkles around the eyes and mouth, deepening and spreading; a harsher beard more difficult to shave off looser folds; the shrinking size of print, leading to a diagnosis of long-sightedness; muscles sagging under flabby skin; veins protruding; the chin no longer forming a unity with the cheeks; the lengthening nose; the head steadily losing its hair; nails thickening and becoming ridged; less reliable hearing; long wakeful periods during the night; loosening teeth; eye-brows growing wiry hairs over sunken eyes … Oh, how he resented getting old! And no doubt Edith too. But one keeps for oneself observation of these myriad signs of decrepitude. One single thing, only one, kept them from despair on the long sad road towards death: the renewal of life, springing up again in their grandchildren. This life they had given was their only source of interest now, true and pure. Life which they had passed on, through them and now beyond them, triumphed, for ever victorious and joyful.

That, at least, remained when tragedy struck and Edith died of a ruptured aneurysm. Hospital. Morgue. Funeral. Loneliness … Alone every morning in the empty apartment, alone for the noon meal, reading the paper, eating frozen food heated in the microwave oven. Alone again in the evening for dinner, with more frozen food, in front of the inane tele. 'Yes, of course, I am getting along all right', he told the children when they called. Alone all day and all night … Paul was amazed at his memories, that he could ever have thought, so long ago, of leaving Edith, so serene, finally had their life together become, so full of happiness. His friends were dropping off around him and he feared death for himself. Old age was a continuing torment.

One April evening, driving back from Lyon where he had been staying with Bérangère, Paul decided to go through Vézelay and spend the night there. In the morning it was foggy, and he walked up along the village streets to the basilica. The old buildings were enchanting in the mist and he admired the sturdy harmony of the uneven houses, the crazy angles of their roofs, the mossy stones in the ancient walls, the house-fronts covered with wisteria, the arched doorways, the walls, the delicate apple-blossom, the gables, posterns, small corbelled towers, mullioned windows, wall flowers glowing in the hollow roof-tiles, forged iron balcony railings and weather-vanes ... He was surprised by this present, so unexpectedly given. It occurred to him that he would never in sunlight have got the feel for the deep-rooted vitality of this place, whose strength challenged the centuries.

Then he entered the basilica, by no means for the first time, but that day its medieval glory inexplicably seemed to enter into him more profoundly. He reflected that his own time, which he had been taught to consider as a period of progress, was really nothing but a parody of richness, empty of true values, however highly it might regard itself. As he walked slowly up the aisles, he concluded that the men who had conceived the perfect procession of these arches, of the sublime features of the Christ in Majesty, possessed true genius. That genius had deserted those who put up at Beaubourg, with huge expense and much publicity, a mish-mash of stove-pipes, or at the Palais-Royal these columns by Buren whose only value was for dogs to piss against ... His meditation continued in a mood of enlightenment. He thought of History, which he rarely did. It surprised him that his contemporaries, self-satisfied and blind as they were, should continue to use the word Middle Ages as a synonym for barbarity, whereas it was the supposed Renaissance which began the decline! Full of these thoughts, enjoying them, he wandered for some time in the nearly empty nave. He could not tell what moved him the more, the harmony and magnificence of the whole, or the exquisite detail. He thought he had exhausted his surprises until he went down into the crypt. Perhaps the beauty of the upper church had prepared him to feel more intensely an invisible reality, for the crypt was plain, dark and humble. There was nothing there except a space divided rhythmically by slight columns supporting the pure curves of the groined vaulting, which, where they met caused a subtle play between shadows and the vague light coming from small high windows and some weak bulbs. There, seated on a hard wooden bench, his feet on the veined rock of the hill polished to marble smoothness by the steps of uncounted pilgrims, he felt a sort of presence, close and yet remote, mysterious, elusive and indescribable. It was not exactly a mystical experience, only a realization what the world's hustle had kept him from sensing until that moment. His life had gone by without his being either a total unbeliever or a practicing believer, but from that day forward he kept within him a feeling of the secret dimension that he had been granted, and the memory of a deep peace which helped him through the last stages of his life.

Time still passed. One day he had a stroke and collapsed in the street. An ambulance, whose three-note siren shattered the evening air, carried him to an emergency ward. He learned there that it is not easy to die in our time of swift medical response. He was injected, examined, given perfusions and transfusions, X rayed, he was saved but not cured. Faced with a paralytic condition which did not yield to treatment, his children decided to put him in a nursing home. More months went by seeming endless to him.

One day, at the end of winter, they pushed his wheelchair along the paths in the park of the home. There he knew his last happy moments after months of confinement in his own room. Every detail of that room, the outlines of the furniture, the blue curtains, the opaque globe of the ceiling light, even the shape of the call-button had imprinted themselves upon his suffering mind. He was becoming confused and he was no longer aware of who was pushing him. He thought it was a nurse, but in fact it was Jérôme's eldest girl, Alice. He had, however, retained his sensitivity, and was able to enjoy the beauty of the outdoors.

They stopped by some bushes. He felt the sun's warmth on his face and on his wrinkled hands. It warmed him even through the wool afghan they had put over his legs. The light thrilled him. The sky was the blue of porcelain. The air was soft, and full of the smells of the moist, working earth. There were cheerful peepings and chirpings. He noticed that while there were no leaves out as yet, the branches were swollen with rising sap and sticky buds. On the ground, among the winter's dry grey leaves, wild primroses were opening their pale yellow blossoms. A robin alighted nearby. Paul Froidvent gazed at his orange throat, his silky body, his tiny round eyes, black as jet beads, and the jerky up-and-down motions of his brown tail. He laughed in delight and the bird flew off. Paul knew that it would be his last spring, and he loved it as he had never loved any of the others. They pushed him back to the house.

The next day the rain returned, and soon afterwards a second stroke killed the old man. But his premonitory vision did not end there, for he was present for all the circumstances of his demise. A nurse notified the head of the establishment and she in turn prepared to notify the family from her business-like office desk with a bowl of hyacinths to make it more cheerful. She looked up the number of Cyril Froidvent, the lawyer, in a card-file. Cyril was in his office, in the act of accompanying a client to the door. The telephone should have rung, but did not. Paul grieved over the sorrow his beloved son would soon feel. He noticed and was touched by the presence on the Empire desk of a photograph of himself in a pewter frame. It was a black and white snapshot that his climbing partner Thomas had taken last year, at the exit of the Marinelli couloir, and it was Edith's favourite. Deeply tanned, his face glowing, Paul was laughing, showing his very white teeth. The client also noticed the picture.

'What a fine looking chap!' he said to Cyril.

'Yes, that was my father. He was a wonderful man, I believe, but I never knew him. He died in a climbing accident a few months before I was born.'

Then Paul Froidvent understood that the life he had just lived through, complete in every detail, was not the one he would have, but the one he should have had. And he knew that at the end of his fall, in one more split second, he would be dead.

THE TWISTLETON HUT

The small hut clung to the slope at the top end of the deep Les Étopieux valley. It had been built long ago by an old English family in memory of a son who died in a tragic climbing accident, hence its unusual name.

Not many people went there, for it served only two passes and the Dôme de la Galbière at the end of the long Arnetaz glacier. There was no hut warden, the place hadn't been modernized, and it retained the old-fashioned, primitive, charming appearance of the huts of the heroic age of mountaineering.

That evening it was full, occupied by a cheerful company of six young men and two girls who were planning to ski to the Col de Carveline next day, and were now busy settling in amidst the carefree disorder created by discomfort, altitude, and the unconstrained cheerfulness of the young.

'Who's got some matches?'

'Hey, Martine, put a bit of snow in that soup or there'll never be enough to go round.'

'Where are the candles? I can't see a thing by the light of this wretched little lamp. We'll have a candle-lit dinner!'

'Watch out, for goodness' sake, you put the bacon down on my sleeping bag!'

'Don't nag! It's not as if your sleeping bag was exactly spotless!'

'Looked at yours lately, have you, you great oaf? Anyway, that's no reason to put the bacon down on it!'

'Nearly finished your mending, Dédé?'

'Yes, almost. Pass me the thread. It's there on the table.'

'You certainly are a master craftsman! Wanting to make your skins up yourself and then getting them the wrong way round! Always good for a laugh, you are!'

'Oh, shut up! Pass me the thread!'

'Hey, back from scouting around outside, Nicolas? What's the weather like?'

'Wonderful! Stars everywhere, but cold as Siberia. And there's an icy wind getting up. It won't be warm when we start, but once the sun comes up it'll be dreamy.'

'You can keep your dreaming for tomorrow! The soup's just about ready and the noodles are almost done. Open that can of tomato sauce,

Julien, and could you get a move on and lay the table, Maxime? There are some bowls on the shelf over there, and spoons here. With what we've brought ourselves, that should be enough. I'll put some more snow on the stove to melt, ready for washing the dishes.'

'Hark at her! The Angel in the Hut. We're not in the army, you know! Our time's our own. You want to relax a little, you do! I'm hungry, though. I don't mind laying the table for you.'

It was a very simple little hut. One room, two partitions, a crudely made wooden table and some benches, shelves, a stove, hooks for sacks and equipment. From outside, all one could see was its walls of rough-hewn planks, the sheet-metal roof shining softly beneath the moon, and the two windows illuminated by the lively, flickering light of the candles. The whole place was lost in the immense calm of the snow and night in the mountains.

After dinner they drank tisanes and talked.

'Nice little hut,' said Maxime. 'I've never been here before. Any of the rest of you know it?'

None of them did; all the members of the group sitting round the table shook their heads. Or all but one: Daniel, the eldest. The senior member of the party, twenty-five years old.

'Yes, I do,' he said. 'I've been here twice, and the second time was no joke, believe you me. This evening it's okay, it's normal, we're having fun, we're all here together. But last time, when I was on my own ... actually it gives me the shivers just to think of it!'

'You coward! You mean just being alone had that effect on you?'

'Yes. Well, no ... I was alone that particular evening, but I'd already slept here the year before, with a friend, and we took part in a rescue operation next day. It – well, it made quite an impression on me. It was the first time I'd seen a climbing accident at close quarters, so of course, finding myself back here I couldn't help remembering it.'

'I don't get it,' Pascale interrupted. 'Are you talking about two different times, or what?'

'Pascale gets the point quickly, see?' remarked Gilbert, 'Only you have to explain it to her slowly first.'

'Right. I'll be more specific,' said Daniel, beginning again. 'I first came up here five or six years ago. That's when the climbing accident happened. And it was the next summer, at the end of the season, I came back on my own. Now I'm here with you lot, which makes the third time. Following me so far?'

'All right, all right, I get it! You can go on.'

'Right: well, the first time was when we tried that rescue. It was a sad story. Four lads who'd set out to do the Dôme de la Galbière by way of the couloir. They weren't very experienced or very fit. They'd started too late in the day, and they hadn't made fast progress. Furthermore, thinking they were being prudent they pitched it, so they lost a lot of time. Well, in the middle of the afternoon, when they ought to have finished the climb long ago and should even have been back down again, they were caught by a snow slide. They were relatively lucky. The slope's smooth and there aren't any ice falls in it. They shot over the bergschrund and found themselves at the bottom of the snow cone, but they'd been knocked about a bit. Two of them were only bruised and shaken, not feeling too good. The other two were injured and in shock. So the two who could walk got them settled as best they could and then, naturally, came down to raise the alarm. They reached the hut that evening. I was there with Petit François. You remember him – François who wore glasses? Night was falling, so nothing could be done that day. The general opinion was that it would do no good to start out on the long slog down right away. We'd have arrived in the first hamlet in the middle of the night, we'd have had to knock to wake people up and telephone, and the helicopter couldn't take off before daylight anyway. We decided the best thing to do was look after the two who had reached us, rest for a few hours and then get up very early. François would go down on his own to raise the alarm, and I would climb up the glacier with the stronger of the two who'd come down, taking what we could in the way of blankets and food to the injured men while we waited for proper help to come. So that's what we did. It took us some time to get up the glacier by head torch. There were crevasses everywhere. Still, we got there at dawn, before the helicopter, but it was too late anyway. They'd both died of their injuries, or cold or shock or stress, I don't know which, or all of them together. It looked as if they'd been dead for some time. They were in the position in which the others had left them. Their faces looked calm – all the same, what a waste. Well, that's life.'

'Not a very cheerful story, I must say!'

'I never knew you'd had an experience like that! Will you show us the place tomorrow?'

'If you like, but in fact that's not the story I was going to tell you. I was going to tell you what happened a year later. I was still here in the mountains. I'd had a splendid season, and now it was nearly time to leave.

The Twistleton Hut

I still had two days left, and I was on my own, so rather than kicking my heels down below I thought I'd go up the mountains again. Not to climb, just to be there. An evening and a night in the hut, and maybe just a little walk up above it in the morning. I'd been around the whole range that summer except this bit, so of course I wanted to come up to the Twistleton Hut. It's pure and wild up here, just what I wanted. I wasn't thinking about the accident much any more. Time had passed, and a lot of other things had happened. But memories did gradually come back as I walked up. It's a long way and not much fun, particularly at the end of the season. Gravel-covered ice, ravines, grey glaciers, moraines, remnants of dirty snow. It's only when you get up here you feel good, perched on a kind of promontory at the end of the world. And I did feel good in one way. I mean, this was what I'd wanted. Here I was in the middle of the mountains. I had peace and solitude, because I was completely alone here, not a living soul in sight. But it was no good: try as I might to convince myself that I had exactly what I wanted, I think I felt that if offered the chance I'd have been somewhere else. And as I was saying, I began feeling closer and closer to the events of the year before. Every detail brought them back to me. The wooden door that had opened when the others arrived. Their strained faces. The aluminium saucepan we used to heat soup for them. The places where we slept. And then next day, our anxiety when we woke up, our departure, and then coming upon that tragic scene on the slope. Well, I didn't spend such a pleasant evening as I'd expected. It was all right, that's the most I can say for it. After eating my evening meal I put on my duvet and went out to watch the sunset and see the little lights coming on in the distance, down in the valley. And when it was almost dark and pretty cold I came in to go to bed.'

'Where did you sleep?'

'Over there, on the right. At least I had plenty of blankets, being on my own. I may have been dropping off to sleep when I heard a sound. Well, sounds. Over by the door. I thought at first there was someone coming. I heard footsteps, or at least it sounded like footsteps. Boots being scraped at the door. The little metallic sound of an ice axe being put down. Oh, I don't know ... anyway, sounds. A knocking at the door. Could have been the wind. I waited for the door to open, but it didn't. That scraping sound. I didn't have the courage to get up and go to see what it was. I stayed under my blankets, apprehensive, almost panting. And then there was a knocking, like something knocking on the roof. Or maybe tapping at the window, very softly. I could hear my own heart beating too. My breath was coming fast. I wondered if I was going crazy or what. I've never believed in ghosts, but I was scared all the same. At one moment I bit my hand to stop myself crying out, because the noise was still going on and getting louder. There was a bumping sound, and rustling all round the hut. Could it be the wind? And then the sound of boots being scraped at the door again. And something like the noise of crampons dropped on the stone slabs outside. Cracking, breathing, murmuring noises. I was panic-stricken. The sweat came out on my forehead. I've no idea how long this went on. Hours, I think. At one moment I put my pillow over my head because I thought I'd seen a light. I honestly did think I must be going out of my mind. Eventually I went to sleep like that, underneath the pillow, so what with that and the fact that it was so late before I did fall asleep I never heard my alarm watch go off. I'd put it on the shelf above the partition. It was broad daylight when I opened my eyes and threw off all that bedding. The sun had risen, and a golden sunbeam was slanting in through the window. Everything was in its proper place, neat, solid, serene. I wouldn't have exchanged the wealth of every palace in the world for that ray of dazzling sunlight with the motes of dust dancing in it, and the bright splash it cast on the coarse-grained, knotty floor. I got up and went out. It was wonderful weather, with the air like crystal. Of course I remembered my terrors of the night before, but I couldn't understand them any more. It's amazing what darkness and solitude can do to the most level-headed person. Well, I walked all round the hut. There was obviously nothing wrong. The sheet metal of the roof was warming up in the sun and steaming slightly. It must have slackened and shifted in the night and the cold. I noticed the tracks of some small animal on a patch of snow out behind the hut. So that explained everything. The metal roofing, the wind, an animal, and me being totally stupid. The things imagination can do when you let it! I had a wonderful breakfast. Everything was clear and sharp as spring water. I said goodbye to the mountains just above the hut, and then I went back down to the valley slowly, drinking in my last impressions of the Alps. There you are, that's my story, so another time you needn't ask if I've ever been to the Twistleton Hut before!'

'Goodness, what an awful night! You must have been scared stiff!'
'I've still got gooseflesh.'
'I don't think I could have stuck it out. I'd have died of fright.'
'Look, I wasn't exactly proud of myself! I told you so. But it was all explained in the end. I mean, there's a reason for everything!'

'Eek!' cried Martine. 'I think something just tapped on the window pane!'

Everyone roared with laughter. They needed to relax.

'For goodness' sake, don't you start now! Anyway, this time there are enough of us to scare any ghosts off. Okay, everyone, we have to get up early tomorrow, so I suggest we go to bed now. Sweet dreams, sleep tight, mind the bugs don't bite! There are no such things as ghosts!'

This last and entirely erroneous statement set the ghosts who had followed the whole conversation shaking their heads in exasperation, as they leaned their elbows on the outside window sill.

'Incredible!' muttered one of them. 'Humans! Will they never learn?'

THE RED SENTINEL

Night was falling. The shadows of the month of Messidor cast patches of brown over the farms and fields, but against the sky the snowy mountains seemed to be irradiated by the strange, clear light that follows sunset. The föhn had been blowing over the Chamonix valley since morning, roaring and howling in the firs, breaking branches and getting on the nerves of both the livestock and the local population. At this time of day everyone had gone to ground at home, closing the windows, but the noise of the wind was still everywhere, and its warm gusts, making their way through the slightest chink, sent the thin flame of small oil lamps flickering.

At the Gavraz farm, Catherine Gavraz and her son were sitting in silence by the huge hearth where a few embers still glowed. There was no point in talking. They had quite enough to occupy their private thoughts. Day after day brought nothing but new anxieties, and tomorrow might turn out even worse than yesterday. Only night brought temporary relief, promising welcome peace and relaxation in dreams.

Suddenly they heard a few brief knocks at the door between two gusts of wind. Catherine stopped spinning hemp. She instinctively compressed her lips and folded her hands, exchanging a glance of alarm with her son. He had already risen. His tall, broad frame hid the fire, darkening the room.

'I'll see who it is,' he muttered.

He went to the door, lifted the latch and opened it, relieved to find only a woman and two children outside. But on seeing his massive shape in the dusk and his red jacket with the tricolour cockade pinned to its lapel, the woman who had knocked could not suppress a small start of alarm.

'What are you doing here, citoyenne?' asked Gavraz gruffly. 'And what do you want with us? The roads aren't safe. You'd better go home, quick.'

So saying he scrutinized their visitor, a thin woman, no longer young, with a large black shawl over her head and shoulders. The children too were dressed like peasants, although they wore stout leather shoes on their feet. Gavraz guessed what the situation was, and his guess was confirmed when the woman replied, in a toneless voice, 'Home? It's a long time since we had any home, citoyen. I knocked at your door because I saw a light. I was hoping to find shelter for my grandchildren.'

She stopped, clearly embarrassed by having to make this request, but a fleeting smile illuminated Gavraz's face.

'You could have done worse,' he said. 'Come on in and sit down in the kitchen. Wait, leave your bundle here and join us by the hearth. You too, children. I'm François Gavraz, and this is my mother Catherine. Don't you worry about my jacket and cockade. I wear them because that's the way the times are now. In this outfit I don't attract suspicion and I can come and go as I please more easily. You may have heard that Commissary Albitte[1] pays a reward of five hundred francs in the name of the Republic to any citizen who denounces a private individual, even without proof.[2] At that price, tongues wag fast and no one's safe. So who are you, then, citoyenne?'

'I am,' said the woman, 'or rather I was – oh, how do I know who I am now? I *was* the Marquise de Bréhal. I'm travelling with my grandchildren who – ah, such dreadful memories! – who have been orphans for several months. I'm trying to save them. I throw myself on your mercy, Madame and Monsieur. I have nowhere else to turn, and you are obviously good people, but I know the price of what I ask. Giving shelter to poor fugitives to save their lives means endangering your own. So I will ask you only to give us a bit of bread and show us a barn where we can sleep.'

'No such thing!' said Catherine Gavraz, speaking for the first time. 'I don't know just how we can help you yet, but it shall never be said of the Gavraz family that they turned away unfortunates who came knocking on their door. Come and sit down at the table, all three of you. We have only a frugal meal, but it will help to satisfy your hunger.'

She unhooked the pot of soup hanging over the hearth, and took some wooden bowls out of a cupboard. Then she went to the larder and came back with a piece of cheese and a loaf of brown bread, which she placed on the walnut table next to a jug of milk and an earthenware bowl of wild cherries.

As the Bréhal family satisfied their hunger and thirst, no one exchanged another word. Despite their weariness and the suffering that had left its mark on their faces the two children, a brother and sister aged around twelve, devoured the food with the hearty appetite of youth. When the meal was over the boy stifled a yawn.

'We'd better put these young folk to bed!' said Gavraz. 'I don't mean to question you, Madame, but I can guess you've been walking a long time, and you must have had to travel by night to avoid the local patrols. You can tell us about it in a minute, though only if you want to, and then we'll think what's to be done next. But now, you follow me, children! Kiss your grandmother goodnight and off with you into the bedroom. There are enough straw mattresses and blankets for everyone, in spite of the requisitions. At least you'll have one night in safety, and pray heaven there may be many others.'

Catherine Gavraz went to help the children to bed, and then returned to sit by the hearth with her son and the Marquise de Bréhal.

'Thank you!' breathed the Marquise. 'Oh, I thank you with all my heart. I was so frightened when you opened the door just now. I thought I'd stumbled upon a patriot anxious to please the authorities and have us thrown straight into prison, just as our goal seemed within reach. Instead I have found real kindness here, as so often on my journey. It's such a comfort to meet so many good people, even when evil is abroad! It gives me hope for the future.'

'Where do you come from?' asked Gavraz.

'Where?' she replied thoughtfully. 'Should I say from the other end of the world? Should I say from Hell? Words from the past don't describe the present reality. Well, I will tell you that we come from the Nantes area. Do you know what's going on there?'

'Nothing good, I fancy, like everywhere else.'

'Nothing good, indeed. And we were only passing through. All the unrest, the denunciations, the poisoned atmosphere that was beginning to spread had decided my son and daughter-in-law to abandon everything and go away with their children and me. Yet what crime had we committed, except to be born as we were? We never chose our birth for ourselves, but for that reason alone we had become pariahs. Even though my son was enthusiastic about the new ideas. Why, the boy now asleep in your bedroom next door is called Émile, in homage to Monsieur Rousseau and one of his books! Like so many others, my son approved of the abolition of privileges and hoped for the coming of a new dawn! But his generosity was equalled only by his ingenuous nature. When you interfere too abruptly with the delicate little wheels in a clock, the whole mechanism of the clockwork is thrown out. And surely society is far more fragile than a clock. You can't just wave a magic wand and change everything that was patiently constructed over a long period of time. You can't usher in a new world by the simple exercise of reason! Oh, what Utopian ideas – and how cruel it has been to learn these things! But I'm wandering from the point; I'm only telling you what I keep saying to myself. Well, back to my story. We stopped at an inn near Nantes, and we were arrested there after some kind of denunciation, I don't know what. I was lucky enough to save the two little ones by offering a bribe. But oh, my poor children! Have you heard of what they call Republican marriages? Do you know what they are?'

'Marriages without benefit of clergy, maybe?'

'Alas, no, far worse. There's a Commissary of the People called Carrier[3] in the Nantes area. They say he alone has the blood of over ten thousand innocent victims on his hands.'

'Even worse than Albitte! Who'd have thought it possible?' murmured Catherine Gavraz, crossing herself.

'Carrier's "Republican marriages" mean tying a man and a woman together naked and throwing them into the Loire to drown. That's how my son and daughter-in-law died in the month of Frimaire,[4] and I haven't even any tears left to weep for them. I don't know how I managed to travel half-way through France after that, sometimes in rickety vehicles, sometimes on foot, trying to save the children, find them a safe place in a world where there may still be a little love left. I won't tell you the whole tale of our journey. It would take all night! So eventful, so full of terrors! I meant to cross the frontier by night near Geneva and reach Lausanne and Turin, where I may hope to find friends. But there were troops everywhere. A good cobbler who sheltered us in an attic for several days and made us new shoes advised me to go up the river Arve. He said that beyond Chamouny you come to a village called Vallorcine, and then Switzerland is very close. It's my last and only hope.'

'Oh, Madame, the army is at Vallorcine! It's true that all manner of people have escaped that way, aristocrats, priests who wouldn't take the oath, bourgeois folk and many working people too. Yes, indeed, they got into Switzerland or Italy over the Grand St Bernard pass. But now there are soldiers all over the place, and our valleys are so steep and narrow you can't climb out of them just anywhere. In fact you were lucky to get this far without being stopped.'

'Oh God, then what can I do?' exclaimed the Marquise de Bréhal. 'I didn't know the worst excesses of the Revolution had spread to the mountains. I hoped to find some kind of peace still reigning here.'

'Little chance of that,' said Gavraz. 'But I can see from your story it may be even worse in other regions. However, there are people calling themselves patriots everywhere. Anywhere there's something to be had. They come down on us wherever they can impose their law. Indeed, when the French troops invaded these parts,[5] we Savoyards didn't think much of the Piedmontese soldiers who withdrew without trying very hard to defend us, and the annexation of Savoy was proclaimed at once.[6]

And the French promised us the moon: no more levies, no salt tax, no conscription into the militia! Not to mention guarantees of religious freedom. They told us the future would be rosy and we'd live a wonderful life here in the mountains. "The National Convention brings you liberty!" they cried. They even wrote it in books, and there were those who believed them. Gentlemen in towns organized "clubs". They planted Trees of Liberty everywhere. And there was a vote,[7] but it was rigged, because nine out of ten still preferred the King of Sardinia. But what could be done? We were in a trap. Only patriots voted, and some of them voted fifteen times over! That's how we came to be French!'

'Anyone with illusions didn't keep them long,' added Catherine Gavraz. 'First, for all they said about religious freedom, they started expelling the priests at the beginning of the next year, or maybe it was the end of their own. I get all confused! I think they brought that calendar in on purpose to confuse us, so nothing would be the same as before. They've even changed the names of some of the villages. But fancy sending the priests away! Poor men, they had to leave the country within a week or face transportation to Guyana. And it was *our* dignity that suffered, Madame. We had to live like brute beasts, we had to be born without baptism, die without the sacraments, be buried like dogs. And who was going to care for the poor now? This was in the month of Ventôse. For nights on end before they left, the priests heard confessions and tried to comfort us. They gave us Easter Communion in advance. And then they left.'

'Yes, we lost them all. Our curé here, Father Joseph Revillod! And the Reverend Effrancey! And Abbé Jacques Tissay! And our assistant priest Pierre-Joseph Paccard! And François Poensin, assistant priest at Les Houches. I knew him well. And so many others too, in the valley and elsewhere.[8] I myself saw Claude-François Amoudruz leaving – the architect of Saint-Gervais. He and a hundred mountain men managed to get past the guns at the Petit St Bernard pass and reach the Col du Bonhomme after the Megève revolt,[9] when the Sardinians came back, but not for long. Everyone who didn't think like a patriot was arrested or had to flee. That's their idea of liberty!'

'And then, Madame, not content with attacking men they started attacking things. We still went to church to pray; they closed the churches. They took the bells out of the church towers. Commissary of the Republic Simond had them laid in the dust at road corners to humiliate them, and us too. You see, we peasants are proud of our church bells, Madame.

They've been baptised and anointed, they have names like people. We knew the sound of every one of them. Our bells rang out the Angelus morning, noon and night, they gave warning of fires, they summoned us to church, they mourned our dead. Some said they could avert lightning. And now we saw them cracked, cast aside, lying in the dirt. We've heard that six thousand bells from this département were sent to Chambéry,[10] maybe to make cannon and kill men!'

'This was still in Commissary Simond's time,' added Gavraz. 'Well, that was bad enough, but when Albitte arrived he attacked the belfries themselves. In the month of Ventôse he gave orders to have them destroyed, razed to the ground. He sold the chapels. He burnt the wooden statues of the saints, he burnt the books, he stole the sacred ornaments. Those things were the wealth of our churches, so they were our wealth too.'

'Our whole life was disappearing.'

'We needn't tell you the rest of it. They said they'd abolish taxes, but they keep imposing new ones. They go around requisitioning things everywhere. They take blankets, sheets, tablecloths, napkins, shirts, even cabbages and potatoes! They requisition oats and hay and straw, cows and bullocks, horses and pigs. They cut our trees down to build ships for their navy. And on top of all that they invite us to make "patriotic donations", and if we don't we're under suspicion!'

'And then they descend on our homes. If a house is shut up they force the doors open with beams to get inside and take anything they can find. They dare to talk about the rights of man – but men never had fewer rights than now. You're always in danger of fire and the sword. It's terrifying, it surely is.'

'Not counting the men their armies devour. The king of Sardinia had professional soldiers, men who'd chosen that way of life and drew a soldier's pay. But under the Republic anyone may have to serve in the army, depending how the lots fall. Then you have to go away and leave your farm. And what did we ever do that means we must obey these Parisians who meddle as they please in the government of Savoy, conscripting our own flesh and blood? That's why the people rebelled at Megève. That was a year ago, and I can tell you, there's been unrest and fighting here too!'

'And what with all this, trade and farming are in a bad way. Food's in short supply. Prices are rising. They take our men, they take our goods, and no one trusts their paper money, those assignats.[11] We wish we had our good solid Piedmontese currency back again! In fact you have to use it in secret when you need something, or else you have to barter, but you can be arrested for that too.'

'If it were possible for you to help me,' said the Marquise de Bréhal, 'or if you could find someone able to do so, I would pay you for so great a service in better currency than assignats. There are still some gold pieces sewn into the hems of our clothes, and I have two diamonds of a very fine water. I'd willingly give you all I still possess to know that my grandchildren were safe in a free country!'

'Ah, it's not a question of money,' said Gavraz. 'There's something much more difficult we have to think about. You came here to our home. You could have knocked on another door, where they might have denounced you and stolen all you had into the bargain. Mountain folk are no better than anyone else. There's wheat and chaff among them, good and bad, the same as usual. Well then, this is the 28th of the month of Messidor, and no sign of any change for the better in Paris, or Chambéry, or Cluses. I've been thinking about all this as we talked. And I'd like to help you, but one can't trust many people these days. There's my brother-in-law, of course, my sister's husband. He has the farm next to this one, and he knows his way around the mountains better than I do. He often goes up there with the crystal hunters. But he has five children; he ought not to run any risks. It's different for me. I'm a widower. I had the very best of wives, as my mother will tell you, but she died in childbed with our son, who would have been your Émile's age by now. God himself must have sent you here, and I'm ready to guide you. If anything should happen to us, my sister will take care of our mother. As you see, it's not a matter of money, it's a matter of the dangers involved – for you, for the children and for me. There's the danger of being seen and arrested, and the danger of walking for a long, long time and being overcome by fatigue, and the danger of the snow and ice.'

'I myself am ready to try anything,' said Mme de Bréhal. 'And the children are strong. They too have suffered so much from this nightmare that they'll do all they can to make one last effort to escape it.'

'The only way would be by the Montanvert and the Géant,' said Gavraz.

'Ah, yes, that's the way Moutelet escaped!' said Catherine Gavraz.

'Yes, after he chopped down the Tree of Liberty at Servoz. What a man! He managed to escape when he was about to be arrested, and in very strange circumstances, I can tell you. But he was on his own, and in the prime of life.'

'I am ready for anything,' repeated the Marquise de Bréhal.

'Then here's what I suggest. Try to get a good night's sleep, and the three of you must rest tomorrow too, but in the barn, in case anyone comes here. Tomorrow will be Nonidi. If Monsieur Bourrit is up at the Montanvert with his workmen, studying his project for a Temple of Nature,[12] he'll come back down in the afternoon so as to be there on Décadi as the law requires.[13] So at dusk we'll climb to the Montanvert ourselves and spend the night there. The next day, which will be the 30th of Messidor,[14] we'll set out over the glaciers. There was a lot of snow last winter, and since then too, so the cracks should be well stopped up. We must pray heaven for fine weather. I think the föhn's dying down already. And we need frost. If all goes well, you should be in the Aosta valley on the 1st of Thermidor, and you'd be sure to find friends there.'

'God bless you!' said Mme de Bréhal. 'Give me your hand! Yours is a noble heart.'

As they had agreed, the fugitives spent the next day hiding in the hay in the barn. Now that they were so close to safety, they trembled at the thought of a last-minute setback. The church tower was being demolished in Chamonix, and the dull noise of picks resounded through the valley, echoing from one side of it to the other, reminding everyone how threatening the present was and how uncertain the future.[15] Late in the afternoon, Gavraz came for the Bréhal family. He had a stout haversack and some iron-tipped sticks, which he gave his companions.

'You must follow me in silence,' he said. 'The forest's quite close, and once there we'll be under cover. We don't run too much risk of meeting anyone at this time of day, but if we do, leave the talking to me. Once we reach the Montanvert we'll be safe from other people, and there'll only be the dangers of the mountains left. I went to see my brother-in-law this morning. He's a good man, he can be trusted. He told me the route we should take. It will be a cold night, and that's all the better for us. Are you ready? Then we'll be off.'

He kissed his mother, who was standing in the doorway to see them off, tears in her eyes. Soon they were in the forest.

'How many leagues do we have to go?' asked Mme de Bréhal.

'It's no use measuring the distance in leagues; we'll be following goat tracks. But say a few hours' walk with the moonlight to help us, and all should be well. You follow me, little one, and your brother will come after us with your grandmother. If you feel tired, tell me. But you must keep on walking as well as you can, because remember, this may be the end of all your troubles.'

The children, matured by their recent experiences, behaved with a gravity beyond their years, and did their best to follow in their new friend's measured, precise footsteps. The path was steep but easy to follow, and they came to the end of it in three hours.

'That's a good part of the way behind us,' said Gavraz, 'but tomorrow's journey will be longer and more difficult. We'll eat and sleep here. There's a stone hut that Monsieur Blair had built – an English gentleman, he was. It's no palace, but we'll have a roof over our heads and be out of the wind!'

Striking his tinder, he lit the dark lantern that he had hooked to his haversack.

'My God, what a strange landscape!' murmured Mme de Bréhal, casting a timorous glance at the Aiguille du Dru and the Charmoz rising to the sky in the clear light of the moon.

The children, who had walked on in silence looking at nothing but the path, also seemed alarmed by the vast mineral world they had entered. Gavraz realized that his companions needed cheering.

'Go in, go in!' he said. 'We're in luck; there's fresh, sweet-smelling hay inside, and here's our dinner. My mother roasted a chicken, and there's bread and cheese, so make yourselves at home! Other people have trodden the path we're taking and arrived safe. For instance, shall I tell you the story of my friend Moutelet?'

'Oh, yes please!' said little Émile.

'His real name is Marie Couttet,' continued Gavraz, 'but he's usually called Moutelet, which is our local word for a weasel, and as you'll see, he can wriggle out of anything. As I was telling your grandmother yesterday, Moutelet had the audacity to cut down the Tree of Liberty in Servoz. He was seen doing it and denounced, just as you might expect these days. But he was on the alert, and when he got home to Les Rosaries, near Les Praz, he saw a picket of soldiers coming to arrest him. Well, it was too late to run for it! So he hid in one of the big baskets we use on the farms, covering his head with hay, and his mother carried him out of the farm on her back. The soldiers were taken in, and let the peasant woman go right past them with her burden. She carried her son as far as the forest. But then the path to the Montanvert, the one we've just climbed, was so snowy that Moutelet feared his footsteps would be seen. So what do you think he did? He put his clogs on the wrong way round, tying them in place with string, and he hobbled up like that, leaving what looked like the footprints of a man coming down! A clever trick, eh? Up at the Montanvert, he put his boots on the right way round and escaped over the glaciers, the same way we'll be going tomorrow.'[16]

'But who told you this story? Has he been able to come back?'

'Not yet; it's too dangerous. No, we heard it from the Abbé Joguet, a priest from Chêne who had to leave for Italy with the rest of them. After a great many trials and dangers, he came back over the mountains in spring. He arrived at Les Houches on the 9th of Floréal,[17] and spent three nights with us, talking, listening, comforting us and hearing our confessions. Then he left for Megève, and now we hear he's exercising his ministry in the Ugine mountains. A saintly man, and very brave![18] It was from him we heard news of Moutelet!'

'And do all the people who try to get away succeed?'

'Sad to say, no. One priest was pursued by soldiers and caught and killed near Charamillon. They say that ever since then a spring has flowed there, and the priest's soul murmurs in it. The shepherds call it the Spring of the Bird because of its song.'

'My God!' said Mme de Bréhal.

'But I'm frightening you, and I meant to amuse you! Have a little more cheese. We'll need all our strength tomorrow. And I can tell you pleasanter stories, like the tale of the Abbé Tissay, who was arrested at Le Tour and imprisoned in a barn. He sawed through a plank and got away to the Valais. Then there was the Reverend Effrancey of Chamonix. We couldn't help laughing at *his* story. He stayed with us longer than was wise, and they came looking for him too. So a local innkeeper hid him at her place, but the soldiers descended on one of their requisitioning raids. Well, she dressed him up as a kitchenmaid in a gown, apron and cap and stood him in front of a tub full of dirty dishes with a dishcloth in his hand. "Get a move on, girl!" she cried as the soldiers came into the inn. "Oh, you lazy, clumsy, good-for-nothing creature!" And our curé certainly wasn't very handy with a dishcloth, that's a fact. "Look at this useless girl!" said the innkeeper to the sergeant. "Deaf mute, she is, and simple-minded too, doesn't even earn the food she eats!" And she slapped the curé's face. Well, the soldiers were well and truly bamboozled. The sergeant even said, "Don't be so hard on the poor girl!" And they left without the slightest suspicion!'[19]

For the first time since the day before the children laughed, almost happily, and Mme de Bréhal sketched a smile.

'And did your Reverend Effrancey get away afterwards?'

'Yes, indeed he did,' said Gavraz, pleased with the success of his story. 'Now, we must sleep. This hay isn't a very luxurious bed, but we must make do with it, and I hope you'll soon have better. I brought up a blanket – here, spread it over you, and try to rest and relax.'

The night passed without any alarms. The dawn of the 30th of Messidor came at last, and after a swift breakfast the fugitives went on their way. Although the air was keen at first, the sun soon warmed it. The Mer de Glace was in a granular condition, offering a good grip, and a little higher up some patches of snow made progress even easier.

'We're not the first to have come this way recently!' remarked Gavraz, noticing footprints. 'Someone was obviously here the day before yesterday, when the föhn was blowing and it was so warm. We're in luck; they've left us a path. I wonder who it was? No doubt we'll never know. There were only two of them, so it wasn't a patrol, probably fugitives. Anyway, they knew the mountains; they went just the way my brother-in-law told me we should take.'

They were indeed in luck, for the deep, well-hardened tracks of the footprints greatly eased their progress. Once pass the Angle, the tracks led to the right of the séracs of the Géant, and without them, determined as he was, it is unlikely that Gavraz would have succeeded in his venture. As it was, all he had to do was help his companions to follow the footprints and make sure they did not fall. Even so, the journey was almost too much for the children. Mme de Bréhal proved strong and energetic enough to keep an eye on Émile while Gavraz helped the girl. The long snow slopes that followed turned out to be the most difficult part of their journey. As they became wearier in the heat of the afternoon, the little procession made only slow progress. They had to keep stopping to rest, and now and then Gavraz carried the little girl.

'Courage!' he said. 'Keep your hearts up! Liberty is up at the top! This is no time to weaken!'

The difficult way forward seemed interminable. Now and then, towards the end, the children and even Mme de Bréhal fell to their knees in the snow. But as the sun sank low the little party reached the Géant pass.

'You're safe now!' Gavraz told them. 'This is where Piedmont begins. We'll spend the night where we are. It won't be as comfortable as at the Montanvert Hut, but I think we can find a little shelter. Tomorrow I'll start on the climb down with you, and when you're on a beaten track again I'll leave you to go the rest of the way alone. Well, now we must think of dinner!'

'The gratitude we shall always feel for you – ' Mme de Bréhal began.

'Now, now, let's not talk about that! After all I've heard of your misfortunes, the happiness it gives me to know I've brought you to safety is greater than any I ever felt before. I tell myself that after succeeding in such a thing I, François Gavraz, shall not have lived in vain. After all, years go by in the same humdrum way, but it will make me proud all my life to think I've been granted the chance to do some good for once.'

Overnight, the cold of the evening gave way to milder temperatures, heralding a change in the weather. Sure enough, next morning the sky was overcast. They hastily began the descent, which was made harder by the weariness and the stiffness the fugitives felt after their arduous journey the previous day. A little after noon, just as the downward climb was becoming easier, they heard voices and saw a Sardinian patrol. The two groups met, and Gavraz left his protégés in safe hands.

'Come with us!' suggested Mme de Bréhal, thanking him with deep emotion.

'No, no,' said Gavraz. 'I must go home. But you will never forget me, or I you, and that's what counts.'

He set off back up the mountains. A slight drizzle was beginning to fall, and it was followed by mist and snow. He found the footprints again when he reached the pass, but they were rapidly disappearing under a layer of sleet. He turned off the track too soon, and found himself in an endless labyrinth of séracs the size of cathedrals. He climbed back up, looked for another way, and got lost once more. After a few hours he despaired of finding his way, and dug himself into a snow hole for the night.

'I might try another route,' he told himself in the morning. 'I'll never get out of these crevasses and ice blocks. My brother-in-law told me that when he was out with the crystal hunters once, they came down over the pass up there. What did they call it? The Col du Midi. And then I think they went over the Rond Glacier. Anything would be better than this chaos. I'll have to go back up quite a long way, but perhaps it will be worth it.'

He climbed up again, but could not get his bearings. While he thought he was making north at an oblique angle, he was actually going west. He reached the Combe Maudite. After long hours of walking, he found a steeper slope in front of him and climbed it, not without difficulty. On reaching the top, he thought he was going down into the valley while he was actually making for the Brenva Glacier.

The Red Sentinel 153

'I must keep going,' he thought, 'or I shall freeze on the spot.'

His long red jacket and his hat were encrusted with crystallized snow. Icicles hung from his moustache. Fatigue overwhelmed him. He found himself facing yet another slope, and now he had not the slightest idea where he was. All he knew was that if he stopped now he would die, so he must go on as long as possible. Slowly, he climbed steep slopes of snow and rock. Night fell. Sleet was swirling incessantly around him, and the wind was howling.

'I'm lost,' he thought. 'Well, since this is my fate, so be it. But thank God the others are in safety by now!'

He leaned back against the rocks, and very soon the frost took hold of him. Slowly, he was covered by the snows of Thermidor.

But when the fine weather returned, a tall block of red granite stood where there had been no such block before. In a mysterious and mighty work of petrifaction, the forces of nature had united to turn Gavraz into a great, vertical rock with clear-cut lines, like a figure that seemed to be keeping watch over the mountains. And when later, much later, an English climber opened up a route there,[20] the name that naturally rose to his lips at the sight of that strange, tall rock was *The Red Sentinel*.

NOTES

1. Antoine-Louis Albitte (1761–1812), a representative on mission to the army of the Alps, introduced a reign of terror in the Ain and Savoy areas.
2. A measure adopted on the 19th of Nivôse, Year II of the Revolutionary calendar (8 January 1794).
3. Jean-Baptiste Carrier (1756–1794).
4. Carrier carried out his functions until the 20th of Pluviôse, Year II (8 February 1794).
5. 22 September 1792.
6. 27 September 1792.
7. 14 October 1792.
8. Cf. F. Descotes, *Les Émigrés en Savoie, à Aoste et dans le pays de Vaud*, Chambéry, 1903.
9. Cf. C. Grosset, *Histoire de Megève pendant la Révolution française*, Annecy, 1869, repr. Marseille, 1979.
10. Cf. F. Gex, *Autour des clochers de Savoie*, Chambéry, 1928.
11. The decree making assignats the official currency was applied in Savoy on the 27th of Thermidor, Year I (14 August 1795).
12. The project was approved by the municipality of Chamonix on the 10th of Floréal in the next year (29 April 1793).
13. By an order of Albitte issued on the 30th of Prairial, Year II (18 June 1794).
14. Friday, 18 July 1794.
15. The church tower was rebuilt at the beginning of the 19th century through contributions and the voluntary labour of the people of Chamonix. It cost 3,280 livres and was finished in 1807. Cf. P. Payot, *Au royaume du Mont Blanc*, Bonneville, 1950.
16. On returning to Chamonix after the Revolution, Moutelet distinguished himself by

The Red Sentinel

single-handedly laying out a mule track from the Planards to the Montenvers. The Compagnie des Guides of Chamonix gave him an annual gratuity of 50 francs for this achievement.

17. 28 April 1794.
18. After being arrested and taken to Cluses, the Abbé Charles Joguet was shot there on 14 August 1794 at the age of twenty-nine. Cf. J-M. Lavorel, *Cluses et Faucigny, étude historique*, Annecy, 1888.
19. Cf. *Chamonix, une vallée, des hommes*, Saint-Gervais-les-Bains, 1978.
20. The first of three routes devised by T. Graham Brown on the south-east slopes of Mont Blanc, the Sentinelle Rouge was opened on 1 and 2 September 1927.

EXPEDITIONITIS

Hi Wosdack! Long time no see! How are your feet doing?

Oh, O.K. Nothing lost ... Minor problems.

And the lecturing tour: still on it?

And how! No alternative! Got to pay things off! Nothing but! ... Its sheer drudgery ... You heard the story?

More or less ... What really happened?

Oh, one thing after the other ... The usual run around. Well perhaps a bit more than usual ... It was something between a heavy and alpine style expedition. Everyone has been eyeing that South-West ridge of Gramaslu for a long time. And its ages since we first asked Lenap for permission to try it. You know how things are there. You have to get a permit and pay an exorbitant fee. Anyhow, we eventually got it; for post monsoon, last autumn. We were lucky, because the Swiss-Jap expedition trying the route in June-July failed.

You mean the one in which Schunderer and Hataki got the chop?

Yep! So it was a good start for us ... We were eight. There was Giusto, Billy, Snussen, Kiodor, Hirida, Zabulon, Nephtali and me. Along with ten Sherpas and a liaison officer. Problems started straight off.

How come, straight off?

From the moment we saw the Sherpas. You know the rules: they had to be equipped with the same material as us. Material, my arse, they have more than we have. They have been bargaining over it for years, and anyhow they are quite rich enough to buy what they need. That's precisely the problem. We were unlucky enough to get a real bunch of rip-offs. They refused the gear and demanded the equivalent of five hundred quid in its place. Take it or leave it. When I think how we have been saving up for this trip ... We had no alternative but to stump up. Hullo there, Mr Bank Manager!

Didn't they understand?

Like heck! They couldn't care less. Many Sherpas today have a nice sum put away. They are an enterprising clan. On one side they are in a position to exploit the climbers and on the other the local porters who they get to carry their loads for a song ... We, on the other hand, had to lug up our sacks since we couldn't afford the porters. But even that wasn't enough. The ruddy Swiss-Jap expedition had been throwing money around: a budget of a million dollars! We were just a bunch of tramps passing through ... No way could we get any respect. The approach march was hell. They whipped everything they could. They went on strike. We almost had a fight.

And me who thought Lenap was a little corner of Paradise.

Nowadays paradises change fast. It only needs a few loud mouths to start shouting the odds ... Anyhow, we did eventually reach base camp, where by dint of digging through the tins and Coca bottles we managed to find solid ground to fix our tents. In fact it wasn't bad ... I must admit we were a bit surprised to see our Sherpas make some effort to set up camp. We soon understood why: they had every intention of staying put for the month and not budging. It was a right little Holiday Home for Sherpas. A real rest cure ... Anyhow, those are the risks you have to run in this sort of thing ... At least we were at the foot of the mountain we'd been dreaming about, all in form and rearing to go. The very next day we set up Camp I.

Good weather?

So so, to start with. Fine in the morning, snow in the afternoon. Sometimes pretty windy. One knows its never going to be really easy ... From the start Kiodor had the shits, but he didn't complain for he knew there was no room for weak links with the Sherpas having dropped us in it. And we knew it could get a lot worse ... So everything was normal, if you see what I mean ... The main problem was the bottom slope, right under a pile of séracs which then had to be traversed. Spooky! I've never seen such a vile glacier. You put a ladder in place and next day it was at the bottom of a crevasse. It took us a week to install a passage and move on. It was at Camp IV that Zabulon got a pulmonary emphysema. You know how it is. You have to move fast and lose altitude. But as it was night we couldn't get him down straight away ... Poor Zabulon. At least he didn't suffer for long ... And then we had a period of bad weather which forced us back down to base camp. It was just above Camp I that Snussen got caught by a falling sérac.

Real bad luck, wasn't it?

Yeah, real bad luck. So back at base camp we started rethinking things. We were only six now. So we decided to go and see the Spanish-Canadian expedition which was camped not far away and see if we could join up with them for the *voie normale*, rather than to go on taking risks trying to get onto our South-West ridge. They agreed, indeed they were highly pleased as they had been having the same trouble with their Sherpas and three of their party were ill ... So next day we were to set off with them, except our liaison officer instructed us by walky-talky to descend. He maintained we had permission for the South-West Ridge, not the Normal Route, and he had to refer back to the Ministry to see if it was going to be possible. He added that if we didn't, he'd see we never again got a visa, and indeed perhaps no one else from back home. We'd no choice but to go on down. And wait. A whole bloody week. A week of fine weather, what's more ... Ruddy hell! But we had to get something done. For ourselves of course ... But also the sponsors and the firms which has supplied us with material ... Not to speak of paying off our debts. So, you can imagine: a week like that ... And eventually the reply came: no. Mark you, I learnt later that the liaison officer had indeed telegraphed to the Ministry that we wanted to join the Spanish-Canadians, but saying that they did not want us. I wonder why he did that, the shit. Just to land us in it, I bet.

You certainly weren't having any luck!

Nope ... So we found ourselves like caged lions, permission refused and with a week of good weather lost. And with no other possibility but our south-west ridge. We were so pissed off we had to do something. We said that we at least owed that to Zabulon and Snussen. So we went after it again.

Well done!

Obviously the good weather wouldn't last. Not that it was really bad. But it snowed each night and it was extremely cold. It must have worsened Kiodor's condition, for he hadn't recovered properly, even during our enforced rest. He died at Camp V, pretty suddenly, from complications brought on by his gut problem. He was completely emptied out, poor chap ... We carried on, as we were now getting quite high. Even so, we needed a Camp VI and a Camp VII, from where Nephtali and me, who were climbing together could go for the summit. It was minus thirty. And an unbelievably strong wind: freeze the bollocks off a brass monkey. And that day the snow started falling about midday, earlier than before. A full scale storm. We were at 7,910 metres. Scarcely 50m from the top. Gramaslu is virtually an Eight-Thousander, you know. Giving up then was the hardest thing I have ever done in my life.

Had you managed to film up to then?

Yes, thank goodness. In fact it was that which had delayed us ... But what's the alternative?

Sure!

We spent the night at Camp VII again. But the same shitty weather next day ... It was the end of all hope. It was pretty awful getting back to Camp VI where the others were stymied, with Hirida who was suffering from migraines. He had to be got down. We packed the tents and started off together, all the five of us who had survived. Hirida's head aches were due to a cerebral oedema. We were knackered ... Completely knackered, I tell you! The temperature was as low as our morale. We managed to reach Camp V where we were stuck the whole of the next day. The snow was now driving horizontally. We had to lose altitude for Hirida. But what could we do? He died there. It was a real Verdun ... Mark you, I don't think Hirida missed much. It was only a miracle that I was saved at Camp IV, which we managed to reach ... We were in two tiny tents, Billy and Giusto, me and Nephtali. During the night, Nephtali went to the other tent where the stove was. He was dying of thirst and wanted a brew. I vaguely dozed off again but was woken up by a feeling of being choked, of being crushed even, I was breathing snow and was suffocating. With difficulty I managed to get out of the tent which had half been torn out, half buried under an avalanche. The slope above hadn't seemed dangerous. But it had snowed so much ... I yelled, I searched everywhere. The other tent had been carried away. The rest of the night was a real nightmare ... So it was all alone next day that I managed to finish the descent. With partly frozen feet, in fact pretty badly frozen ... We had had such a run of ill chance that I was sure I was going to be carried away by the seracs. But no. Luck was with me! I got out!

My God, what a terrible story!

You can say that again! I'll miss out the rest of it as they were trifles compared with the loss of my mates. The return was sad, boring ... I only passed 7,472 trekkers ... Then at Matkandu after I'd paid off the Sherpas they stole the box containing what little money remained. And they threatened me. I had to take refuge at the Embassy to save myself, and I only came out when it was time to leave, in a car with diplomatic license plates ... Its rotten that country now ... I tell you, its finished, spoilt. But they have such beautiful mountains!

You ought to publicise all that.

Not likely. I'm not an idiot, I'd never get a visa again ... Above all I can't say anything in my lectures. I tell the public what they want to hear: a fabulous country, the solidarity of a mountain people, their delightful customs ... Fortunately, it was me who had the photo spools in my sack. And we have been able to make the film. Its called *The Avalanche*. It's a meaningful title, you understand. Not just the snow avalanche, but also

Expeditionitis 159

the avalanche of problems we suffered. One can't refer to all the disasters we had and name it *The Emphysema, the oedema, the runs,* etc. That wouldn't sell. And so as the title isn't *The South-West Ridge of Gramaslu*, it doesn't matter whether we made the summit or not ... You must come to one of my lectures, I'll give you a ticket. But, I tell you, what is hardest is to be the only one remaining to make all these appearances. I have still got two more to do in the Paris region. Afterwards I go straight on to Brussels, Strasbourg, Sarreguemines, Maubeuge, before coming back to Paris for two more. Do you want to come?

Sure. In any case it would be good to see you again. We could go out for a meal.

With pleasure ... But I warn you, I'm off again soon. We've had the permit for a while. Only a 7,500m, but a real tough one! We're four. We're hoping to do it alpine style in winter ... I have to be back in Matkandu a fortnight Friday. And this time no problems!... We'll do it, shit or bust!

THE TEMPTATION OF PHILIBERT AVRIL

There was once a time when the demonic powers had appalling difficulty in seducing men and women: in beguiling them, captivating them, getting a firm grip on them and finally dragging them down to the sulphurous depths of Hell. The conquest of a single soul demanded efforts that can scarcely be imagined today. It called for a strategic campaign, complex plans that were always going wrong, cunning manoeuvres, sudden violent attacks, campaigns, ambushes, skirmishes and furious battles. All for a victory that could never be sure until the end.

In those days, it must be admitted, people thought it was perfectly normal to be loving husbands and wives and bring up large broods of children, teaching them the values by which they themselves lived. In those days they also thought it perfectly normal to work hard and well, really putting their hearts into it. That was a time when masters and servants ate at the same table and always remembered to leave something over for the poor. A time when people indulged in honest, cheerful amusements at home with their families or in their local village communities. A time when, believe it or not, thousands of monks who had never read Freud spent all their days and a good part of their nights celebrating the glory of God and praying for their fellow human beings. Imagine trying to conquer souls in so unfavourable a climate! Even in those hard times, of course, there were always a few soldiers mercilessly slashing each other to pieces, a number of villains who would cut the hamstrings of honest citizens and then rob them, bandits who broke into convents, stole the sacred vessels and raped a nun here and there. Such conduct did help to bolster up a certain faith in human vice. But these cases were the exception rather than the rule. It was a positively exhausting task finding any chink in the armour of charity and goodwill that protected most living souls. You had to lay siege to one for years on end if you were to lead it into temptation. All that trouble to make some honest blacksmith take to the bottle, just so that he might come home drunk one night and maltreat his maidservant! All the wealth of imagination you had to deploy to introduce lascivious images into a pious hermit's dreams! The sheer length of the struggle to make a farmer, once only slightly miserly, become avaricious to the point where he would appropriate a poor widow's field! On such occasions, the denizens of Hell would give themselves up to loud rejoicings in celebration of their triumph. Triumph? Well, sort of … for when they thought all was won, guess what was more likely than not to happen? As death approached, the apparently irrevocably damned would start thinking about the state of their souls. Soon they felt regret, then contrition, then penitence. They called for a priest, confessed their sins and made reparation, over and above the wrongs they had done. Then, with their minds at peace and feeling much more cheerful, they departed this world to go straight to Paradise! As I was saying, those were terrible times. It was enough to drive a conscientious demon who took a pride in his work and kept an eye on his productivity round the bend.

But as we know, all this has changed. It took time and trouble, mind you. There was wholesale mobilization of the infernal forces to achieve that end, at the personal instigation of the boss himself. A bureaucratic system bogged down in routine had to be completely overhauled. The powers of darkness called on the creative brilliance of all their minds, and then special committees undertook a rational study to investigate such suggestions as had been proposed, from the constructive to the downright dotty. Simulated human beings were used in trials. Next came redundancies and restructuring. All the demons had to go on retraining courses. The investment of labour the whole process entailed was vast, but it brought results! Within a few centuries, the old trends had been reversed.

Take love, for instance, Lilith's specialist area. She concentrated on corrupting its image, shattering the old myth of life-long affection and replacing it with the bait of ephemeral carnal lust, mirages that brought only insecurity and distress.

Mephistopheles put his mind to making humanity worship the sciences with such idolatry as to consider them self-sufficient values, not just the means of coming to a better understanding of the Creation. Once most people saw them as prime causes they brought forth dangerous fruit, so that men and women became bogged down in worldly comfort. They even discovered the means of directly or indirectly destroying all natural life, and it was far from impossible that they might eventually achieve that supreme aim.

Then there was Astaroth, who succeeded in diverting the noble qualities of the human mind into ideologies so contrary to the most elementary common sense that anyone would have thought him bound to fail. But no: he managed his ideologies with such fiendish skill that they produced astonishing results, triumphantly establishing themselves on the planet so firmly that in less than a century they had done more harm than all the uncoordinated savagery of previous millennia!

Asmodeus set about developing and dispersing the various evils engendered by money. Again, his success exceeded all expectations, no doubt because in number and power the banking and financial institutions had to a great extent replaced the temples where worship was once offered to the True God.

It is a fact that Beelzebub lent his colleague a hand here, taking on the apparently minor but in fact essential talk of undermining the foundations of the Church so that mankind, deprived of faith, hope and even charity, found itself in a vacuum, without any spiritual aid or support, a prey to discouragement, egotism and doubt. Victory was not yet complete, of course, but hopeless as the venture seemed it had its moments of glory, and to be honest, at present it is not doing at all badly.

In fact the situation is now very promising. There has been an unhoped-for reversal of fortune. A few bulwarks of resistance remain here and there, and perhaps I may tell you some other day about the indignation unleashed in the infernal regions when the sport of climbing was first invented. On the whole, however, all is well, and there are no longer any supply problems over souls to fuel the spiritual furnaces. The demons sow, they reap, they gather in and store their harvest. Everything is as it should be.

For this very reason, in all the satisfaction of knowing that their mission is accomplished, demonkind at the height of its powers resents the few occasions when it is still thwarted. The tale I am about to tell you is the sad story of Philibert Avril.

Haven't you heard of Philibert Avril? In that case you've never climbed up to the Minvielle Hut at the top of the Fromont Glacier in the Cirque d'Ourtoulane. It's a long way, of course, a five-hour climb. Perhaps you're one of those who like to drive to the bottom of an outcrop and do single pitch lower-offs, preferably with the television there to film you. Well, never mind. Let's hope there are other reasons why you've never been up to the Minvielle Hut.

Philibert Avril is the warden there from June to September. He works as a woodcutter for the rest of the year. He is a sturdy young man of nearly twenty-five, clear-eyed, with a direct gaze and a smile always hovering around his mouth, strong as an ox and gentle as a lamb, and he is passionately devoted to his little hut and his own part of the mountains. The moment the season begins he starts taking things up there, checking everything, repairing the metal sheeting on the roof, airing mattresses and blankets, sweeping the knotted wooden floor, waxing the pine tables and putting up little gingham curtains with tie-backs at the windows. Then he contemplates his domain and says to himself, smiling happily, 'Right, they can come now! They'll be comfortable here!'

And his clients do come, sometimes simply for the pleasure of seeing the place again and getting what they know in advance will be a very warm welcome.

'Hi, Phiphi,' they say, taking their heavy sacks off their shoulders.

'Good to see you again!' says Philibert Avril. 'You're in luck, this is a good season! But you've walked up all this way; you must be hot. Sit down and make yourselves comfortable. Now, what would you like? A nice cup of tea? Some lemonade? It's on the house!'

And off he goes, attending to everyone's needs, serving and clearing away, cooking, talking cheerfully, singing. The fact is, his hut is a little paradise. And that comparison, which sprang spontaneously from my pen, explains why it is so difficult for the powers below, whose projects I described at the beginning of this story, to accept such a situation. Philibert Avril never raises his voice in anger, never shows ill humour, never overcharges anyone. He does everything with such attentive cheerfulness that even bad-tempered climbers – and there are such people – are won over by the happy atmosphere and come down the mountain better folk than when they went up it.

Furthermore, Philibert Avril knows his way around the mountains and is generous with sensible advice to one and all, helping them to avoid inconveniences and even accidents.

'The Toubin peak is in fine condition at the moment, and there's a good track for the approach. This is the right time to do the Fabre-Autin route on the Aiguille Misette; it'll be easy to get across the bergschrund. The North Face of Mont Bouyer? No, I wouldn't really recommend it just now; it's hard ice and overhung by a cornice, but have you ever done the traverse of the Dentelles d'Eycely? Well, why not try it? It's nice and airy, a splendid climb and in good condition this year. I think you'll enjoy it.'

In the evening, without appearing to do so but with gentle authority, Philibert Avril gets all his guests off to bed early, and then goes to the kitchen to prepare for breakfast next morning. He finishes the washing up, stacks the bowls, grinds coffee in an old, well-worn wooden coffee mill, fills the kettle, puts out the ceiling light, and – dare I tell you this? – once back in his own little room he kneels humbly on the floor, recites a decade of his rosary, and prays that his guests will sleep well and have a good climb next day. Philibert Avril is an almost unheard-of phenomenon in modern times.

Could the demonic powers leave such a man alone to devote himself to such practices, do you think? Obviously not. They kept watch on him, they studied him, they realized that he had a natural resistance to occasions of sin, and they decided to pay him some serious attention. A special committee of experts on temptation held a meeting, for this was a grave case.

The first to speak was Lilith, princess of the succubi, a lascivious fiend whose methods were ruthless but usually efficient. She was particularly proud of her success in seducing a sixth-century stylite who had spent over four years meditating on top of his column, and who then came down from his pedestal to abandon himself to unrestrained debauchery in her company in the low-life quarters of Antioch. But Lilith had many other successful missions to her credit, and she always went straight to the point. The fact was, she knew only one method of temptation, but she knew that one method inside out.

'You let me get my claws on that bloke! He won't know what hit him!' she said. Her language was seldom elegant. 'I know his kind. The innocent, naïve sort, doesn't know what life's about. I can deliver the goods in no time at all.'

'But that wouldn't be much fun,' protested Moloch. 'We don't often get a chance to amuse ourselves. Why not make use of this one? Let's make it more complex. Look for his weak spots, find out where he's sensitive. There isn't a human being alive who isn't susceptible to pride.'

'Well, our man isn't, not so as you'd notice,' sighed the lame devil Asmodeus. 'He doesn't take himself seriously, never talks about himself, never even thinks about himself. His mind is entirely set on doing his duty and serving others. Those are the very worst sort! Why don't we think about the seven deadly sins, and the resources they offer? Pride ... well, as I was explaining, our man is humility itself, though I'll admit that given a little subtlety, you can sometimes get surprising results in that area. Sloth? No, Philibert Avril's a glutton for work and enjoys it. Envy? I fear he may be the kind to think himself happier in his modest little Minvielle Hut than if he were director of the entire Hilton hotel chain. Anger? Whatever anyone says he just smiles with the greatest goodwill – yes, I know, disgusting! Avarice? No good; once he has enough to live on he asks for nothing more. He takes no care for the morrow, doesn't even have a savings account or a credit card. So what's left? Gluttony? He'd take the bread from his own mouth, and be glad to, if there wasn't enough for his customers. That just leaves us with lust, which Lilith has already discussed, but he respects himself. One day he'll marry some nice girl, love her with all his heart and in the gentlest possible way give her any number of children to be brought up in the paths of virtue, and *then* we'll have to start all over again with them. So before that happens I really do think we should try to – '

'That will do!' Beelzebub interrupted. He had taken a break from his own activities on purpose to attend this debate. 'You have no imagination at all. I agree with Moloch: if we want a bit of fun it's no use being too hidebound. We mustn't just try a single method, we must be innovative. Let's put him in some untenable situation and see how he reacts. Very well: while I was listening to you lot, I had an idea: the man loves his hut, am I right? He's invested a lot of himself in it. So let's attack him through that hut. You just wait and see if anger and envy and pride don't all suddenly surface to do their work and hand us the man. On a plate!'

This conversation took place in winter, and before long soon a horde of fiends, large, small and medium, came down on the Cirque d'Ourtoulane like the wolf on the fold.

A few months later, in early June when the pastures were full of flowers, Philibert Avril thought it was about time to go and prepare his hut for the summer season. Going up to the Fromont Glacier he felt very light-hearted, in spite of the weight of his sack. Every year he experienced this moment of intense pleasure on returning to the unspoilt world of the high mountains. Moraines and patches of snow gradually replaced the short grass. Then came a long walk over a compacted snowfield with brown streaks that revealed to his practical eye the presence of crevasses. Fluffy clouds floated in the bright expanse of sky. The shadows were short and clear-cut. All was for the best in the best of all possible worlds. On the flat stretch before the final steep path, Philibert whistled a jaunty tune.

Soon afterwards, however, he froze in shock. The shutters of his hut were hanging from their twisted hinges, the window panes were broken, and the door, swinging loose, had allowed a drift of dirty snow inside. Philibert said nothing but hurried on, and then, with dismay, viewed the disorder in the hut. It was obvious that vandals had ransacked it very thoroughly. The tables and benches were overturned, the mattresses gutted, the blankets slashed, and all the kitchen equipment was strewn everywhere, dented or broken. The old mountaineering photos he had pinned up so carefully on the walls were torn to shreds, and the pieces lay scattered on the muddy floor. It was a pitiful sight, but Philibert Avril felt no anger. He took off his sack, sat down on the threshold with his face in his hands, and let two large tears flow slowly down his tanned cheeks. Then he pulled himself together, raised his head and said out loud, 'Oh, dear Lord, what a trial! I suppose I was too happy. Give me the strength to forgive the louts who did this. They can't have had any idea how it would hurt me. And please give me strength to create order out of this chaos, so that I can entertain my clients all the same. They really need this hut, you see.'

Closing his eyes, he added, with a smile that was less sad already, 'Well, they say God helps those who help themselves. So God and I will try to do something about the mess!'

He did not see the fiery glow that lit up space for a moment, but he caught a strange, unpleasantly modulated screech. It was Beelzebub saying, 'Foiled, by Mephistopheles!'

The fiends had indeed failed. Philibert Avril reopened his eyes, took a deep breath and set to work at once, sorting out what could be repaired and what could not, standing the furniture up again, sweeping away the snow, covering the open windows and doorway as best he could. Then he hurried back down at nightfall, making a mental list of everything he would need to order next day to repair the damage: wood, glass for the window panes, blankets, fabric, plates, glasses, nails ... oh yes, and he mustn't forget wire and candles.

And in this way, coming and going, employing his own efforts, sawing planks, spreading mastic on the edges of window panes, sewing up mattress covers with his beefy hands, he had repaired the worst of the damage within ten days. On his last journey up he even brought some rhododendrons to make little flower arrangements for the tables and make the room look festive. Guests arrived, and he entertained them with even more amiability than usual to make them forget any slight discomfort.

Another committee meeting was called in Hell. 'What did I tell you, you idiots?' enquired Lilith. 'Be innovative! Make it complex, you said! Well, look where that got you! Trials and tribulations simply make that kind of bloke stronger. I could have told you so. He's earned himself indulgences! He's made progress on the road to heaven! This is too bad! There's no time to be lost. Just let me get at him!'

'Not so fast!' Asmodeus interrupted. 'Too much haste could spoil everything. I think we should indeed agree to entrust this mission to you …'

All the demons present nodded their heads up and down in a gesture of pensive acquiescence.

'But,' continued Asmodeus, 'we mustn't take this too lightly. For one thing, it's fine weather on earth just now, in the Alps anyway, and there are twenty or so climbers sleeping in the Minvielle Hut every evening. Whereas what you want is to be alone with Philibert Avril.'

'You bet,' Lilith agreed.

'And for another, it's quite some time since you exercised your charms on human beings. I mean, they don't need you these days in order to succumb to any number of vices. You'll have to brush up on the taste of the day, see what makes a man randy now, get in the groove, as they say up above. If you turn up in the last costume you used – if I'm not mistaken, it was a pleated pink tussore gown, a pearl necklace, silk stockings, court shoes with a buttoned strap and a sweet little cloche hat trimmed with a ribbon bow – well, forgive me, but turn up in that outfit and you'll look like someone's dear old granny, which isn't exactly the desired effect.'

'I suppose you think you're funny,' grumbled Lilith. She might be four million years old, but she did not like being compared to a grandmother.

'Calm down, for badness' sake,' said Moloch. 'We only want to make sure you hold all the trumps.'

'And that,' Asmodeus went on triumphantly, 'is why I've been collecting information. I repeat, you have to appeal to the tastes of the day, nothing run of the mill, something really in line with the imagination of the period. So what's the dream woman of the late twentieth century like? That's what we need to know! And with that end in view I've got hold of some of the illustrated reading matter they call strip cartoons up there. These strip cartoons have more or less replaced literature. They faithfully reflect the deepest expectations and feelings of the present day. In particular, they show some very detailed pictures of women. I fed them into my computer, and it's produced the perfect, typical profile of the girl you must impersonate if you are to correspond precisely to the dreams of an alpine hut warden.'

'Tell me more,' said Lilith, rather intrigued.

'You need to wear a pair of tiny shorts,' explained Asmodeus. 'Close-fitting. Really minute. Bare legs except for lace-up boots, and woolly socks drooping over the boot tops.'

'But I'll be cold,' protested Lilith.

'Never mind that,' said the fiend impatiently. 'If you want to succeed, you just do as I say. I will now continue. Your bosom will be large. Excessively large. A fine pair of knockers, if you know what I mean, and bulging out of a silver-studded black leather bra. You wear a large metal watch on your left wrist as an accessory. Now, what else was there? Oh, no hat. Ringlets of red hair tumbling carelessly to your shoulders. A sensual, full-lipped mouth … yes, that's about it.'

'Okay about the sensual, full-lipped mouth,' agreed Lilith, 'but the rest is com-plete-ly crap! Subtle suggestion is what gets a man, not putting everything out on public view. I object to being got up like some kind of savage. Anyway, the whole outfit strikes me as inappropriate for a mountain climate.'

'I do agree that men have reverted to a very primitive state,' Moloch admitted. But we have to take the situation as we find it. Remember that time you went off to the Neander valley to make trouble in a tribe there? Well, if we're talking about refinement, tastes today are about as high as they were then. In view of which I predict that you'll be sure to score in the outfit I suggest.'

'And you'll have to put up with the cold,' added Asmodeus, 'since you'll be going up there when there's no one else about, which means in a storm.'

It was thus in a storm that Lilith set off for the Minvielle Hut two weeks later. To be more precise, she set off first in rain and then, as she climbed higher, in snow. Her breasts, weighing some six kilos, did not quite balance the weight of the eleven-kilo purple rucksack that Asmodeus had finally persuaded her to carry. The outfit originally envisaged had been supplemented by a harness in the year's top fashion colours, a combination of turquoise and fluorescent orange. A small, striped chalk bag dangled from her rear. The entire costume was extremely uncomfortable, particularly when wet, but thorough study of modern strip cartoons could leave no one in any doubt of the efficacy of such a get-up.

Soaked, frozen and exhausted, Lilith arrived at the Minvielle Hut at nightfall. She then let herself drop in the snow and began uttering feeble cries.

Philibert was alone, busy reading an old number of a climbing magazine by the light of an oil lamp. He suddenly raised his head and listened to the sounds outside. A weak, almost smothered cry came distinctly to his ears. He leaped up, put on his anorak and ran to the doorway.

'Hullo!' he shouted. "Is there anyone there? Do you need help?'
'Help, help!' groaned Lilith.

Philibert hurried towards the voice, and saw a human form lying slumped on a patch of snow about a dozen yards from the hut.

'Help!' repeated Lilith. 'Have pity on an unfortunate creature in distress! Do not turn a poor girl from your door!'

This was not exactly the way she should have put it, but with her diabolical nature Lilith could not imagine that some homes were open to all comers, and the one she wanted to enter was particularly hospitable. In any case, Philibert Avril took in the situation at a glance. He raised the exhausted girl to her feet, put his strong arm round her, helped her to climb to the hut, and himself brought her in under his roof.

'Good heavens, what an outfit to wear!' he exclaimed, on seeing the girl he had rescued in the light of a lamp. 'I don't believe it! Really, the ads the sports gear manufacturers use will persuade people to buy anything! I've seen some oddities in my time, but nothing like this! Don't you have anything else to put on?'

Lilith very obviously did not have anything else to put on. She had observed her instructions scrupulously, down to the very last detail. The contents of her sack, which her host emptied on the table in the hope of finding a sweater, consisted chiefly of a purple polyamide rope, two bottles of champagne, some highly spiced food, a copy of that notorious seventeenth-century Latin work of eroticism the *Alosia Sigea*, in its 1678 edition, and a mixture of slings, karabiners and nuts to add local colour.

'I never saw such a badly packed sack!' sighed Philibert.

'Well, it's not my fault,' protested Lilith, seeing her chance to embark on the tale she had already prepared in advance. 'I started out with some people I met by chance, you see. They said they'd show me what fun climbing was. So we shared out the climbing gear and the food and drink between us any old way, and you see what I got landed with. The others had an argument on the glacier and then they just went off, leaving me alone. I was badly scared, and so cold and frightened ... and I hurt myself! Look!' she added, bending her supple waist to show a gash running down the back of her shapely thigh. 'I had to walk and walk for ever such a long time! I was afraid I was lost.'

Limpid tears welled from her big, long-lashed blue eyes. Philibert Avril was bowled over.

'You poor child! Abandoned like that! How could anyone do it? There are some frightful people around! But don't worry, you've nothing to be afraid of now. I'm here with my little hut to help you forget what a bad time you've had. We must look after you!'

Lilith could scarcely suppress a victorious smile. It was in the bag! A mere routine job, hardly even any fun!

None the less, matters did not go exactly as she expected. Pulling himself together, Philibert had shaken off the effects of his surprise and recovered his usual efficiency. In no time at all Lilith's voluptuous appearance, so conscientiously designed for her by Asmodeus, had been counteracted by simple comforts that entirely banished the atmosphere of carnal lust she liked to create around her. She was soon swaddled in a woolly blanket, with another draped clumsily around her shoulders and bust. Her hair was wrapped in a towel smelling of soap and toothpaste, and there was a steaming cup of Bovril on the table in front of her.

Momentarily taken aback, she decided to play this new game and confront her adversary on his own ground. Philibert was sitting opposite her, watching her drink her Bovril with a kindly smile.

'I really would like to know more about climbing,' she said. 'I seem to have seen the worst side of it today.'

She laughed, showing pearly white teeth, and Philibert joined in.

'For instance,' she asked, 'what are those funny things in my sack for?'

'Well, that depends.' And Philibert, who like many climbers, especially men, loved technical questions, took it upon himself to explain the function of a descender. He was unstoppable on the subject. He gave a brief outline of the history of rappeling, picked up the end of a rope, coiled it, demonstrated manoeuvres. Lilith listened with fascinated interest. Soon her slender fingers, slipping into those of the expert, were trying to imitate the loops of the rope. Clumsy at first, she soon proved a quick learner. A comfortable atmosphere was established. Philibert felt increasingly happy to have had such a pleasant companion fall from the skies (as it seemed) on a gloomy evening which he was preparing to spend alone.

Lilith sat down again, bent her head gracefully and finished drying her red ringlets, finally throwing them back like a halo around her small face.

'Why, she's enchanting!' thought Philibert, who had not previously thought of her in any light but that of a waif stranded in the mountains.

'I'm feeling really hungry!' said the girl. 'And since I went to all that trouble carrying up the champagne we might as well enjoy it.'

'I've already eaten,' Philibert objected. 'And you're tired; you need something hot inside you. A good plateful of potatoes – I put them to cook just now – a piece of cheese, and that'll soon help you get your strength back.'

'All right, we'll pool everything,' said Lilith obligingly. 'Do something for me, will you? Put the second bottle somewhere cool when you go to the kitchen, and bring back a couple of glasses. I need cheering up after the tough time I had today, and it's no fun drinking alone.'

Philibert obeyed with a kind of tenderness. His little protégé should have her way! Leaving the hut, he went to put the second bottle in a nearby snowdrift, and then came back to get busy in the kitchen so that he could serve his guest an appetizing meal. The pink champagne sparkled in their glasses, and they began talking again. Lilith wanted to know all about her host, and he took pleasure in recounting the uneventful circumstances of his life; while they were of great importance to him, no one else had ever taken any interest in them. No, he wasn't a native of the mountains. He was from Tournus, and his parents came from Noirmoutier. One day, as a child on a colony holiday, he had discovered the Alps. He felt sure a boy of thirteen can feel a great passion which will last all his life – at least, that was what had happened to him. When he grew up he came to work here, and now he had the job of looking after the hut during the summer. He loved it, and thought it stood in the most wonderful site in the world. Of course she'd seen nothing this evening, in such bad weather. But tomorrow, if the sun came back … no, she mustn't laugh, as if he were exaggerating the magnificence of his mountains. She'd be able to see and judge for herself. The Cirque d'Ourtoulane was an amazing place!

Lilith smiled radiantly, apparently drinking in every word that fell from her companion's lips. She had allowed the blanket to slip down on her curvaceous shoulders like a shawl, revealing her pearly neck. Leaning towards Philibert, she in her turn began softly confiding in him. She spoke of her life as a lonely orphan, her work in a big city, all the traffic and noise and stress, and then this chance of a mountain holiday, something she'd dreamed of so long. After the day's adventures, she was really glad to be here this evening. With a surge of gratitude, she placed one hand over her new friend's, and felt the quiver that ran through him. A tender moment followed. Lilith spread her fingers in an imperceptible caress. Philibert was gazing admiringly at her. They smiled. Philibert lowered his eyes, and Lilith clasped his hand more gently with her own.

'Lean over,' she murmured. 'I want to tell you a secret.'

Bending her head towards him, brushing him with her light ringlets, enveloping him with her amber perfume, she whispered in his ear that she had never in her life felt as happy as she was here with him, close to him.

'I feel just the same,' Philibert replied honestly.

'Do something for me?' she said, caressing him again with her fingertips. 'I'm still thirsty, and we've finished the first bottle of champagne. Would you go and find the other one?'

The smile that accompanied these words was irresistible.

'All right,' said Philibert, utterly bewitched.

But Lilith had just committed a strategic error, although she had no idea of its gravity. If her request had not required the young man to take a few steps or make a movement, she would have won her victory. However, she had asked Philibert to go outside, and there he suddenly was, out of doors in the deep night of the mountains. Snow whipped into his face, and a gust of icy wind made him stagger as he bent down and felt about in the snow for the buried bottle. Then he stood up, suddenly feeling perfectly sober, and took a deep breath of cold air.

'Goodness!' he said. 'What on earth did I think I was doing? I do believe I was losing my head. Good heavens, I'd have done anything, however stupid. And that poor child, so pure and simple, taking shelter with me after all her sufferings, without the faintest idea about anything. Good God, what a lucky coincidence she happened to fetch up here! I hate to think what might have happened to her anywhere else. I must find some way of breaking the spell, but without hurting her feelings, of course – without upsetting her.'

'What a long time you've been!' smiled Lilith, seeing him come in again. 'Do pour a drink for us, quick!'

'Right away,' said Philibert. 'But really, I'm so scatterbrained – I don't know what I was thinking of. It was the cold outside reminded me. I haven't even given you something to keep you from catching a chill yet, and you easily could have caught one, you know. You poor thing! Let's hope it's not too late. Here, I'll open the bottle and then get you something.'

The cork popped merrily. Going to his medicine cupboard, Philibert found two powerful sleeping tablets and placed them in front of his companion. Lilith, who was paying more attention to the game as a whole than its minor details, never suspected anything. Drawing the young man down beside her, clinking glasses with him, she automatically swallowed the drug as she drank. Then she placed her light head on her friend's shoulder and whispered pretty nothings, to which he replied with all manner of remarks about the mountains, the snow, the sky, the stars. But soon she felt strangely torpid: her head nodded, she uttered several disjointed words and tried in vain to resist the drowsiness overwhelming her. Philibert took her in his arms and laid her on a bunk, with a pillow under her head. He wrapped her in blankets, looked at her affectionately and dropped a loving little kiss on her forehead. If she had been in any state to register what was going on she would have felt some satisfaction in realizing that her defeat was not total, since before he too went to bed Philibert shook his head thoughtfully and then took a sleeping tablet himself. However, the game was over for now.

Lilith did not wake until very late next morning. The sun was shining again, and after making their way through the fresh snow the first customers arrived, filling the hut with a cheerful buzz of conversation. Philibert looked after them all, now and then casting a solicitous eye at the shape lying on the bed. Then, on returning from the kitchen, he found her gone. Ingloriously defeated, Lilith had vanished in silence. Philibert was rather surprised, but when he realized she had gone sighed slightly, and told himself that after all, this was the best solution.

Lilith's failure was an extraordinary sensation in Hell. The same man, the insignificant warden of an alpine hut, a person of no importance at all, had braved the Satanic race with quiet audacity twice running! It made you wonder just how far the infernal powers had really been regenerated! The rebel must be made to acknowledge his masters! He must be punished, and punished severely! There was such a stir that it came to the ears of great Lucifer himself, and then Lucifer had to be told the whole story. He nearly choked with fury. What was the meaning of this? He had never known such a bungled job. He clearly had no collaborator worthy of the name who could be relied on for minor details! How in Hell did he come to be landed with such incompetent subordinates? Fiends who couldn't think up anything but the most elementary set of pitfalls! The seven deadly sins, and that was it! Had they even a nodding acquaintance with historical theology? Did it never occur to them to look for inspiration to the Middle Ages, when people agreed to draw up lists of serious sins with a view to trying not to commit them? Oh no, of course not! Never thought of accidie, for instance, did they? No use looking so stupid, they had *not* thought of it, and that was that ... No, to be sure, accidie did not feature in the *Dictionary of Catholic Theology*. But had they so much as consulted the *Dictionary of Spirituality*? Paris, Beauchesne, 1937, vol. 1, columns 166– 169, if anyone was interested! Accidie, perhaps the most dreadful of sins – now fallen entirely into oblivion! No one even took any notice of it, it was readily pardoned, it was even regarded as an excuse for all other sins. Yet it had been the subject of much debate in ancient times! Cassian, St Bonaventura, St Thomas Aquinas had written wise dissertations on the subject. Accidie! In other words sadness, despondency, boredom, indifference, grief, moroseness, disgust, melancholy, uneasiness, anxiety, spleen, depression, black despair, the blues, and so on and so forth ... all conveyed by that one word accidie. These days, who even knew that accidie was a grave sin? No one at all. But that was the way to attack a recalcitrant soul! That was the way to make it fall! And since he, Lucifer, had such useless minions he would see to the matter himself, on his own. Where was this Minvielle Hut? Come on, where was it? He, the boss himself, would take command of the manoeuvre, and anyone wishing to make progress in their prentice efforts at temptation could watch. They'd soon see!

Lucifer took his time, compiled files, worked on his plans. September came with its light mists, brisk air and early snowfalls. There were fewer guests at the Minvielle Hut now, and Philibert was thinking of closing it for the winter when one afternoon a stranger appeared alone in the doorway, asking if he could spend a few days there without disturbing anyone. No, he didn't want to go climbing, certainly not; he just wanted to look around the neighbourhood a little. And he'd like to borrow the corner of a table to work on, having brought some papers up with him. Board and lodging were all he required, if he wouldn't be in anyone's way, of course.

Philibert was quite glad to have company, but the stranger turned out a taciturn character. He was a man of about sixty, going grey at the temples, balding in front. Although he wore an air of apparent affability, there was nothing attractive about his face. His complexion was sallow, his mouth twisted in a deeply lined face, and he had a large nose, its contours made slightly bulbous by age, upon which he wore a pair of metal-framed glasses. His slack eyelids drooped over sombre eyes, he had large ears with pendant lobes, and the general effect was of a faintly displeasing and indeed unattractive physiognomy. He wore a tartan shirt, its crumpled collar open above a supermarket sweater, shapeless corduroy trousers, and always a red scarf. He stooped, and when he was working, seated sideways on to the table, he rested his head on his left hand, emphasizing the wrinkles across his forehead. His fingers would then touch his nose with an automatic movement, caress the top of his glasses and go on up towards the top of his skull as he sat there absorbed in lengthy meditations.

It was difficult to say just how he occupied his days. He came and went without a word, walking for a few hours in the moraines, then coming back to immerse himself in his files, sometimes thinking, sometimes feverishly consulting a few pages on which he wrote figures. His presence, without being actually annoying, was not agreeable. No one else came up to the hut now, and although he did not like turning the man out, Philibert was thinking of telling him the season was over and he must shut the place up.

Then one evening, after filling his pipe, the stranger, who had written his name in the visitors' book as Ferlussi, decided to strike up a conversation. Tapping the table with his fingers, he asked the warden, 'So what are you thinking of doing next year?'

'What ... well, how would I know? I expect I'll make a few improvements, as usual. Reinforce the shutters, do something about new mattresses. Oh yes, and I was thinking of putting better lighting in.'

'In where?'

'Well, here, of course.'

'Here? But surely you've been told. The development plan does away this hut, of course.'

'What?' shouted Philibert. 'What development plan?'

'Why, that's why I came up here – to work on it on the spot. Most of the work was done in spring, of course, by helicopter and from aerial photos. Everyone's talking about it. I can't believe they haven't let you know! Come on, you're pulling my leg! Surely you've heard of the Cirque d'Ourtoulane development? I mean, it's due to begin this autumn! The idea came from President Mitterand himself. He wants to give his name to various projects, and since he intends to open them himself while he's still in office, the work has to go ahead quite fast.'

Philibert went pale. The entire conversation seemed unreal to him, but he began to feel dreadful anxiety. He took a deep breath.

'Please tell me what you're talking about,' he said, making an effort to keep calm.

'I told you, just now! The President wants to build two large residential and tourist complexes for popular sports, or at least what they call popular. One by the sea, the other in the mountains. The seaside project is going to take in the entire area around Mont-Saint-Michel. The mountain project is planned for the Cirque d'Ourtoulane.'

'But Mont-Saint-Michel is a conservation area!' stammered Philibert, searching for logical arguments. 'And it's much too high up here, at two thousand seven hundred metres!'

'Conservation area! You must be joking. Wasn't the Louvre a conservation area when its square was demolished to build the Pyramid? The state can do things beyond the power of individuals, that's all there is to it. The state takes no notice of laws passed for mere plebs like us. As for the altitude here, that won't make any difference either.'

'But without fitness training ... I mean, heart problems ... oxygen ...'

'It was the idea of the altitude they liked,' Ferlussi calmly explained. 'To appeal to public opinion – the eternal snows and all that. Even at two thousand metres you can't be sure of snow these days. Up here the place is sure to be fully booked even in the off season, if the advertising campaign's well handled. They expect to pull in the retired, people just coming up to retirement, the unemployed on the dole, student groups, business committees, congresses, seminars, recycling courses, who knows what else! But of course they aren't just counting on the snow. They're relying on the attractions of sport and sporting spectacles. All the slopes will be specially equipped. There's to be a huge ring-shaped climbing wall at the centre. Yes, this is going to be a real twenty-first century resort! There'll be the most up-to-date communication links between the roundabout as you enter, the heliport, the hotels, the condominiums, the ski slopes, the climbing area, the jogging course, the medical and paramedical complex, the skating rink, the swimming pool, the disco, the relaxation area, the ice stadium, the congress centre, the gymnasium, the snow therapy centre, the fibrocement luge tracks, the centre of social culture, the Summitarium and the rest of it. Because that's far from all. They're even going to build a mosque.'

'This has to be some kind of a joke!' said Philibert weakly.

'Well, if you call a project involving capital to the extent of several hundred billion francs a joke, we certainly aren't speaking the same language.'

'But I tell you, it's impossible! The local mayor will never allow it. And ... and the ecologists won't either.'

'My dear Monsieur Avril,' replied Ferlussi, 'don't be so naïve! For a start, your new mayor has agreed.'

'I'll have you know that the new mayor is the old mayor's son, and the old mayor held the post for thirty years. And everyone elected the son because he thinks just like his father, so we're as sure of him as his predecessor. They're upright, honest men!'

'Of course they are, of course they are! Calm down, you're getting into quite a state. I never said they weren't honest! And you mustn't think there've been any backhanders, no, not at all … well, hardly any. I only mean there are subtler, more effective ways of going to work. Like settling local authority debts, promising a new town hall, a swimming pool, a sports stadium and multi-purpose hall, a Third Age club, a golf course, how would I know? You see, all this is progress for a local authority worth its salt. The golf course was a great hit with your mayor. Not to mention the new local taxes the resort will bring in – oh yes, they were the clincher! No, there won't be any problems; the mayor's agreed. And even if he hadn't, well, I'm sure you know his opinion wouldn't have weighed very heavily in the balance beside a Presidential decision.'

'But this is crazy! What about the regional council?'

'The regional council has voted in favour … look at it this way: the project will create jobs! And just between you and me, that's the way to silence any objections. No one would dare oppose a project promising to encourage job creation, or he'd be branded a reactionary without a social conscience.'

'But listen, Monsieur Ferlussi, we all have jobs around here anyway. There are farmers, craftsmen, businessmen … we may not be rich, but we lead free, happy lives.'

'Young man, what does it matter that the project is going to do away with as many local jobs as it creates new ones? Job creation sounds good, and that's what counts! Proper jobs that show up in the statistics, not little self-employed occupations. They'll have to go anyway: the motorway has to be fitted in somewhere, and that somewhere will be the old farmland and the alpine pastures. The car parks must go somewhere too. Local trade will have to give way to bigger firms, of course, but that's progress, that's development for you!'

'But listen, like I told you, the ecologists will never allow it. They'll see all hell let loose first.'

'Yes, I take your point, the ecologists were a problem,' agreed Ferlussi. 'But there's a way of getting round all these things. There've been negotiations, transactions. No, no, don't go imagining things! I don't even believe it was necessary to offer to provide party funding. As I'm sure you know, finance is always a problem for political parties. I mean transactions of an entirely different kind. For instance, the ecologists have been given a guarantee – well, a provisional guarantee – that none of the sites rather dearer to their hearts than the Cirque d'Ourtoulane will be touched. And between you and me, the Cirque d'Ourtoulane isn't widely known except by a few rather reactionary specialists. So the ecologists will be allowed to keep the Carlaveyron site. For the time being, anyway. Well, look at it this way: I'm not about to go into detail, but I can assure you that everything's been amicably settled with the ecologists as well.'

'I don't believe you!' cried Philibert.

'Oh yes, you do. It's because you believe me you're getting into such a state. But my dear Monsieur Avril, I'm only a small cog in the machine. When I contemplate this wild, unspoilt natural landscape I do sometimes feel compunction at helping to destroy it, but I'm only an employee. I'm sure you can see I'm not personally about to make a fortune out of this kind of speculation. It won't bring me any honour and glory either. I have my own small interests to think of, of course, like everyone else. I was made redundant from my last job when they cut down on staff, and it's not so easy to find a new post once you're over fifty. I have a wife, I'm trying to support my children through their studies, and then there's the car, monthly mortgage payments and so forth. Getting offered this job was an unexpected piece of luck. I'm telling you this just by way of explaining that you mustn't think we're all evil or I'm your enemy. We're perfectly normal people, not monsters.'

Philibert sighed, sadly. It had been a convincing plea.

'There, you're seeing sense now,' said M. Ferlussi. 'Here, let me show you the plans, and perhaps they won't seem so bad after all. I don't have them all here, of course. There are any number of files down in the offices. Still, take a look at this.'

And he unfolded maps, tracings of drawings, sketches, pictures, drafts, proofs, perspectives, axonometric projections, diagrams and graphic designs.

'As you'll see,' he explained, 'the idea's based on investment in the mountain product to provide added value. The installation of all this equipment should help us to forestall competition from other parts of the alpine area.'

'You mean it's a race – a headlong race to perdition!' said Philibert indignantly.

'I don't know about perdition, but it's certainly a race. Not that there's anything new there, though you could say the competition is intensifying. We're all caught up in it now. Perhaps no one actually intended it this way, but once the machinery's been set in motion, it would be a clever man who could stop it or even slow it down. Look, don't you think that's pretty? It's going to be the fast food outlet – the cafeteria and pizzeria. This design was a great hit, and your mayor's brother-in-law has been promised the franchise. The brother-in-law who went to work in the city but didn't do well there, I mean. Such little details help to oil the wheels, you see. Well, that's the way the world goes round. But just look at the lines of the building! With its futuristic shape, it will always feature among the most unusual architectural projects of the late twentieth century. It's to be built of concrete, no exterior finishing, but – wait for it – painted bright orange with purple stripes. The model was made by an artist who's still an unknown, but he's a friend of the President. Personally I like the project. And just think, the plans provide for the place to serve ten thousand meals a day!'

Philibert made no comment. At a loss, he gazed at the papers gradually being spread out on the table as if in implacable witness to the veracity of the news that cut him to the heart.

'And then there's this!' Ferlussi continued. 'Just take a look at this one! What a line that building has, too! What a splendid profile! It's the Summitarium, near the climbing wall. Made of tinted glass and stainless steel, but there'll be a pine door-frame added to the concrete at the entrance, for local colour. They're being careful to respect the alpine atmosphere, you see. They haven't decided yet exactly what the Summitarium is going to be for, but they'll find some purpose. It's a good attention-grabbing name; it'll help the advertising campaign for the resort. Nowhere else will be able to boast a Summitarium. A brilliant idea, the brainchild of an architect from Singapore.'

Philibert sighed again.

'Do you like children?' enquired Ferlussi. 'They'll have the time of their lives here, with a special area all to themselves along the lines of a little Parc Astérix or a Mirapolis or Disneyland, if you see what I mean. The general idea is to develop their sense of originality and beauty – stimulate their intelligence. There'll be games, attractions, a mini-climbing wall to get them started on the sport as young as possible. Climbing's big in the market economy and the media these days, so enthusiasm for it has to be cultivated among the population as a whole. See these stylized roughened concrete gnomes? Amusing, aren't they? And the finishing touch will be the resort mascot, a big orange plastic rabbit, inflated and deflated six times a minute by special pumps.'

Philibert's face was set. Ferlussi spread more files over the table.

'What else can I tell you? Oh, here's the document stating that the

Cirque d'Ourtoulane isn't on the UNESCO list, so it's not a World Heritage site. And this is the one making the site an IDZ – that's for Integrated Development Zone. Here's the agreement from the Sites Commission. This one's the plan for a six-level multi-storey car park. There'll be a giant cable-car railway, the longest in the world, linking the resort with the valley, but there will still be a three-lane highway too, and that was something of a headache, what with problems of access, viability, the road, rail and waterways network, avalanche risks and so forth. You should feel proud of the place! The Cirque d'Ourtoulane will be a superb demonstration of mankind's present high degree of ability and advanced technology. It will be held up as an example all over the world. After all, what did the place have to offer before? Rocks, frozen water, and that was it. Well, we'll soon be changing all that, I can tell you!'

Glancing sideways, Ferlussi thought the other man's face showed too little emotion, but on closer inspection he noticed that Philibert's jaw was imperceptibly quivering. He thought it a good idea to press his advantage home.

'Then there was finance – that was a major problem too. I don't know if it interests you, but I have all the data here ... let's see, several letters from Martial Hardricourt, chairman of Citydev International. You must have heard of him. Same age as the famous Norbert Piéta, but a more attractive personality, less arrogant; I think you'd like him. A self-made man of the most remarkable kind. He started from nothing, and now his offices occupy the whole of the Fréron Tower in the La Défence business centre on the outskirts of Paris. In a way, you could call him the driving force behind the whole project. I don't know just how he came to decide on the Ourtoulane Circus, but I heard he's a skier and once came here by helicopter to ski off piste.'

This was Ferlussi's trump card, for Martial Hardricourt really existed in flesh and blood, and it was Hardricourt's services to himself, Lucifer, that were at present leading him into sin and damnation. As all writers know, here's nothing like a touch of the real thing to lend verisimilitude to a fiction. In preparing his files and forging his documents, Lucifer had reproduced the authentic letterheads of the Fréron Tower offices and the signature, deliberate and precise, of Martial Hardricourt. All this strongly suggested veracity, and Lucifer dwelt on it with pleasure.

'It was he who founded the SCI property company, you know – the Société Civile Immobilière. It's in charge of the work and has shouldered responsibility for building the development. On a relatively small budget at first – as usual, SCI turned to the big investment banks for financial backing. The banking pool is headed by Aloys Abraham & Co. of London, and the syndicate spreads the risks between its members, although in this case, when the project has such firm state support, you couldn't say the risks were great. Martial Hardricourt has real vision. He suggested the site, and it met the President's requirements very well. He studied the road links, took into account the relative proximity of an international airport, had the micro-climate analysed, everything. He's going to launch a vast publicity campaign. Charter flights will bring in prospective customers, and those who buy will get the price of their tickets refunded. Look, this diagram sums up the structure of the entire syndicate and its subsidiaries. Note the important part played by Rychner Property Bank and Flayac Brothers Ltd., two subsidiaries of the Hickman Group – you'll have heard of it, the group that's just bought up our Banque Gressier. The French property market is ten years behind its British counterpart; hence the prominence of so many British firms in our operations. Oh yes, they include the Broadmoor Corporation – I don't think I've mentioned that yet – directed by Baltazar Ripamonti. Another remarkable character! An Italian immigrant to New York who started out delivering pizzas and is now one of the richest men in the world. Everything he touches turns to gold. There's a famous senator on his bank's board of directors. It may be a mafia-type operation, but it's an interesting outfit, in fact fascinating! Such men are the real adventurers of modern times.'

Philibert did not reply. Ferlussi decided to strike once more before delivering the final blow.

'And finally,' he continued, 'last but not least, as our friends at the other end of the Tunnel would say, there are the stars associated with the complex. Big names are an indispensable way of promoting the operation! They've recruited the Swiss skier Heidi Rösti, three times world champion. And the mountaineer Florent Kervallez, known to a wide public under the name of Yeti, at the age of twenty the only man to have climbed the fourteen eight thousanders twice without losing his life! And the cliff star William Caxton, known as the Monkey, the only acrobat in the world capable of climbing grade nine! And the rock and wall climber Yuri Zapopov, known as the Big Tsar, who fills competition halls to capacity and makes as much money as a pop music star! They should set a real trend! Their names alone will be enough to launch Ourtoulan's Circus, as the site will be called in future. Well, that's the way the minds of the gullible masses work.'

There was silence. This could be the crucial moment. Black despair was obviously well and truly implanted in the victim's soul, and could now be expected to transform itself in the simplest and most natural way into violent reactions ruled by avarice and envy. The matter just had to be handled properly and then, if Philibert entered into the bargain about to be offered him, he would be in the Enemy's clutches for ever. Lucifer was well aware that in the circumstances, not one man in ten thousand could have resisted the opportunity.

'Well, that's the lie of the land,' he said calmly, 'and there's nothing to be done about it, but don't despair. You'll lose your present job, of course: the question is whether you can find a niche in the new structure. I don't mean a really top job, but still, something very much better than being warden of an alpine hut. I can't suggest the post of director of tourism – that's already marked out for someone or other's nephew, I forget his name. But there are other quite gratifying and profitable openings. Sports director! Leisure director! Or wait a moment – you've got an attractive physique, a handsome open-air kind of film-star face, what about public relations? Liaising with the press and the media? Frequent television appearances ... you could be almost rich in a few years' time. And then I imagine they might reward you for your hard work with the franchise of a shop. "Avril Sports" – I can see it already. Or maybe a little rustic-style restaurant. Why, you could call it the Minvielle Hut, and you'd have come full circle!'

Philibert rose to his feet. While Ferlussi did not hope for instant agreement, he noticed with malicious satisfaction that the other man's face, impassive a moment ago, now bore all the marks of violent anger. However, he did not break into imprecations, but contented himself with picking up both ends of the heavy wooden table at present strewn with papers. He raised it over half a metre into the air and furiously let it drop again. Pieces of paper fluttered through the air and fell on the floor. But Philibert Avril had already gone to his sleeping quarters and slammed the door. He did not want anyone to see him shedding tears.

And he shed them copiously, head buried in his arms. His entire universe had just collapsed into a void. And even a void was better than the mindless concrete of Ourtoulan's Circus! How could he doubt what he had just heard? It was the way of the modern world, a world for which he was not made. In revulsion and great distress, he decided to get away. Such anger overcame him at moments that he wanted to assault the abominable Ferlussi, messenger of all these evils, now probably sleeping peacefully in his bunk, assault him and smash his head in. He even envisaged setting fire to the hut and burning the remnants of his old happiness and the emissary who had brought dismay and ruin on him in the same holocaust. However, he curbed this impulse, and deciding to do no harm to anyone but himself he left, abandoning everything.

Foreseeing such an eventuality, Lucifer had posted two minor demons answering to the names of Pazuzu and Azazel at the doorway of the hut. Their mission was to keep watch on the desperate man and report what he did and said to whom it might concern. The fiends set off in pursuit of Philibert, and had difficulty in keeping up, so fast did he hurry down the glaciers and moraines leading to the valley in his intention of leaving the Cirque d'Ourtoulane for ever.

It was still dark when he reached the village, but he did not linger there, going home only for a moment. When he came out again he did not put the big iron key he had used to unlock the door back under the beam over the doorway, but threw it violently into the river running nearby. So he did not plan to be back. This news seemed important enough for Azazel to set straight out on the road to hell. The trap had worked perfectly.

Philibert Avril had got into his little car. Pazuzu clambered into the back seat. With growing certainty, the fiend deduced that they were making for Paris, an unexpected but promising development. Everything was going very well. Up in the mountains the alpine hut warden was his own man. Now, hard-pressed by events, he was making for one of the big cities of the material world. The last of his strength would evaporate under the influence of conflicts of interest and power, in a place where crowds of human beings milled around with their fictitious requirements and where money reigned supreme.

In fact, as he drove towards Paris Philibert was thinking only of getting away from a place where he could no longer bear to be, and making one final appeal. It was not that he really hoped to prevent the development of the resort, but at least he wanted to hear from the lips of someone responsible just why such things should happen. He had remembered the name of Martial Hardricourt. He felt an urgent need to see the man, talk to him, hear him explain why mankind should wage war on nature, on the ridiculous pretext of making it available to more people.

After driving around the bewildering road system of the La Défence business area for a long time, getting lost, he parked his car and made his way on, seeming to pass interminably from car parks to shopping malls, from corridors to escalators, lost in the vast labyrinth of a human hive where everyone but himself had a place. He walked on by the artificial light of halogen lamps and neon strips, asking his way, always coming to new series of corridors, halls, levels, ramps. He finally came out into daylight, made his way on between great geometrical constructions, and reached the Fréron Tower.

The offices of Citydev International occupied a tall, grey, rectangular building with hundreds of square windows reflecting neighbouring structures in undulating distortions. On the far side and level with the third floor, cars streamed permanently along a roadway intersection with yellow cranes towering to the sky above it. The place felt very strange to Philibert. He entered a huge hall paved with shining marble and spoke to a receptionist, asking to see M. Martial Hardricourt. Was he expected? No. What was his name? He gave it. What was his business? It was about the property development on the Cirque d'Ourtoulane site. The receptionist asked him to wait.

Ill at ease, he sat down on a leather sofa, from which vantage point he contemplated, with some surprise, a large metallic sculpture that seemed to have been made from the rejects of a blacksmith's forge. The one familiar note in the place was struck by a series of enormous pumpkins enthroned on all the low tables, like a tribute from Mother Earth to the new cities of steel and concrete. No doubt the decorator who placed their rounded forms here had thought he was giving the place an audaciously modern touch, but to Philibert the pumpkins conjured up nothing but a homely kitchen garden, linking him to a simple and familiar world.

Time passed, and suddenly a receptionist came over to say that M. Hardricourt would see him in a moment. He was then introduced into the inner sanctuary of the building through a complex system of doors and gates operated by magnetic cards, and told to take one of the lifts on his right up to the thirty-second floor, where a secretary would be waiting.

When he entered Martial Hardricourt's huge, light-filled office, Philibert was no longer sure what he was going to do there. The occupant of the place was a man in his forties with an intelligent, open face. He looked at his visitor with surprise.

'Now, who are you, I wonder?' he asked. 'I thought I knew your name when they mentioned it, but you're not the person I was expecting to see. And as a matter of fact, I have nothing to do with the project you wanted to discuss.'

'My name is Philibert Avril,' said Philibert, 'and I'm sorry to trouble you, but something terrible has happened. I've heard you're a skier. Well, I'm the warden of the Minvielle Hut in the Cirque d'Ourtolane, and it's about the new resort.'

'Well, yes,' said Martial Hardricourt – thinking of some business he really did have on hand – 'yes, it's a fact that I'm involved with two projects for high altitude resorts at the moment. They'll open up some remarkable new opportunities for skiing: fourth-generation or fifth-generation models, both of them. You could call them resorts for the twenty-first century.'

'That's what I heard,' sighed Philibert. 'But listen – it will be an eyesore! It will be right out of keeping with the mountains.'

'Ah, so that's it!' said Martial Hardricourt. 'I admit I wouldn't have agreed to see you if I hadn't thought you'd come about something else. But you seem a pleasant person, and since you've come so far let me briefly explain my views. I don't hope to convince you, since you must belong to that small number of people who want a world that never changes, always preserving the past – a wonderful past, perhaps, but it's over now. Human history entails movement. It must progress. There has to be change.'

'But not at any price!' protested Philibert. 'We seem to be caught up in an endless spiral. I do know a bit about the way all these investments work, though. You always have to make new investments to pay for the last lot. You have to sell more and more things, find more and more customers, and persuade them to get so deeply in debt that business can go on. The local authorities are caught up in this endless game too. They don't mind devastating their most beautiful sites. That hasn't happened yet where I come from, and I'll admit that when it only affected other people and I wasn't directly concerned, I didn't pay enough attention. But when I was suddenly confronted with this disaster – well, I was shattered.'

Martial Hardricourt looked at Philibert with a friendly smile.

'You know, people always exaggerate the impact of our operations,' he replied. 'Do believe me when I say I'm sorry you feel like that. But listen, what are a few alpine pastures to the positive aspects of development? It's not just a matter of money. Think of today's living conditions, with most of the population crowded into huge cities, traffic problems, the break-up of family life, so many people living alone as a result, the ever-growing burden of bureaucracy, pursuing citizens even into their private lives, the shock of a constant barrage of world news from the media. It's hardly surprising our contemporaries are under stress. Modern life gives them little respite. And respite is what we're offering, to adults and young people alike, when we provide places where they can relax.'

'Then it's the whole system that's rotten,' said Philibert.

'Don't judge so hastily,' continued Martial Hardricourt. 'For instance, think of the advantages of sport. Sport lets people work off aggression which otherwise might well express itself in violence, even war. I agree that there's a good deal wrong in the world of sport today, even including some unsavoury financial dealings. But at least you could think of it as a safety valve. And like the sea, the mountains offer a variety of sporting activities, the kind of thing that only our developments will make generally available. It would be élitist to say otherwise.'

'And where's the harm in that?' replied Philibert. 'Take the few enthusiastic climbers who reach my hut after walking for hours and really appreciate what they find when they get there – well, if you call them élitist, I say good for the élite! Elites exist; why despise them? The people I'm talking about know there's no pleasure without some pain or effort, and their pleasure is great because they've earned it. I wouldn't say as much for the human herds attracted to these developments of yours. You're manipulating puppets who are simply following fashion. And anyway the sites you offer them will have been disfigured. They haven't deserved to see them and they hardly *will* see them. Myself, I prefer people who can make a personal effort and will pay for it in the only coin that interests me: imagination, effort and courage. Call that an élite if you like; it won't worry me!'

'Well, you have your reasons and I have mine,' replied Martial Hardricourt. 'But you won't deny that the big business ventures of today make the wheels of the market economy go round, and the whole country depends on the market economy. See what happened to the Eastern bloc. Look at the absurd economic management of Third World countries. And are the sites of special natural interest in those countries protected? No, they are not, and the deterioration is even worse there. Here in the West we may not have many natural resources, but thanks to intelligent activity and our efforts in the industrial field, we've been able to expand them. Some mistakes have been made, I agree, but people are still happier in our countries, and that, Monsieur Avril, is progress.'

'Again, I can't agree there,' said Philibert. 'No doubt there's some truth in what you say, but there's a harmful side to it too. Everyone seems to go on and on about progress, but I think they've got the wrong idea. Look,

The Temptation of Philibert Avril

I'm only an ordinary man from the mountains, but I read, I try to understand things and learn, and I can tell you that the sort of progress you mean is nonsense – an idea quite recently invented. People just take it up like a lot of sheep, without thinking. Anything new is called progress, and progress is supposed to justify it. I'm not saying technical improvements are a bad thing. But do they really count for much when you look at it seriously? I mean, is destroying nature progress? And you can't deny that nature *is* being destroyed at an extraordinary rate, not just here, all over the world. The ozone layer, polluted lakes and rivers – polluted seas too, come to that – accumulations of garbage, disappearing forests, animals becoming extinct ... that's the real end product of what you call progress. I've thought about the pros and cons, and the way I see it, there are more cons. The secret of human happiness is in people, not in technical improvements. I should have lived in the thirteenth century! I might have had to wash in cold water and go around on foot, but I'd have done it in a world where real values were safe ... Oh Lord – you see, all this has been such a shock it's started me questioning everything. And I only came about the Cirque d'Ourtoulane.'

'But I really don't know anything about this Cirque d'Ourtoulane!' Martial Hardricourt assured him.

'Well, whatever you call it – the place where you're going to build a new resort at two thousand seven hundred metres, anyway.'

'No one's building anything at that altitude, I really do assure you!'

'Then I just don't understand what's going on,' sighed Philibert. 'What I do know is that the world is going the wrong way. Believe me, I don't bear you any personal grudge. If it wasn't you doing it, someone else would. There's a general tendency that way, and it makes me despair. But don't, please don't confuse it with the notion of progress. What really matters lies elsewhere, and it's being stifled – I'm certain of that.'

At this point a bespectacled young man came into the room very quietly, and discreetly placed a folder on a filing cabinet. Martial Hardricourt made a gesture of thanks and glanced at the quartz clock on his office wall. Philibert realized that the interview had gone on long enough. Anyway, everything there was to say had been said.

'Thank you for seeing me,' he concluded. 'We don't agree, but I'm pleased to have met you and glad you agreed to talk to me. I won't forget your kindness.'

The two men shook hands warmly, and Philibert left. Far from reassuring him, his conversation with Martial Hardricourt had merely increased his distress, for he had found his opposite number in the dispute not an enemy but a normal, sincere human being with coherent and logical ideas. They had nearly convinced Philibert Avril himself. He remembered what Ferlussi had said about the 'real adventurers of the present day'. Undoubtedly the changing and management of the world was closer to the spirit of adventure than any attempts to beat the record for climbing Mont Blanc there and back again, or winning an ocean race to the greater glory of some charcuterie manufacturer or bank. And behind Martial Hardricourt, Philibert sensed the presence of a whole society sharing the same opinions, values and goals.

Lucifer had been right to construct his stratagem by dwelling on modern life and modern developments. He had not foreseen the sudden surge of feeling that led Philibert to Paris and confronted him in even more realistic fashion with twentieth-century conditions. But in detaching his victim from a world preserved as if in aspic, he had set him on the path to inevitable destabilization. It hardly mattered to Philibert Avril now whether Ferlussi or Martial Hardricourt had told the truth about the Cirque d'Ourtoulane, or which of them had been lying. The stakes were much higher. Sooner or later, given the present system, the whole alpine area would be criss-crossed with roads, mechanical lifts, pylons, property developments, and it would be increasingly given over to uncaring crowds with no respect for it. The equilibrium that Philibert Avril might have maintained was gone for ever, as a result of his understanding of what would inevitably destroy it. Until now he had lived happy, with hardly a care, hearing the many noises of the outside world as a distant murmur. Now the world had come to him and pierced him to the heart.

A prey to bitter thoughts, he wandered among the buildings and towers, the contours, angles and curves of the architecture of La Défence. In fact, its forceful lines moved him. He realized it had been a good idea to preserve the old urban structure of Paris but build a new city at its gates, a city for the modern age, answering new and bold criteria. But it did not contain what was essential to him. Even a glance at the new buildings confronted him with innumerable and still unanswered questions.

He realized that he was hungry, and made for the glass façade of a restaurant. He had had nothing to eat or drink since the previous night except for a coffee on the motorway. The afternoon was getting on, and the last lunch-time customers were finishing their meals. They were grave gentlemen discussing grave subjects, undoubtedly talking business. As they saw it, the mountains and indeed the entire universe could be reduced to terms of markets. The waitresses were clearing and wiping down tables and sweeping floors, and they received the late arrival unsmilingly, serving him abundant but anonymous and insipid food. Philibert ate quickly, preoccupied by the ideas churning around in his mind. He was aware that something unusual was going on inside him, but he had difficulty in understanding what it was, and he had no idea what change of fortune, good or ill, it might bring.

He paid his bill and left. Then he went on walking, amazed by the reflections of the sun on tall, blue façades of the buildings. Suddenly he happened to catch sight of the place set aside for God in this city of concrete and glass, whose new cathedrals celebrated not the Spirit but the reign of money, human power and terrestrial glory. By chance, at the bottom of a flight of steps, he came upon a curious little vault, dimly lit and furnished as an oratory under the pompous title of Relais Jean XXIII. Philibert sighed and returned to the empire of banks, information technology, insurance and oil companies. He climbed the Grande Arche, passed through a political exhibition of obsolete militancy, and contemplated the sea of roofs extending to the horizon. This was a place where millions of people governed, made decisions, managed industries and prospered or were merely content to survive, but they were none of them free; they were all accomplices. Philibert had been watching them since morning: they looked calm, well nourished, well clothed, well washed and cared for, but a light was missing from their eyes.

He came down again, and sitting down in the middle of the angular flight of fifty-four steps leading from the forecourt to the Arche, he leaned his head against the wall of white marble and thought. Grey clouds had invaded the sky, which was lit up occasionally by a pale gold sun. At his feet, as if alien to him, the human ant-heap swarmed and went its way, indifferent to his own despair. The wild mountains were condemned; no doubt the entire planet was condemned. And what could he do, isolated, helpless, powerless, in this exploding world? He stayed there for hours, telling himself that every battle was already lost in advance. Then, suddenly, he thought of the one possible battle that could still be fought, the spiritual struggle. An idea came into his mind. He had occasionally entertained it before. Now, though the notion seemed slight at first, it gradually acquired strength and was inflated by a breath like that of the evening wind beneath the Grande Arche. When Philibert finally rose to his feet, night was falling and he had come to his decision.

Down in Hell the fiends were preparing for a suitable celebration of the victory that had just been won. The demons had been laughing their heads off at the vain resistance of the poor mortal who thought he could stand up to them. They had enjoyed themselves enormously going over the strategic skill of the campaign, the many traps Lucifer had set, and the way they inevitably snapped shut. Azazel kept telling anyone who would listen about the victim's desperate flight. Lucifer, chuckling with satisfaction, was accepting praise of his expertise and his experience of human weakness from one and all. A great banquet was being made ready. Vast tables, black and shining like pitch and lit by flaming torches, bore a whole range of strange dishes and bottles with sulphurous aromas. Fiends both male and female took their places with wild laughter. They were beginning one of those sinister orgies of evil debauchery that alone can amuse the infernal powers.

Roaring rose from the abyss as more crowds of demons came up to join the feast. This was the great, dark festival held to celebrate the irrevocable loss of a rebellious soul.

Lucifer rose, intoxicated by his victory, and swelling his hairy torso he brandished a heavy basalt goblet in both hands, the signal for the satanic festivities to begin. Howls of delight greeted his gesture, and the orgy began.

Suddenly, however, the weighty bronze double doors isolating Hell from the outside world opened to urgent pressure, and Pazuzu entered, out of breath.

'Stop!' he shouted. 'Stop everything! We've lost!'

'What?' thundered Lucifer.

'We've lost! It's all over. We failed!' gasped Pazuzu.

'Mind what you say, you little vermin,' cried the great demon. 'I don't believe a word of it! You're lying. Philibert Avril gave way to despair. He's abandoned everything. We know he has. His hut, his home, his country. He'll never be back. He's done for. Destroyed. Crushed. Let's celebrate! It's a triumph!'

'I tell you it isn't! exclaimed Pazuzu. 'I saw him! I was watching! He only spent a single night in Paris. Then he set off again, his eyes bright with hope. And do you know what he thought up? Do you know where he is at this moment? Do you know what he's doing? He went back to the

The Temptation of Philibert Avril 192

Alps, he went to the Grande Chartreuse monastery and he asked to be admitted as a novice. All he did with our traps is draw lessons from them. He's found a way to get back to his mountains and spend his life there humbly, the hard way, in the middle of a wonderful landscape of forests and rocks covered with a thick cloak of white snow in winter. And there, among his brothers, meditating, reading and cultivating his garden, he will celebrate the glory of God and pray for the world ... Oh no, you didn't win – *He* did!'